Savannah

or

A Gift for Mr. Lincoln

*Also by John Jakes
in Large Print:*

Charleston
American Dreams
North and South
Heaven and Hell

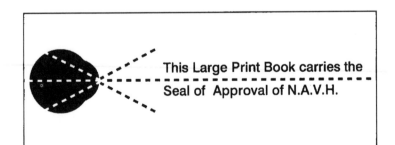

This Large Print Book carries the
Seal of Approval of N.A.V.H.

Savannah

or

A Gift for Mr. Lincoln

John Jakes

WHEELER
PUBLISHING

Published in 2005 by arrangement with Dutton, a member of Penguin Group (USA) Inc.

Wheeler Large Print Hardcover.

The text of this Large Print edition is unabridged. Other aspects of the book may vary from the original edition.

Set in 16 pt. Plantin by Christina S. Huff.

Printed in the United States on permanent paper.

Library of Congress Cataloging-in-Publication Data

Jakes, John, 1932–
    Savannah (or) A gift for Mr. Lincoln / by John Jakes.
      p. cm.
    ISBN 1-58724-863-8 (lg. print : hc : alk. paper)
    1. Georgia — History — Civil War, 1861–1865 — Fiction.
2. Sherman, William T. (William Tecumseh), 1820–1891 —
Fiction. 3. Sherman's March to the Sea — Fiction.
4. Savannah (Ga.) — Fiction. 5. Generals — Fiction.
6. Girls — Fiction. 7. Large type books. 8. Biography — Fiction.
9. Historical Fiction. 10. War stories. I. Title.
PS3560.A37S38 2005
813′.54—dc22   2004059567

for
Carole,
her book

As the Founder/CEO of NAVH, the only national health agency solely devoted to those who, although not totally blind, have an eye disease which could lead to serious visual impairment, I am pleased to recognize Thorndike Press★ as one of the leading publishers in the large print field.

Founded in 1954 in San Francisco to prepare large print textbooks for partially seeing children, NAVH became the pioneer and standard setting agency in the preparation of large type.

Today, those publishers who meet our standards carry the prestigious "Seal of Approval" indicating high quality large print. We are delighted that Thorndike Press is one of the publishers whose titles meet these standards. We are also pleased to recognize the significant contribution Thorndike Press is making in this important and growing field.

Lorraine H. Marchi, L.H.D.
Founder/CEO
NAVH

★ Thorndike Press encompasses the following imprints: Thorndike, Wheeler, Walker and Large Print Press.

Many are the hearts that are weary tonight,
Waiting for the war to cease;
Many are the hearts looking for the right
To see the dawn of peace.
> — "Tenting Tonight on
> the Old Camp Ground," 1863
> Words and music by Walter Kittredge

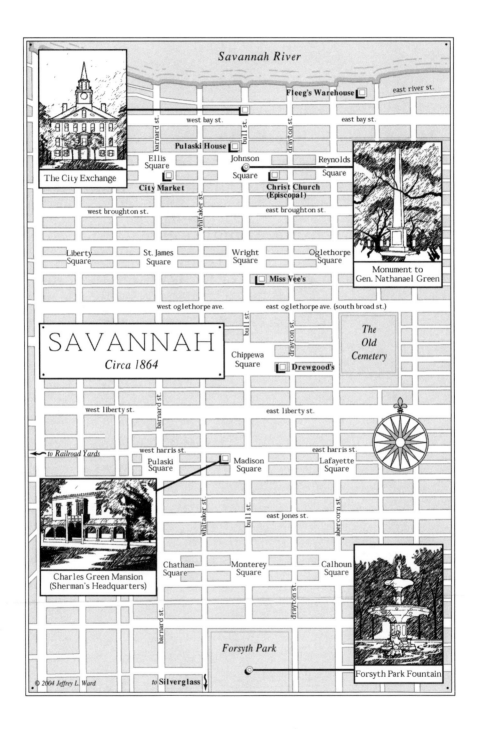

Savannah River

Fleeg's Warehouse

east river st.

west bay st.

east bay st.

barnard st.

bull st.

drayton st.

Pulaski House

The City Exchange

Ellis
Square

Johnson
Square

Reynolds
Square

City Market

Christ Church
(Episcopal)

west broughton st.

whitaker st.

east broughton st.

Liberty
Square

St. James
Square

Wright
Square

Oglethorpe
Square

Monument to
Gen. Nathanael Green

Miss Vee's

west oglethorpe ave.

east oglethorpe ave. (south broad st.)

bull st.

drayton st.

The
Old
Cemetery

SAVANNAH

Circa 1864

Chippewa
Square

Drewgood's

west liberty st.

barnard st.

east liberty st.

to Railroad Yards

west harris st.

east harris st.

Pulaski
Square

Madison
Square

Lafayette
Square

whitaker st.

bull st.

east jones st.

abercorn st.

Charles Green Mansion
(Sherman's Headquarters)

Chatham
Square

Monterey
Square

Calhoun
Square

drayton st.

barnard st.

Forsyth Park

Forsyth Park Fountain

© 2004 Jeffrey L. Ward

to Silverglass

Preface

Between the burning of Atlanta in November 1864 and the burning of Columbia in February 1865, there occurred one of the most remarkable yuletides in American history.

Late in November, William Tecumseh Sherman, nemesis of the Confederacy, launched out from Atlanta in a campaign still written about in books and studied in military colleges. He cut his lines of communication, literally disappeared off the Union's war map and, with his army of sixty thousand, marched across Georgia to the Atlantic.

It was a march rife with pillage and arson, civilian suffering and martial excess. Sherman professed a hope of shortening the war by "making Georgia howl." Those caught in his path called him the new Attila.

Yet when the Yankees reached the sea in December, a curious interlude followed. Sherman captured and occupied Savannah and remained there throughout the holidays. It was a Christmas like none that had ever been and none that ever would be: not quite war but not quite peace, forever remembered by those who lived it and those who came after.

Through the eyes of a few — Yankees and Confederates, men and women, and one special girl — this narrative spins a tale of that Christmas.

Thanksgiving Afternoon, 1864

Little Ogeechee River

Thanksgiving was a holiday not much observed in the failing Confederacy. It was suspiciously Northern in origin, but more important, Abe Lincoln had lately promoted it to boost home-front morale. Anyway, there was precious little to be thankful for. The air was biting. Last night it snowed, although the white dusting melted away by noon. The tidal waters had a flat, cold sheen; thick windrows of spartina grass on the islands dotting the marshes had lost their summertime brilliance. The worst was unseen: Somewhere out beyond the autumnal forests and farmsteads was the trampler, the looter, Sherman.

Two youngsters, together with a starving pig named Amelia, whiled away the afternoon beneath a straggle of sable palms on the bank of the Little Ogeechee, just where the Grove River flowed in from upstream. Neither youngster came from a poor family, but you wouldn't have known it, given the patched and threadbare state of their clothes.

"You having anything good for dinner?" asked the boy, Legrand Parmenter. He was fourteen but looked older because of his bony height and craggy jaw.

The girl, twelve, pulled her patched shawl more tightly around her shoulders. The girl's name was Harriet Lester; all in the neighborhood, including her companion, knew her as Hattie. She was approaching the doorstep of womanhood but was not quite there yet.

"Same as yesterday," she said. "Blue crabs I caught this morning with mullet heads. Mama's boiling them. I have to pick the crabmeat before we can eat."

"Don't act so peeved about it. You're lucky. We get possum."

A silence. Food was a prickly subject. After the hateful Union general drove the citizens of Atlanta out of their fair city early in November, then torched it, conditions along the seacoast had deteriorated to previously unimaginable depths. Railroads no longer ran. A few provision schooners sneaked down the Savannah or the Ogeechee, but what little they carried was fought over by mobs in the city's public market. Hattie and her mother, Sara, were never in town to get any of it.

In front of Hattie and Legrand, the river curved prettily through rice lands long ago cleared of tupelo and pine and palmetto. Behind the children lay square fields where generations of Lesters had dug out stumps, burned brush, built dikes and trunks; a house; and a rice barn. Hattie's great-grandfather had named the place Silverglass late one afternoon at candle-lighting, when the confluence of the

12

Grove and Little Ogeechee shimmered and shone like enchanted metal. The county seat, the charming old city of Savannah, lay roughly ten miles northeast.

The boy seemed to have that place on his mind: "Beauregard's put a new general in charge of city defenses. Hardee." Legrand seemed to be dancing around something important but so far hadn't said it outright. He'd been nervous and fidgety ever since he came calling. He'd get to it — maybe.

"Old Reliable." Hattie pulled a face. "Mama says he can't be too reliable — he's only scraped up ten thousand troops, and the Yankees are coming with six times as many."

She studied a limp white ribbon tied to the tail of her beloved Amelia, a young sow, rust red. Amelia's dwindling weight created a deep anxiety in Hattie. She frowned and drummed her peculiar shoes on the hull of the overturned rice boat where she sat. The shoes consisted of strips of canvas attached to thin soles of poplar. A pair cost thirty cents in town, made thunderous noise on pine floors, and were FULLY GUARANTEED TO LAST UNTIL VICTORY IS OURS. Leather shoes, like so many familiar things, had gone to the soldiers at the front.

Legrand continued to ponder and fidget. Hattie jumped off the rotting boat and poked at Amelia's ribs. "Oh, damnation."

Legrand Parmenter's eyes bugged. "Are you allowed to say words like that?"

13

Hattie tossed her thick yellow curls and flashed her periwinkle-blue eyes. "I guess I can if I do, Legrand. Everything's topsy-turvy."

She explored Amelia's ribs again. The pig rebelled, snorted, and ran off. A green heron stepped through the reeds below the bank, then lunged and speared a fish.

Legrand said, "The birds around here are better fed than people."

"Or pigs. Amelia can't eat acorns and snakes forever. She'll starve to death 'less we find some food."

Legrand eyed the western horizon, a vista of lemon-colored marsh and sky tinted by the pale sun. "If General Sherman's boys don't kill us first."

Hattie showed her fist. "If I lay eyes on General William Tecumseh 'T-for-Terrible' Sherman, I'll give him a sockdologer, see if I don't."

Legrand couldn't help laughing. "Oh, you're going to punch him, are you?"

"Do worse if I could. Night before last, I dreamed I captured a dozen of those blue-bellies. I knew a magic spell to change them into eggs. I climbed all the way to the roof and dropped them off one by one."

"Phew. You're a da— er — blasted little rebel, all right."

"Well, I should hope so." Hattie's expression changed to one of pensive melancholy. "Pa died

14

for Georgia, even though he never went into battle."

Legrand inched over to stand beside her, although he wouldn't risk slipping his arm around her; she inspired a combination of adoration and wild terror. In the bulrushes bordering a man-made canal on the other side of the river, a marsh hen sang. The vast Atlantic, some ten miles east, filled the air with the unromantic but familiar scent of salt and tidal mud. Legrand said, "Did I tell you James ran off Monday?"

"Your patroon?" The old term meant "boatman," a slave usually considered the most important on a rice plantation.

"Uh-huh. Guess it doesn't matter much — our barge is wrecked, like yours, and there's no crop to float to market. James promised to cut us a pine tree for Christmas, confound him."

"Do you have any colored folks left?"

"No."

"We don't either," she said. "I found our Sam and Cora camped not a mile up the Grove Road. They were nice and polite, but little Braxton stuck out his tongue at me, and Sam said I couldn't order them back home — jubilee's come and they didn't belong to us anymore."

"That's all you hear: jubilee," Legrand agreed.

"Pa depended on his nigras, but he was always nervous about it. He told me once that

15

when Governor Oglethorpe started the colony, way back, he made slavery against the law. Didn't last long — people here wanted to be like the fancy South Carolinians."

"The ones who got us into this fix." Another hesitation. "Do you know something?"

"Legrand, don't be annoying. I know lots of things. What is it you've been busting to say all afternoon?"

He looked very stiff and important. "Mayor Arnold is writing up a proclamation. First of the week, he'll ask all able-bodied men to rally to defend Savannah."

"Who told you?"

"Mr. Sappington."

"Why, he's a hundred and ten years old. He couldn't defend anybody."

"You're wrong. He's half that age — plenty young enough to serve."

"Then hurrah, we can't have school without the teacher." Hattie lifted her skirt an inch and did a quick dance in her odd shoes. "What's it got to do with you, Legrand? You're not an able-bodied man — you're a boy."

Legrand flung a stick into the river where it skipped once, then floated peacefully, turning and turning on the outgoing tide.

Hattie retrenched: "I made you huffy."

"Yes, you did. I'm as able as the next body — a lot more fit than those old grandpas who march around the squares in town with canes and broomsticks instead of guns. People take

16

me for sixteen — seventeen sometimes." He jammed his big-knuckled hands on his narrow hips. "When the call comes, I'm going."

"To war?"

"Well, I don't mean to some cave."

"That's what you came to tell me?"

"It is. If we have to defend our land with our blood, we will," he declared with a sententiousness that went right over Hattie's head because she was envisioning a red blossom on Legrand's shirt as he sank and expired with a Yankee ball piercing his heart.

She wanted to sob; she didn't, because she hated bawl-babies. She wanted to throw her arms around him, but it wasn't seemly for a girl to do that, no matter how flushed and dizzied with patriotic passion. Poor, dear Legrand — he was a mere male, but he was also her special friend.

Barely whispering, she said, "How soon will you go?"

"Any day now. Before Christmas, for sure. Nobody knows how soon Sherman will get here, or if he will. Nobody knows where he is until he arrives, and then people can only guess where he's going next. My pa says there's never been such a crazy march — poling off from Atlanta, telegraphs cut, even Old Abe and those other Washington monkeys" — he bellowed in a fair imitation of a great ape — "they don't know where he is until and unless he announces himself with artillery and cavalry."

Hattie shivered, and not from the cold this time. Though she and her mother regularly worshiped at a little Congregational chapel nearby, Hattie felt she wasn't on the best of terms with the Almighty. She must rectify that for Legrand's sake.

A bell *clang-clang*ed. Hattie said, "Time to pick the crabs." Amelia had settled herself belly-deep in the sand and appeared to be sleeping. Hattie poked her. The porker reluctantly heaved to all fours, awaiting further instruction.

"You're welcome to stay and share some, Legrand."

"No, I have to go on home, but thanks."

"I think you're very brave."

He preened and puffed up considerably. Hattie scratched Amelia's head, then pointed off across the weedy rice squares to the distant house. All the trunks in the rice dikes had been closed after the fields were drained for lack of hands to tend a crop. The wind felt stronger, sharper.

Impulsively, Hattie grasped her friend's hand. "We can't win, can we, Legrand?"

"I don't think so," Legrand answered, the contact of hands reddening him. "I think there are too many Yankees. But we can put up a devil of a fight before they drive us down."

All at once Hattie remembered Christmas. In the course of the last four years she'd experienced diminishing expectations for the increasingly popular holiday, but this one promised to

18

be the worst. Sherman was coming. And Legrand was going off to fight him.

Silverglass Plantation

The children and the pig walked the checkerboard of rice dikes toward the plantation house. At one point a dike had collapsed. Legrand easily jumped the gap, but Amelia balked and retreated. Hattie rolled her eyes, picked up the pig, and leaped.

She teetered on the far edge; dirt cascaded into the gap from under her wooden soles. Amelia wriggled out of her arms and ran squealing toward the run-down dwelling half concealed by tall magnolias. Hattie's father had planted those trees but hadn't lived to see them mature to their current magnificence.

Hattie's parents, Ladson and Sara, never fooled themselves into thinking they stood on the top rung of the social ladder, but neither were they dour-faced crackers who raised peanuts in the hinterlands and came to Savannah only to shop and truculently crack the whips that lent them their name. The Lesters, from Liverpool originally, were a long time in Georgia; nearly a hundred years. They were respected and, before the war, prosperous.

Ladson Lester was a planter who never stinted on physical labor and who kept neat books when he wasn't indulging his one fatal vice: consumption of beers, ales, wines, and spiritous liquors. Long-suffering Sara loved him and tried to save him. She took him to church every Sunday and to temperance meetings and tent revivals put on by itinerant preachers. He would swear he'd conquered his demon and would remain pure and clear-eyed for several weeks, but then he'd sneak away and enjoy one of his "bracers," as he called them, and he'd be off on another tear.

All the Lester men, Ladson included, were considered strong-willed, assertive in one way or another. People claimed this was because Liverpudlians were cheeky, like Parisians or Berliners. Whether the trait traveled down five generations, and across sexes, is debatable, but there was no doubt that Hattie Lester had a quick tongue and a forward manner. Stiff-necked individuals who disliked those qualities in a girl called her saucy, unfit for proper society.

Georgia at the outbreak of the War for Southern Independence was a conflicted place. Yes, she was stoutly Confederate and sent her men to fight and bleed for the cause, whether it was preservation of slavery or the right of secession or both. (More than 140 years later, this issue is still debated.)

Yet Georgia's fires of rebellion never burned quite so hot as those in neighboring South Carolina. Georgia had a streak of Unionism, sometimes deeply buried in the bosoms of her English and Irish and Scots and German settlers. Ladson Lester, for example, doubted the wisdom of splitting America in two, and he harbored a heavy guilt from owning other human beings. This in no way softened his patriotism or reduced his willingness to serve. In the summer of 1861, he joined a local regiment, the Yamacraw Mounted Rifles, presumably destined for glory on distant, and as yet unknown, fields of battle.

Each man had to furnish his horse and gun. Ladson bought his horse from a neighbor known for sharp dealing. Ladson didn't have a good seat; on the third day of drill, he felt compelled to improve his confidence with a generous bourbon bracer. The horse threw him and broke his neck. He died before Sara could reach the drill field. A story went around that the neighbor said Lester should have known better than to buy a horse named Old Bucky.

After Ladson's death, Hattie and her widowed mother continued to live in the house built by Ladson's father, slaves, and Ladson himself when he was eight years old. Sara Lester strove to keep the plantation going, but she lacked her husband's talent for organization and attention to detail. She hired an overseer who proved to be a thief. He lasted just eight months. She worked in the flooded fields herself, only to fall ill and nearly die of a miasmic fever.

Disaster piled on wartime disaster. Sherman's feared army of Westerners rampaged into Georgia from Tennessee, overcame and destroyed Atlanta, and then turned east. The effects were sharply felt at Silverglass. The slaves grew pertinacious. They slipped away by ones and twos until Hattie and her mother were alone except for Amelia, whom they couldn't bring themselves to barbecue to satisfy their hunger.

The house built by Hattie's grandfather stood on a brick foundation. The siding was longleaf pine, peeling now but painted regularly when Ladson was alive, as a sign of the owner's respectability. The two-story dwelling had piazzas on the east and west, and large windows open to sea breezes but covered when necessary by shutters that kept out hurricane winds and other intruders. Two large rooms opened off the downstairs hall. Two spacious bedrooms flanked the stairs on the second floor. It was to this house that Hattie and Legrand made their way with Amelia trailing.

Grandfather Lester, as was the custom, had built a covered walk from the residence to a small cookhouse, the cookhouse set apart as a precaution in case of fire. The pigpen was a short distance from the cookhouse, built against the wall of the big rice barn. Down the dirt track leading to the city road, six abandoned slave cabins were falling into ruin among some water oaks.

Hattie and Legrand cajoled Amelia into her pen. Hattie shut and latched the gate. "Come in and say hello to Mama." She led the way to the cookhouse. They found Sara at the old iron stove, her cheeks shiny from the heat. After a sojourn in the nippy air, Hattie was soothed by the warmth of the kitchen, although, as usual, the place was in terrible disorder.

Sara poked a long spoon into the pot of boiled crabs. "Hello, Legrand. Will you join us for dinner?" Sara had a sweet, round face, straw-colored hair she had passed along to her daughter, and a wan complexion compounded of too little nourishment and too much worry. Once, Hattie's mother had been a willowy beauty; lately she was rushing toward haggard middle age. It made Hattie sad.

Legrand said politely, "Can't, Mrs. Lester, but I appreciate the invite. Pa trapped a possum for us."

"A possum. How delicious." Hattie knew her mother loathed the smelly long-nosed creatures, whose meat was favored by the vanished slaves. But Sara was Sara; she would never embarrass a guest. Her late father, a Congregational parson, had taught her that, among many virtues.

"Any news from the front?" Sara asked as clouds of steam arose from the pot.

"Last we heard, the Yankees were aiming for Milledgeville."

"Oh, horrors." Sara pressed a hand to her

well-shaped front. The capital was the symbol of Georgia's sovereignty, the home of important state offices and institutions.

"There's big news right here, though," Hattie said. Despite Legrand's visible embarrassment, she described his decision to serve on the defense lines when called.

"You're indeed a brave young man," Sara said. "We'll pray for your safety."

Legrand thanked her, wished them a happy day, and set off down the dirt track to the main road. Sara hugged her daughter. "Let the water cool awhile. Then you can pick the crabs."

"Are they cooked?"

"Thoroughly."

"Good." Hattie couldn't stand it when blue crabs were dropped in a pot of scalding water; they made a plaintive noise as they were boiled alive.

She left for a short visit to the outdoor necessary. She might have liked to change her sweaty frock, but she didn't have a better dress in her wardrobe; Sara's spinning wheel was broken. She'd sewn Hattie's dress out of multicolored scraps from her ragbag.

A sudden hail from the cookhouse brought Hattie rushing outside again. On the dirt track, a dust cloud rose in the fading daylight. A carriage. Sara stood on the cookhouse porch with a hand shielding her eyes. Hattie ran to her.

"Who is it, Mama?"

"I can't tell. I surely hope it isn't our nasty relative come to torment us again. He doesn't seem to understand the meaning of no."

Hattie put her arms around Sara's waist and watched the dust cloud billow.

Silverglass Plantation, Continued

A cold gust from the river parted the dust cloud and revealed their unexpected guest. It wasn't the nemesis Sara feared, her uncle by marriage, but Miss Vastly Rohrschamp of East York Street, the city. Miss Vee was Sara's best friend, a classmate from their boarding days at Pouncefort's Genteel Young Ladies' Academy down in Sunbury.

The visitor's first name suited her; despite wartime shortages, she weighed, by Hattie's best guess, at least 270 pounds. Her brown eyes resembled raisins stuck in a plate of dough, but she was uncommonly pretty even so. Miss Vee was patriotic: She refused to pay four hundred or five hundred dollars Confederate to some gouging milliner who offered bonnets imported illegally from shops in Bermuda or the Bahamas. Miss Vee had made her own hat, wheat straw bleached to remove its yellow cast and decorated with chicken feathers that whipped in the wind of her furious driving. She called a stentorian *whoa* to the lathered beast drawing her carriage and waved.

"Hello, hello — there's the most awful news. I rushed out to tell you."

Sara ran to the carriage to help her friend alight. The carriage was an old Stanhope gig, its dark green paint faded, the pearl striping too. Miss Vee's late father was a gentleman physician, and the gig was a gentleman's conveyance. It was less suitable for a woman as seriously large as Miss Vee. The nag in the traces looked exhausted from hauling her bulk.

"Awful?" Sara repeated as she danced this way and that, ready to assist yet wary of being crushed if Miss Vee fell on her. "Tell us, for heaven's sake."

"As soon as I catch my breath."

Miss Vee came out of the gig backwards. Sara braced herself; Hattie kept her distance. Miss Vee landed successfully, without assistance, and drew a huge handkerchief from her sleeve. She fanned herself as though suffering a heat spell. Hattie couldn't understand the affection her mother felt for the scatterbrained woman, but the bond was certainly strong. Miss Vee survived in town by giving piano lessons in the house Dr. Rohrschamp had left her.

Sara repeated the invitation extended to Legrand. Miss Vee declined; she was dining later with parents of a pupil. "Then at least come into the parlor," Sara said. "Hattie will entertain you while I brew some tea."

"Heavens, you have real tea?"

"Ersatz," Sara said with a rueful smile. "It's a wonderful recipe, though — holly leaves and twigs sweetened with a dot of molasses."

She dashed off to the cookhouse. Miss Vee took Hattie's hand, her multiple petticoats rustling. Miss Vee's dress, of sufficient size to cover a baby elephant, was made of good domestic homespun; not for her any dry goods smuggled through the blockade. The dress was prettily striped in a vertical pattern of blue on white, the direction of the stripes doing little to minimize the visitor's size.

As they stepped inside, Miss Vee said, "So many books. I am always astounded by the number of books your dear mother collects." From the hall onward, the dim interior of Silverglass was crowded with hundreds of volumes in all shapes and conditions, piled everywhere. Hattie didn't feel it necessary to say that most of the books were acquired before the war brought hard times and penury. Hattie moved Victor Hugo and William Gilmore Simms off the parlor sofa and invited the guest to sit.

"Oh, gladly. It's a long way out here." Two sofa legs creaked ominously under her weight. She took off her straw hat and laid it beside her. For herself, Hattie cleared a rocking chair of privately printed copies of the sermons of her maternal grandfather, Reverend Chider.

The state of the household frequently put Hattie in a funk. Like her father, she was an orderly person. Sara had many admirable qualities, including a kind heart, but she also had a disregard for housekeeping. The room felt less like a parlor than like a used-book store. Upstairs, under Sara's bed, more books were concealed: McGuffey primers and hornbooks Sara had used to teach Silverglass slaves to read and cipher. These were never mentioned to outsiders, not even to Miss Vee.

Of course, teaching slaves broke a long-standing state law, but Sara wasn't easily deterred. She insisted that regardless of when the Confederacy gave up, the unlettered black souls Lincoln had freed with his proclamation would need basic skills to survive. Ladson Lester had nervously given his wife permission to conduct her lessons in the slave cabins. There, by lamplight, Sara had taught the vanished men, women, and children — including obnoxious Braxton, who'd stuck out his tongue at Hattie.

Miss Vee cast a wistful eye at the mantel of the brick fireplace; it was the one spot free of books. "I do so admire that photograph of your papa," she said. Next to a daguerreotype of Sara's parents, Reverend and Mrs. Chider, a similar photograph presented Ladson Lester as he was in 1860, a year before his inglorious death: a solemn oval face, a head already bald, a mustache full and down-sweeping, as though much of his hair had migrated south from his pate.

Hattie nodded in agreement; she loved the picture, though it hardly reflected the father she remembered — the man whose blue eyes sparkled, who sang cheerfully as he worked, who hugged his wife and daughter with jolly abandon. Miss Vee responded to the picture for a different reason. Back in school, Sara confided, Miss Vee had been "disappointed in love," her heart permanently broken. She envied women more fortunate than herself.

Soon Sara arrived with a tray, an assortment of cups, and a blue pot from the kiln of a local potter. She poured three cups and passed them around. "Now, what is this awful news?"

"Milledgeville," the guest announced, as though someone had died. "Milledgeville has fallen."

"Oh, no."

"Oh, yes. Two days ago, Sherman's left wing took the town. The lad who rode to Savannah with the news said the barbarians had already moved out again, across the Oconee River bridge, coming this way, surely."

Hattie spoke up. "Our neighbor Legrand Parmenter was here a while ago. He said Milledgeville was in danger, but we didn't know it had been captured."

"Captured and vandalized. Atrocity after atrocity. The weather was frosty, like today. The Yankees chopped up church pews for firewood."

Sara shuddered. "Dreadful."

"There's more." Miss Vee leaned forward; again the creaks, and Hattie thought one end of the sofa sagged. "They looted the treasury of stacks of unsigned Confederate notes and lit their cigars with them. They carried fine books from the state library and threw them in the mud. They held a mock session of the legislature that lasted all night. That debauched devil Kilpatrick" — Hattie recognized the name of the infamous general of Union cavalry — "drunkenly orated on the merits of various whiskies."

"Where was Governor Brown while this was going on?"

"Fled, who knows where? The cowardly legislators too. That isn't the worst." Miss Vee's tone inspired a thrill of fear in Hattie. The day had become dusk; they needed to light the fatwood in the hearth to drive out the shadows and the chill.

"The vandals burned the state prison. The governor had already offered the inmates amnesty if they would enlist to fight. Some did; many did not. The Yankees set fire to the place, and the remaining inmates were released to run amok. There are" — she lowered her voice — "Sara, should your daughter listen to this?"

"This is wartime, Vee. Hattie is quite grown up. Please proceed."

"Well, all right. Between the escaped criminals and Sherman's plundering horde, I am reliably informed that no decent woman in Milledgeville was safe, not even in her own home. Women of all ages were — outraged. Do you know what that means?"

"I have heard the expression." Sara's reply

was sober, unemotional. Hattie had a vague idea of what Miss Vee was trying to say. She didn't quite understand the mechanics of men and women together, but she'd been around live-stock most of her life and could fill in the gaps with imagination.

Sara asked, "Did the person who reported this actually witness any such outrages?"

"I don't believe so, but —"

"Then let us hope these particular rumors are nothing more than that. I've never visited the North, although my father did, several times. I don't believe the Yankees are saints, but neither do I believe they're monsters."

"They are men, Sara. Lustful men. For months, perhaps years, they have been denied the wholesome calming influence of mothers, sisters, and sweethearts. Sherman allows them to have their way," she concluded with a finality that brooked no disagreement.

Sara sipped tea. Hattie balanced her cracked cup on her knee, unwilling to drink the dismal stuff; she'd spied a piece of bark floating.

"I appreciate your informing us, Vee. We'll pray that General Sherman can control his soldiers."

"What about the jailbirds running hither and yon? He has no control over them. Certainly some may come this way. Which brings me to the second reason for my visit. I want to offer you the sanctuary of my house. You and Hattie will be much safer in Savannah."

"There's Amelia," Hattie began.

"She is welcome too. Close up this place. Pack a valise, and come stay with me."

Hattie responded with a vigorous nod. The plantation had become fearfully isolated. Sara, however, had a contrary response: "Abandon Silverglass? I don't think I can, not yet."

"Don't wait too long," Miss Vee warned as she finished her tea and prepared to leave.

Sara and her friend exchanged sisterly hugs and kisses. Outside, the carriage horse seemed to cast a despairing eye at the fleshy passenger rolling toward him. Sara assisted her friend into the gig, and Miss Vee drove away, chicken feathers waving.

"She's a dear person," Sara said as they went inside again. "I don't doubt the Yankees have done some terrible things, but I refuse to believe all this talk of outrages. Not until there's evidence." She pondered a moment. "In regard to such threats to herself, perhaps Vee is — um — slightly too hopeful. Do you take my meaning, Hattie?"

"Yes, ma'am, I think so. It was generous of her to offer us a safe place, though."

"Very generous," Sara agreed.

"Can't we go?"

"Only if it becomes necessary. I'll decide."

Which was the answer Hattie expected, and profoundly unsettling. Off in the November night, the Yankees were coming, possibly the convicts too.

Sara saw her daughter's anxious look, patted her gently.

"Help me find a lamp. If we don't pick those crabs, we'll never eat dinner."

November 27, 1864

Near Sandersville,

Washington County

Wagons, he wrote, *hundreds of wagons, inundating the land like Noah's flood or Pharaoh's plagues —*

No. Plumb, his irascible editor at the *New York Eye,* would slash that out, assuming he read it, which assumed eventual reestablishment of telegraph connections to the North. Plumb wanted war dispatches written in short, bleak sentences. Stephen tore the sheet from his pad and tossed it in the ditch behind him. He hailed from the city, where you disposed of trash that way. He licked the tip of his pencil and contemplated a new beginning.

Ah, but bleakness was hard; the passage of this army hour after hour invited fanciful allusions. The left wing was a chaotic, ever-changing spectacle: infantry columns slogging by — the tall, tough, sunburnt "Westerners" from Indiana, Illinois, Iowa, feared in the South far more than Grant's immigrants and shopkeepers; then a dozen sutler's wagons; drovers herding cattle; a band of ragged Negroes, some with babes in arms. They followed the army without purpose or permission; Uncle Billy resented it.

Stephen observed the Sabbath spectacle from a shoulder of the sandy road leading to the county seat. Marauders had carried off most of a hand-hewn fence behind the ditch. The adjoining field ran to a forest of sixty-foot pines; the field had been trampled and rutted by horses and wagons of the army foragers — "bummers," most people called them. The creak of iron wagon tires, the lowing of cattle, the cursing of teamsters, the singing of the black folks, the occasional distant pop of a weapon blended into a weird music. Not, however, the kind of music Stephen appreciated most.

Stephen was a slender, dark-haired chap of thirty-two. Large dark eyes and pleasing swarthy features spoke of his heritage: black Irish Presbyterian father, mother from the Italian community in Rochester. In 1852, their only son had decamped for the wicked metropolis to start his career by sweeping floors at the *Eye* on Park Row.

A dawn fog had lifted, but the sky remained cloudy. Elements of the XIV Corps commanded by Gen. Jefferson C. Davis continued to pass. Stephen had it on his mental task list to interview the unpopular and unfortunately named Jef Davis, but he didn't look forward to it.

From the direction of Sandersville he heard a regimental band triumphantly playing "Tramp! Tramp! Tramp!" — quite a contrast with yesterday, when skirmishers from Joe Wheeler's cavalry, perhaps reinforced by home-grown partisans, had fought for thirty minutes in the streets of Sandersville before being routed. Uncle Billy was in a fury over that, as well as over the earlier delay at Buffalo Creek, where rebs had destroyed a series of small bridges, forcing Captain Poe and his engineers to repair or rebuild them before the army could progress.

Stephen stuffed his pad into the pocket of his travel-worn uniform blouse, jumped the ditch, and untied his mule. After a week on an Atlanta-bought horse that bucked or bolted at every round of rifle or artillery fire, Stephen heeded the advice of a teamster who handled a six-mule hitch; he traded the horse for the less skittish mule the seller had named Ambrose, to mock the hapless Union general, Ambrose Burnside, who had admitted to blundering at Fredericksburg. "Half an ass if not more," the seller said, but Stephen kept the name, quickly concluding that Ambrose the mule soldiered more effectively than his two-legged counterpart.

As he mounted, three officers on horseback appeared. Stephen recognized the major, three years older than himself, who was his favorite on Sherman's staff. He saluted. "Major Hitchcock."

"Captain Hopewell."

Stephen exchanged salutes with two lieutenants accompanying the sturdy, blunt-spoken lawyer who'd been assigned to Sherman in Atlanta, chiefly to handle his voluminous correspondence. Although Hitchcock was born in Alabama, his family came from New England; he'd studied at Yale and practiced in St. Louis. He said, "Are you riding to town?"

"Yes, sir. Did the rebs destroy it yesterday?"

"No, but the general's threatening to apply the torch. He's in one of his tempers. This doesn't help." Hitchcock produced a page of newsprint. "The *Augusta Constitutionalist* urges loyal Georgians to round up Union stragglers and, if surrender is refused, to — I quote — 'beautifully bushwhack them.' Care to read it?"

"I take your word, sir. Do you think the general will carry out his threat?"

"He'll burn the courthouse if nothing else. The rebs sniped at us from the second floor yesterday." Hitchcock observed Stephen's expression. "You don't wholeheartedly believe in this campaign, do you, Captain?"

Stephen answered candidly. "I saw no need for setting fire to Atlanta. Also, everyone says the foragers are badly disciplined."

"I'd argue the first point but grant you the second. The general set out to 'make Georgia howl,' as he phrases it. He wants to be the man to end the war."

"By punishing civilians."

36

"I would keep that opinion to yourself. You know what the general thinks of ink slingers."

Stephen quoted an overheard remark of Sherman's: " 'It is impossible to carry on a war with a free press.' "

"Nevertheless," Hitchcock said, "the general does not make war on women and children."

Only on their homes, livestock, crops, and provender, Stephen thought. But he refrained from saying it. He held his rank by sufferance of the War Department. Uncle Billy detested journalists because certain of them had criticized him for erratic behavior in Kentucky in '62. The *Cincinnati Commercial* had actually called him insane — "stark mad." He fought to ban all newsmen from his army. He lost the battle, and barely tolerated the clutch of reporters who, like Stephen, tagged along with the troops.

A dispatch rider appeared from the direction of Sandersville, bringing a message for the major. Hitchcock perused it quickly. "The general requires my presence immediately. Good morning, Captain." Off he galloped with his lieutenants following.

Ambrose proceeded at a walk while Stephen scribbled phrases on his pad. Suddenly, up ahead, he heard a woman wailing. Not suffering, exactly — protesting. He dropped behind a four-wheeled ambulance, maneuvered through half a dozen plodding steers, and rode up to have a look.

The sight he came upon appalled him. A band

of army foragers had picketed their horses in the dooryard of a large cabin set well back from the road, where the pine forest began. The bummers were a mixed lot: three callow privates, not long off the farm; a homely stoop-shouldered corporal with moles on his cheeks; a giant brown-skinned soldier Stephen took to be one of the Winnebago Indians marching with the army — how had he gotten separated from his Wisconsin regiment? — and finally, a sergeant. The sergeant was arguing with a stout lady at the cabin door.

"I never wanted this war," she cried. "You got no right to punish helpless women who never did nothing to harm you."

"Oh, yes?" said the noncom, his chin aggressively thrust forward. "Let me ask you — where's your husband?"

"Off in the army, but —"

"Did you use your influence keep him home?"

"No, but —"

"Then you did all you could to help the war, and nothing to prevent it. Boys, this is a rebel house. Take whatever we can use."

The bummers stampeded inside while Stephen dismounted and approached the peculiar-looking sergeant. The fellow was tall, well muscled, sunburnt. Over his blue tunic he wore a cape improvised from an Oriental carpet. Huge silver spurs, not army issue, clinked and gleamed. He saluted lackadaisically and grinned, as though friendliness would protect him. Ste-

38

phen snapped a salute in return. "Take off that ridiculous hat."

"Yessir." The young man doffed a black top hat decorated with artificial flowers; his blond hair hadn't been cut in a while.

"Whose horse is that?" Stephen indicated the animal whose open saddlebags bulged with ears of corn, yams, books, a silver candelabra, and a dead rooster. The sergeant allowed as how the animal was his.

"Your name?"

"Alpheus Winks. Eighty-first Indiana."

"Where's the officer in charge?"

"Posted to the invalid corps, sir."

"Pretty far from your unit, aren't you?"

"Foragers are allowed to roam at will, sir."

"And plunder at will. Where did you steal those goods?"

"From reb houses already condemned to be burnt. Sir." The pause before the final word was pointed.

"Well, I don't approve."

Two of the farm boys dragged an old rug from the cabin. The stout lady watched, disbelieving, as they spread the rug in the weedy yard. The Indian ran out with a jug containing some kind of syrup, which he proceeded to pour all over the rug. The stout lady reeled back, gasping.

"That's criminal," Stephen barked. "Mount up and leave this property."

"Sir, we're only carrying out Uncle Billy's —"

39

"General Sherman to you."

"General Sherman's Special Order Number One Hundred and Twenty. 'Forage liberally,' it says. That's what we're doing."

"Yes indeed," said the corporal, standing in the cabin door with a pair of lapis lazuli ear pendants held up to his ears.

Winks looked uncomfortable. "Put those back, Professor. We don't make war on ladies."

"What do you call stealing their possessions?" Stephen exclaimed.

The corporal smirked. "I call it 'a place for everything, and everything in its place.' Mr. Emerson said that. I say the place for reb baubles is right here in my pocket. Just so's you know I'm not a lowlife, I taught the classics at Indiana Asbury College in Greencastle," he advised Stephen.

"Corporal Marcus, don't try to hornswoggle this here officer," Winks said. "You taught in a four-bit, run-down, one-room schoolhouse in Cloverdale. Now put those things back." The stout lady leaned against the cabin wall in a state of goggle-eyed suspense.

Yet the professor hesitated. "She's got a pump organ, Alph. Ought to be worth a few shekels." Stephen quivered with a guilty interest.

Winks shook his head. "We ain't in the business of moving pump organs." He drew his sidearm — an English-made five-shot .44, from the look of it. "Will you git, or do you need encouragement?"

The corporal vanished. Stephen said, "Marcus. I'll remember that name."

"Marcus O. Marcus," Winks said. "Putnam County, Indiana. We're all from there. I have to sit on the professor — he'll steal anything. Thinks he's smarter'n the rest of us too."

A wild bleating announced two of the farm boys waving sticks and chasing a trio of hapless sheep. The third farm boy followed with a burlap sack; judging from the internal noise and commotion, it contained one or more anxious hens. The farm boys hoisted the sheep and burlap sack into a wagon parked by the road. The Indian clambered in to guard their acquisitions. The professor shambled out of the cabin, looking disgruntled.

Winks mounted his booty-laden horse and tipped his flowered top hat. "Pleasure meeting you, sir," he said to Stephen, meaning directly the opposite. They all rode away in the direction of Sandersville, quickly lost in the continual grinding confusion of the advance.

Stephen's face was a curious contrast of a beard already showing black since his early-morning shave and, above it, the scarlet of sunburn and frustration. Winks had a certain countrified charm, but he and his men were thieves. When the North won, as it surely would, the state of Georgia might harbor resentment forever, and not without reason.

The stout lady glared at Stephen and disappeared in her cabin after a last woeful look at her ruined carpet. Stephen wanted to see her pump organ but figured that even asking permission would tar him with the same brush used on the bummers.

December 1, 1864

Silverglass Plantation

A week after Miss Vee's visit, other unexpected guests came rolling up the road, not so welcome this time. "It's the judge and his whole clan," Sara informed Hattie. "Trailing clouds of spurious respectability." Sara loved Wordsworth, had in fact memorized many of his poems, including his "Ode on the Intimations of Immortality," which she readily paraphrased.

Hattie might have behaved during the visit but for an incident an hour before. Outdoors, among the magnolias, a brown canebrake rattler slithered from the spartina grass in hot pursuit of a dune rat. The rat escaped when Hattie inadvertently tripped over the snake.

The annoyed serpent showed off its fangs and rattled its tail. Hattie jumped, caught a strong lower branch of the magnolia with both hands, and kicked up her feet. She hung by her hands and ankles until the rattler lost interest and left.

Red-cheeked, her heart pumping, Hattie waited until her wrists ached unbearably. Then she somersaulted down from the tree. She was sometimes criticized for being a tomboy, but it had its benefits.

When Sara made her poetical announcement, Hattie was still a bit overwrought. She ran to the kitchen window in time to see the Drewgoods tumbling out of their gaudy carmine depot wagon. Adam held the reins. Hattie had always considered Adam the acme of handsomeness, but the judge's last remaining slave was plagued with rheumatism now, slow to bend and walk — an old man unnoticed by his owners except when they gave orders:

"Find a shady spot. Take a nap. I'll call you when I want you," the judge said to Adam, whom Hattie liked better than this whole potful of relatives combined.

Sara and Hattie's connection to the Drewgoods was Ladson Lester's older sister, a portly and phlegmatic lady of forty. In the finest confusing Southern tradition, she'd been handed a man's name, Leonidas. Everyone called her Lulu. She stepped aside deferentially to permit her husband, the judge, to march up to the front entrance.

Judge Cincinnatus Drewgood had been thrown off the Chatham County bench, allegedly for rendering favorable tort verdicts in return for cash. Hattie remembered her father railing against the judge's "peculations, speculations, and Lord knows what other aberrations and abominations." What galled Ladson most while he lived was the judge's studied air of

43

piety. At church, from his front pew — the amen corner, Ladson had called it — the judge always sang the loudest and prayed the longest. Ladson believed his sister must have been temporarily deranged when she accepted Drewgood's proposal of marriage.

The judge was ten years older than his wife, with a little white goatee and big booming voice useful in intimidating defendants. The elbows of his bottle-green frock coat were shiny; a certain false hauteur was much reduced by wartime. Hattie disliked his eyes, of a peculiar, oddly menacing pumpkin color.

"Why, hello, Judge — hello, Lulu — hello, children — do come in," trilled Sara, ever the polite Southern hostess. "Wouldn't Adam like a cold drink of well water?"

"The nigger's all right," the judge said, handing his tall beaver hat to Hattie. There was an elaborate ballet as, one by one, the ladies tilted their steel-hooped crinolines and squeezed sideways through the door. The judge's two older children were nineteen. Merry, the pretty and buxom one, dressed neatly; Cherry, her squinty, small-bosomed fraternal twin, never combed her hair or rouged her cheeks, as if set on spitefully enhancing her drabness. Napoleon, age eleven, a late arrival, was white and pudgy, with a tendency to whine and pick his nose in public. It happened now; Lulu smacked his hand and chided him. Napoleon's eyes flashed murder for a second.

"Things are mighty dire in Savannah," the judge announced as he sat down without invitation. The cluttered parlor was roomy, but occupied by three ladies whose skirts measured eight feet across, each, a crowded feeling prevailed.

"That Yankee devil has passed through Louisville," the judge continued. "He may be in Millen already."

"More than halfway to Savannah," Lulu added as her dolorous contribution.

The judge wrung his hands. "Beauregard wants to confer with Old Reliable, but Hardee won't go to Charleston. Says things are hot here and sure to get hotter. The vandals are liable to arrive before Christmas."

"I hate the holidays anymore," Napoleon declared. "That old Sherman man ruined them."

"Didn't he just," said Cherry. "We'll get no big dinner, no gifts — they might as well tell Saint Nicholas to stay clean out of Georgia."

"I should hope he stays away," the judge said with a sniff. "He's a Yankee concoction. Christmas is the day niggers expect presents from their masters. We exchange gifts the correct way, at New Year's."

Hattie rolled her eyes at this. Napoleon slyly stuck out his tongue at her.

Sara, as per the demands of courtesy, offered the guests some of her precious ersatz tea. Napoleon seized his throat and made a gagging noise. Cherry sniffed and said, "We drink the English kind, from Fernandina."

"Now, now, no bragging," Lulu cautioned. Merry, seated with her hands folded in her lap, looked similarly embarrassed.

The judge said, "The tea was a gift from a client. If it came through the blockade, I have no knowledge of it. We don't welcome contraband in our house, no indeed. Refreshments aren't necessary, Sara. I merely want to inform you of the worsening military situation, and renew my offer."

Sara sat placidly in her rocker, though Hattie guessed she must be starting to boil. The judge arrived with his pleas and his offer with tiresome regularity. Sherman's surprise departure from Atlanta had increased the frequency of his calls. Hattie could feel the tension in the sunny parlor. Since the rattler incident, she was feeling a little snaky herself.

Sara maintained her outward calm. "You have heard my answer, Judge, many times."

"But you have three hundred valuable acres and no slaves to work them. I have access to the capital to buy the property and make necessary repairs and refurbishments. Why continue to burden yourself?"

"Because this is the Lester plantation. For five generations, since the first Lester came down from Virginia in 1768."

"A penniless indentured servant — an illiterate Liverpudlian," the judge said with ill-concealed contempt.

"True enough, but he was a free man after six

years up there. He saw opportunity here. That's why he signed a second indenture."

"Chasing the silkworms — I know all about it."

So did anyone conversant with Savannah history. By the early 1770s, the dream of a fabulous silkworm culture had gone glimmering, leaving nothing but a few dying mulberry trees scattered around the county, and a book of engravings showing lush orchards and lavish estates, produced in England to promote the scheme. The Swiss to whom the first Lester had indentured himself in Savannah disappeared into the trans-Mississippi West, escaping a host of debts but freeing his servant at the end of four years rather than six. The first Lester in America applied for and was granted twenty-five acres, the foundation of the family lands. Slowly the holdings accreted; Hattie's grandfather owned three hundred acres along the Little Ogeechee and Grove rivers. Hattie's father, Ladson, died before he could increase the family holdings, but three hundred was an attractive number to the judge.

Hattie fidgeted at her mother's elbow. Papa always claimed the judge was a mediocre lawyer, but she supposed crooks had other ways to get their "capital," as he called it. He pretended he was helping a relative, but Mama said the judge didn't have much of a law practice anymore and would do anything to get his hands on a new means of livelihood. He wanted Silverglass at a sacrifice price.

And he was persistent: "I am equipped to make this a working, producing plantation again. When peace is restored, the niggers will come back. They're like children: They only want three squares a day and a master who doesn't beat them excessively. It's become altogether too hazardous for you to stay out here alone, you and your" — he screwed up his mouth as though tasting a sour pickle — "lovely daughter. That debased rascal Sherman has no morals or civilities. He released many, many evildoers from the state prison."

Sara nodded. "Yes, we heard."

Hattie clapped her hands. "Do you suppose Jo Swett was one of them?"

Had she uttered a blasphemy or some purple oath favored by Savannah River stevedores, the silence couldn't have been deeper, or more freighted with disapproval. Merry began to weep into her cotton gloves. Lulu sat rigid as garden statuary. Cherry crucified Hattie with her squinty eyes. Napoleon watched his father like a volcano sightseer awaiting an eruption. They all reminded Hattie of the rattler.

She smiled prettily for them. "Do you suppose Tybee Jo would come back? If he did, I bet he'd be mad as hornets."

The judge puffed up righteously. "None of your business, Miss Hattie. You need lessons in deportment. Maybe even a good tanning."

Sara took Hattie's arm. "Apologize to the judge and his family, please."

"All right. I apologize." A deep breath — then an outburst: "But everybody knows Jo Swett was arrested and sent to Milledgeville because he was courting Merry" — Merry boo-hooed forcefully — "and he wasn't good enough for her."

Napoleon stamped to the center of the circle, on the barricades: "Jo Swett was a robber. He broke into old Jew Bettelheim's hardware store and stole a pistol. There was a witness."

Paid for by whom? Hattie wondered. Gently but firmly, Sara said, "According to the paper, Tybee Jo swore the gun was sneaked into his room by someone else."

"He perjured himself when he appeared before me," the judge declared in a wrathful bellow left over from his bench days. "My sentence was just. That boy won't come back. He's trash, and a coward besides."

"Don't forget orphan. And fortune hunter," Lulu said, receiving general approval from the family.

"A coward is incapable of taking revenge," the judge said.

"Jo had a temper, but I liked him," Hattie said.

The judge pronounced sentence: "Sara, this child of yours definitely is ill-bred."

"I'm ever so sorry, I'll speak to her about —"

"Won't do a blessed bit of good. She's had too much education." He gestured at the piled-up books. "Too much reading. Bad for females." In an aside to Lulu he remarked, "The child's twelve going on ninety."

"How true. My poor brother would be heart-broken to see it."

Hattie was ready to heave some books at the Drewgoods, but Sara saved the moment by rising, smoothing her skirt, and saying, "I'm very sorry you drove all the way out here for the answer you've heard before. Silverglass isn't for sale."

"You'll change your mind."

"I don't think so. Are you sure I can't serve you some tea?"

"We are going. I only hope we won't be called back to survey smoldering ruins, or the grave of innocents mercilessly butchered by invaders." His pumpkin-colored eyes flicked to Hattie, leaving no doubt as to which innocent he meant.

"Lulu, fetch my hat." She responded to her husband's command obediently. "Napoleon, run out there and wake up Adam. Good day, Sara." And out he marched, followed by smirking Cherry, sniffling Merry, and last of all, his wife. Hattie twisted her apron.

Sara said, "Well?"

"Yes, ma'am, I was bad. They just make me mad as snakes, is all."

"Unfortunately they never give up."

Hattie waited. Sara paced. At last Hattie said, "Do you want me to bend over so you can tan my bottom?"

"Don't say *bottom;* it's indelicate." Sara frowned in a thoughtful way. "I should do it, though, shouldn't I? Indeed I should, I — oh, stop." She stamped her foot. "Tell the truth, Sara Lester. They made me mad too. You're a brave girl, Hattie. You said what I should have. I wish Jo Swett would come back and settle accounts."

She hugged her daughter, smiling. The smile produced a giggle. Sara covered her mouth and began laughing.

A tear tracked down Sara's cheek, then another. Pretty soon Hattie felt it was all right if she laughed too. Before long they were both rolling on the floor, convulsed, tearful — laughing beyond all control.

December 3, 1864

"Station 7," Jenkins County —

Headquarters, XIV Corps,

Screven County

"They set a fire yet?" said Mr. Davis of *Harper's Weekly,* never looking up. The sketch artist perched on his stool, charcoal stick flying over the pad on his knee.

Stephen watched the anthill of activity along and across the railroad tracks. "Not yet, but I'd hurry up and finish." Mr. Davis continued to draw furiously. Stephen stood at his shoulder; Davis didn't seem to mind.

One Davis generated thoughts of another. The Jefs — General Davis's XIV Corps — were somewhere to the east, demonstrating up toward Waynesborough to alarm Augusta while actually slanting southeast toward a ferry crossing on the Savannah. Stephen was due and overdue to interview XIV's controversial commander.

Five miles from Millen, at the rail junction known as Station 7, he was watching Sherman's men busily rip up rails and ties of the Georgia Central and the Augusta & Savannah lines. The soldiers cursed, as soldiers will, and they sweated; it was a hot Saturday morning. The work was made all the hotter by bonfires of ties. Other gangs heated rails in the flames; then, hands protected by heavy gloves, they ran the rails to nearby trees and twisted them into useless corkscrews — "Sherman's neckties."

Theo Davis leaned back and visually critiqued the sketch that would one day be an engraved illustration. Across the tracks, other soldiers tore apart the interiors of Station 7's depot, two-story frame hotel, and storage buildings. Stephen heard walls being knocked down, floors being axed. Sudden flames gushed from under the depot eaves. "Boys couldn't wait for orders, could they?" Davis grumbled.

Stephen squinted at the clear December sky.

Almost noon. He resettled his floppy black hat on his sweaty forehead. "I have to leave, Theo. Reluctantly."

"Not your favorite subject, old Jef?"

Stephen shrugged. "He's a big bug in the army. Sherman likes him."

"I hear plenty of others wish he'd — um — meet with an accident."

"My editor charged me with talking to him. Any man who kills a fellow officer and gets away with it is news." Jef Davis of Indiana had put a bullet in Gen. William "Bull" Nelson after an exchange of insults in a Louisville hotel. Gov. Oliver P. Morton of Indiana, Davis's friend and a Union stalwart, witnessed the shooting and intervened; Davis was never charged.

"You headed east?" Stephen said he was. "Watch out for Wheeler's scouts, I hear they're thick in those swamps." Stephen thanked him and untied Ambrose from the fire-scarred trunk of a dead pine.

An hour later, having crossed the county line, he had occasion to recall the warning. He was on a grim little road twisting between black water ponds in a dank cypress swamp. With no warning, halloos and a fusillade scorched the air.

He ducked his head, booted Ambrose down the mud track. A swift look back showed four pursuers, rebs riding recklessly with reins in their teeth and pistols in their fists.

Bullets whistled right and left of Stephen. At any moment he expected to be blown off the mule and into the scummy black water. Stephen's revolver was an expensive Belgian-made pin-fire bought at an exclusive Manhattan shop. He'd fired it for practice but never in anger. He managed two shots at his pursuers. All he got for his trouble was an overhanging branch knocked down, and derisive hoots from the rebs.

Just as he thought it might be all up, the road curved, then abruptly widened. Ambrose carried him onto a grassy little island. Marching from the other side came a squad of boys in blue, preceded by their lieutenant, a patrol from the XIV Corps, as it turned out. Stephen reined up, gesturing and yelling. "Rebs. Wheeler."

One volley from the Union patrol, and the butternut boys turned and fled. Thus Stephen arrived, rattled but safe, at corps headquarters some ten miles farther on.

A spotty drizzle set in as he rode through the camp. To reach the headquarters tents, he had to pass the smoky fires of a Negro encampment. Clusters of raggedy runaways watched him with hungry eyes and downcast expressions. He tried to count the black people. There were too many — he guessed two hundred or more.

He presented his credentials to an aide under the canvas awning of the largest, not to say the only, wall tent. "I'll carry in word, Captain, but you're liable to have a fruitless wait. You can imagine that the general has more pressing concerns than pleasing the press."

Stephen stifled a complaint and went into the warm rain to find forage for Ambrose. All he could cadge for himself was hardtack. He chipped a tooth on his third bite. In the dusk an unknown tenor sang "Just before the Battle, Mother." The air clouded with gallinippers, huge mosquitoes that kept Stephen swatting.

The aide sought him a half hour before midnight. "He'll allow you ten minutes." Stephen scrambled off his borrowed camp stool.

The wall tent reeked of wet wool and cigars. Lamps glowed yellow orange. Stephen spied a Sibley stove tucked in a corner, unlit. Brig. Gen. Jefferson Columbus "Jef" Davis sat at a field desk littered with orders, maps, ink pots — the paraphernalia of command. Stephen saluted; Davis returned it. "Sit if you want. Your name's Rockwell?"

"Hopewell. Thank you, sir." Stephen presented an engraved card, to which Davis barely gave a glance. Davis's flat, countrified speech offended Stephen's Eastern ear. A Hoosier hayseed with a thin layer of education in the military was how Stephen assessed it.

No denying the man had a reputation as a competent soldier. He'd been in the army since the Mexican War, even turned down West Point to stay in the field. Middle thirties, Stephen estimated, with pale, calculating eyes. Like so many senior officers, Davis wore a bushy beard that

55

hid most of his mouth, chin, and collar. Reputedly he was a master of profanity, indeed, said to be the champion cusser of the entire army. Stephen jotted the word *overbearing.*

"General, they say the extreme left of the army is a place of honor," he began.

"It is, and it'll remain so. I intend to be the first to cross into South Carolina."

"Is that General Sherman's plan?"

"I haven't consulted him yet."

"Do you believe the march is going well?"

"Absolutely. Our biggest problems are all the lies the enemy spreads about us. That we burn everything in sight. That we roast babies alive. That we capture nigras and shove them in the front lines."

"You have a host of colored people following you."

"Not by choice, by God. I don't want them, General Sherman doesn't want them — they impede our progress and interrupt important work with their incessant pleading for food and shelter." Stephen wrote rapidly. The comments wouldn't be well received at the editorial desk of the *New York Eye.*

Davis thumped the field desk. "I didn't come down here to free slaves. I didn't come down here to be Moses. I came down here to help Bill Sherman whip Georgia to its knees."

Stephen countered with a provocative question politely stated: "Involving able-bodied colored men in that cause isn't acceptable?"

"It may be acceptable to that four-eyed little frog Stanton, but not here. The general considers nigras useful only as teamsters and pioneers" — Stephen had seen pioneer companies felling trees and corduroying roads in fair and foul weather — "I concur."

"What about the men of the Fifty-fourth Massachusetts, may I ask? They performed gallantly at the siege of Battery Wagner outside Charleston."

"A fluke." Davis closed the subject with a dismissive wave.

Antagonized, Stephen was snappish: "Perhaps I should just confirm that the commanding general agrees with you."

Davis regarded him with cold eyes. "Why, do that if it pleasures you, Captain. Bill Sherman doesn't think niggers are any more fit to be front-line troops than I do. But ask him. Just don't stand too close when you do — he's likely to knock your head off. He tolerates you scribblers only because Washington insists. You and your crowd almost cost him his career."

Stephen jumped up. "Sir, I didn't have anything to do with those stories about the general's mental state."

Davis matched Stephen by standing behind the desk, knuckles white on a battle map. "This interview is over. Don't bother sending me a copy of whatever you write — we don't use paper at the sinks."

Before Stephen could retort, the aide burst in.

"General, sir — the guard caught three bucks trying to steal a horse."

"At midnight? What the devil for?"

"One of them says there's an old grandpa who can't walk another mile tomorrow."

"Then invite grandpa to sit by the side of the road and rot. We didn't ask these people to tag after us." Davis gave Stephen a look. "You see?"

"General, I would certainly like to talk with that Negro."

"Permission denied. Hand me my saber."

The aide jumped to fetch it from the general's camp bed. Davis did up his four-button fatigue coat, cinched his sword belt, and hooked the scabbard over it. He marched out of the tent.

Stephen put his notepad in his pocket and left too. Subalterns peeked from their tents as the general strode by, cursing at peak volume. Stephen craved something to soothe his temper — a cigar, a drink. The latter was illegal — sutlers who sold whiskey lost their licenses — but it was not unheard of.

No sutler was awake to sell him anything, so he rolled up in his rubber blanket underneath a regimental wagon. Far off, contentious voices were raised. Someone yelped, fiercely hurt. Stephen reflected that colored people who thought Sherman's army brought the jubilee were seriously mistaken. The darkies wanted to show their devotion to their liberators, but men like Davis gave them the back of the hand.

Stephen softly hummed "Beautiful Dreamer"

to calm down. With his right hand he played chords on his leg and thus, after a while, lulled himself to sleep.

December 5, 1864

Silverglass Plantation

From the north came winter rains and bitter temperatures. From the Grove River road, during a lull between downpours, came two strange figures that alarmed Sara and Hattie until they turned into Legrand Parmenter and a much older companion, a neighborhood carpenter named Grandpa Stubbs.

Grandpa Stubbs's white beard reached halfway to his waist. He protected himself with an old parasol more suited to sunny days. Sara had long ago assured Hattie that the gentleman, no more than forty, was indeed a grandfather because of an unwholesome tendency of certain county residents to marry too young.

"Look at Legrand." Hattie wanted to giggle. "Did you ever see anything so silly?"

"I wouldn't mock him. I expect I know why he's dressed that way."

Hattie realized it then too, and felt ashamed of her witless reaction. She pressed tight to her mother's side as they stood in the open door, watching the two visitors trudge up the muddy track.

Legrand Parmenter was indeed a sight. His basic garment was a clawhammer coat the color of weathered copper, probably a hand-me-down from his older brother Sparks, who'd been born with a clubfoot. Over this, for warmth, he wore a faded blue wool dressing gown, cut in the double-breasted mode and minus all but one button. A ragman's sale item, Hattie suspected.

Somewhere Legrand had acquired a soldier's gray kepi, which he wore at a jaunty angle. Nothing else about him was jaunty. His nose dripped. His knuckles were several shades bluer than his outer coat. He carried a knapsack fashioned from a flour bag. Grandpa Stubbs was all in patched blacks and browns.

"Legrand, Grandpa," Sara greeted them while shivering in the northern blast. Low clouds of dark gray sped across the pearl sky. "This is awful weather for a stroll." As their soaked and muddied trousers testified.

"We're militia," Grandpa said in a belligerent way. "We're bound for the front, yonder." He waved at the west.

"The sector of General Ambrose Wright, on the left wing," Legrand said. "General Hardee's thrown a defense line from the Savannah to the Little Ogeechee, thirteen miles. They've re-cruited clerks and wounded war veterans — they've even got some Dutchmen who were cap-tured and jailed in town."

Grandpa Stubbs expressed his disdain by

blowing his nose in a red bandanna. "Can't speak a word of English, them boys."

Sara stepped back. "Won't you come in, warm yourselves?"

Legrand shook his head. "No, ma'am, haven't time. Just came to pay our respects and say you'd better leave — Beauregard's down from Charleston again, and the word is, no relief column's coming. What we have is all we've got."

"How close is that old Sherman?" Hattie asked Legrand.

"Nobody knows for certain. My family has rooms in the Pulaski House starting tomorrow. I wouldn't stay out here alone, if you don't mind my saying so, Mrs. Lester."

"I don't, Legrand, and I very much appreciate the thought."

"All right, then." Legrand scuffed a cracked boot. "You be well, Mrs. Lester. You too, Hattie. How's Amelia?"

"Cranky as get-out. There isn't much to feed her except what's left of the rice crop."

"Rice for breakfast, rice for lunch, rice for supper — that'll be our menu pretty soon," Grandpa Stubbs predicted with grisly glee. "Ain't no food nor nothing else getting through to Savannah. No Santy Claus this year."

Hattie was bursting with a strange, unexpected loyalty to Legrand, admiration she couldn't express for fear of blubbering. He allowed himself a soulful look at her; the intensity of it jolted Hattie. He tipped his kepi and said, "We'll be off, Grandpa."

" 'Bout time. More blasted rain coming."

And indeed, it began to pour before the two were halfway to the slave cabins and the Grove River road. Hattie wanted to run after Legrand, apologize for all the times she'd teased and scorned him as a mere boy. He was brave. He was a soldier.

She might never see him again.

The rain fell harder, almost hiding the rice barn.

Hattie heard Amelia snorting uncomfortably under the old canvas she had rigged to protect her pet. She and Sara retreated into the house; Sara closed the door, enfolding them in shadows. Hattie wondered, as she never had until this moment, about the worthiness of a war that stole away her best friend.

"Perhaps it's time for us to accept Vee's offer of shelter," Sara said.

December 8 and 9, 1864

Ebenezer Creek, Effingham County

Zip shivered in the December dark. His teeth clicked. He lay curled on his side with no blanket, praying to last out the night.

No chance of sleeping, the army was still passing by: hoofs banging and wheels creaking on the pontoon bridge, soldiers yelling to other soldiers — they had strange, hard accents, these sunburnt white men from the West. Torches and lanterns lit the trees and swamps on either side of the narrow road.

Closer, amid the human dross camped beside the road and ordered to stay out of the way of the ten-mile-long column and the foul-mouthed general who led it, there was other noise: snatches of hymns, sudden cries of "Amen" or "Save us, Jesus." Zip's companion, an old woman named Evangeline, muttered to herself. "Crossing tomorrow. Army be crossed — then I go over an' find my freedom."

As if it were some kind of trinket in a box, Zip thought sadly. A lot of the black people tagging after the army wanted to find their newly won freedom, but like Evangeline, they were unsure about its exact nature or whereabouts. Zip believed he was already free. His former owner, Mr. Cato Tightly of the Augusta Gin Company, a natural-born coward in Zip's opinion, had packed up and boated away on the Augusta Canal, bound for sanctuary with relatives in Hardeeville, South Carolina. This allowed his slaves to run off and look out for themselves.

Zip was eighteen, dark brown, short — handsome in a dignified way. He had no other name so far as he knew; his parents had been sold off to a Texas cotton baron when he was six.

Zip was illiterate, but that didn't greatly influence his ambition. He wanted to be an army pioneer, had wanted that ever since he ran away and found the great blue-clad army, five or six hundred of his own people wandering in its train. The foul-mouthed general permitted younger colored men to become wagon drivers, cooks, pioneers. Zip had watched pioneers clearing trees and corduroying roads so the great blue army snake could slither forward to gobble Savannah. Not only did the pioneers do important work, but if he was one of them, he'd also be among the first to see the ocean, whose immensity he could hardly imagine.

"Wheeler, Wheeler!" The cry went up from behind them, followed by shots.

Zip crouched with his arm around the old lady: "We be all right, keep our heads low. Those reb boys can't do nothing but pick off a few."

As if on cue, a shot hurled a burly teamster from a passing wagon. A young soldier climbed up to control the mules while a second one fired his shoulder weapon into the dark. Evangeline moaned. Similar expressions of terror rippled through the great mass of Negroes on the soggy slope beside the road.

"Drive 'em off, boys — they's only five or six," a soldier cried. Galloping horses re-treated. Evangeline covered her face with gnarled hands.

She was the reason Zip wasn't a pioneer yet. He'd accidentally fallen in with her when he came upon the aggregation of ragged Negroes following the army. On his first evening among them, he accepted some corn gruel from Evangeline, who took pity on him. Like Zip, she was alone; a childless widow, sixty if she was a day. Others told Zip that Evangeline was the kind of Negro the cursing general didn't want following the army: He didn't want women, children, old men. Didn't want to feed them or even tolerate them. One colored boy had tried to steal a horse so an elderly man could ride. The general punished the boy personally one midnight, whipping his bare bottom with the flat of his saber until blood ran. Zip heard that the big general who commanded both wings of the army, familiarly called Uncle Billy, felt the same way, though perhaps he stopped short of cruelty.

The morning after Zip arrived, the march resumed and he discovered Evangeline's true condition: feeble, thin as a stick. She walked with a hand-carved cane, and fell often. Zip helped her to walk, several hours that day, and every day thereafter, letting her lean on him while they pursued the column that advanced ten, twelve, sometimes fifteen miles before making camp, putting up tents, posting pickets, lighting cook fires. At night Zip wanted to entertain Evangeline with his mimicry, but she settled into exhausted sleep almost the minute they stopped. He soon realized he couldn't be a pioneer while caring for the old woman, yet he couldn't leave her. He was temporarily stuck.

Lanterns carried by medical corpsmen threw crazy tilting shadows over the road. The fallen teamster was hauled away to an ambulance. The night grew colder; more shots rang out distantly. The reb harriers on the flanks, Joe Wheeler's cavalry, wouldn't let the ten-mile army alone.

Zip passed the rest of the night in a frigid doze. In the morning he saw Ebenezer Creek, fast-flowing and dark. A railed pontoon bridge had been flung across it two days ago by the Union engineers, soldiers wearing fancy gold badges decorated with oars, an anchor, and a castle.

The army continued to pass over the creek as it had all night: infantry, wagons, cattle. Among the Negroes there was growing excitement. They would soon cross the pontoon bridge too, moving nearer to the ocean where Linkum's ships waited for Savannah to fall.

A large family, a woman and five children, climbed up among the cattle lowing and butting each other on the bridge. A mounted officer caught them. "Fall back, fall back with the rest." They did.

"Won't be too long now," Zip said to Evangeline. " 'Bout the last of 'em comin' up the road, looks like." Ebenezer Creek unsettled him, though; it was wide, flowed fast, swollen by recent rains. Zip didn't know how to swim. Mr. Cato Tightly had never provided instruction in anything except running the gin machinery, and

66

when Zip ventured into the water on his own once, in the reeds along the canal, he immediately sank. He was strong, but he was clumsy in the water, not a natural swimmer.

Hundreds of Negroes lined the creek bank as the last of the rear guard marched over the bridge. Then a horrid thing happened. Engineers started pulling up the nearest railings and planks, then their supports, cross-pieces resting on one of many canvas boats. They ran the wooden sections forward to wagons on the far shore while other engineers jumped in the first pontoon boat, freed the anchor, and cast off. Someone cried, "We needs to cross over."

"No, you can't," shouted an officer supervising the dismantling. "Orders of General Davis. Wheeler's horsemen are behind us. We need the bridge later."

Evangeline lunged away from Zip. "They ain't going to let us go over."

"Come back here," Zip yelled, rather uselessly. Evangeline threw herself in the water and tried to fight the current by flailing about with her stick.

Zip's large brown eyes brimmed with fright, but he didn't hesitate. He jumped into Ebenezer Creek as others were doing. Screaming oaths or pleas, young and old leaped in the water, which was bitingly cold. Zip paddled as he'd seen dogs do, but his heavy factory-made shoes, left and right exactly the same, bought by Mr. Cato Tightly by the gross, slowed him down. He was nearly wild with fear, but he didn't let that stop him.

Evangeline was three or four yards downstream, lashing and kicking like a mad cat but no match for the rushing creek. Zip sank, swallowed water, fought for the surface, spat out the water. He couldn't see Evangeline. Dozens of black people kept jumping in Ebenezer Creek, only to sink and cry for help. A few of the Union engineers angrily pulled some of the blacks into their canvas boats, but the dismantling of the bridge never stopped.

Zip felt the tug and push of the swift current. An old man cursed him and kicked him hard underwater, then swam around him, able to handle the current despite his age. Zip spied Evangeline ten yards downstream, amid a half dozen children who swam like little fish while she continued to flail and gasp. Then she sank.

"Evangeline, I'm comin'," he cried, but in truth he wasn't making any progress, windmilling around in the water, sure that he was just a few breaths away from drowning. Evangeline's bony brown hand was the last part of her visible above the surface. It released the hand-carved cane that sailed downstream like a fast boat; then she was altogether gone.

"Grab on here, nigger," a rough voice said. Zip dashed water from his eyes, saw a young engineer in a canvas pontoon boat. He grasped the wood-reinforced gunwale and hung there, saved until the young engineer's superior, older and wearing yellow chevrons, slammed his paddle on Zip's knuckles.

"Let him go — it's just one more Gol-danged mouth to fill." The noncom beat Zip's hands with the paddle until Zip let go and sank. The canvas boat pulled away. In the breaking gray daylight, the whole creek was a scene of similar struggle and failure.

Zip surfaced, kicked, but he was heavy as stone. The current bore him toward the far bank, where a few of the stronger Negroes lay panting and retching. He sailed into a thicket of low-hanging branches. Wild hope surged; he grabbed branches with both hands. The branches broke.

He clawed the bank, fruitlessly digging mud that fell into the creek. He heard snorting horses, quarrelsome voices:

"You see what he is? He's a coon."

"Shut your clapper, Professor. I wasn't brought up to let a man drown."

The Yankee leaned down, extended his left arm. "Hey you, boy. Hold on here."

Zip rolled his eyes and gargled incoherently.

"I said grab hold."

The mounted man seized Zip's wrist and almost yanked his arm off. Zip's head lolled back and he glimpsed his benefactor: yellow hair hanging over his ears, a tall black hat decorated with purple and yellow posies.

Zip gradually rose from the water, his benefactor grunting, the horse pawing mud and

whinnying. The stranger cursed. "I'm tryin' to save your black hide, least you can do is help. Do you think I want to do this?"

The pale daylight faded, and Zip faded with it, clinging to the wet arm of the angry Samaritan.

December 10 and 11, 1864

Silverglass Plantation

The soldiers came early Saturday morning, ten of them, mostly youngsters. Only three wore uniforms, holes in the elbows, buttons missing. Sara and Hattie watched tensely as the corporal in charge sent the others to the dikes by twos and threes. They attacked the earthen berms with shovels, digging through to let the water pour in. Sara ran to the corporal.

"Stop. You're destroying private property."

The corporal, eighteen if that, snapped back at her. "Ma'am, we're following General Hardee's orders. Flood all the rice plantations so the only routes into town are the railroad causeways. Less to defend."

"I don't care who ordered it, I demand that you leave."

"Ma'am, I was taught never to lay hands on a lady, but you'll force me if you don't stand aside."

Sara remained where she was. Fatigue and

71

desperation grated in the corporal's voice. "Ma'am, you'd better listen. The Yanks are only five, six miles from the city. We got no time to argue." He pivoted to yell at two soldiers struggling to raise a sluice gate Ladson had built. "If she's jammed shut, smash her."

Near to tears, Sara retreated to the back piazza. From there she and Hattie watched the systematic destruction of Silverglass. Muddy water gushed through cypress trunks and new ditches in the dikes. The corporal and his crew took less than two hours to submerge all but two acres surrounding the house. The familiar regularity of the square fields disappeared, replaced by shimmering upside-down images of the pine and cabbage palmetto forest. Sara's garden was spared, and the barn, and Amelia's pen, although Hattie had to run out and soothe her terrified pig.

Next morning Hattie woke at dawn to hear a rumble of cannon in the west. *Oh, Legrand,* she thought, clutching the coverlet to her chin.

She had no appetite for the small portion of boiled rice and the half cup of ersatz coffee Sara served for breakfast. The day was gloomy and growing cold. Without preamble, her mother said, "It's time we moved into town."

"The Parmenters are already there."

"I know. We must get ready."

Cannon reverberated in the sky. The windows whined.

Hattie saw no point in making her bed as she

did every other morning. Instead, she walked around her room for a last look at her few possessions, each a storehouse of memories. Some lay in a red-and-white-striped toy chest her father had hammered together and painted: a cloth book on creating shadow puppets with your hands; a rusting tin steamboat that could be floated or pulled; three rag dolls of assorted sizes; a lumpy stuffed pig, cotton flannel dyed red, that Hattie had sewn as one of her first attempts to master the skills required of a young woman; a Japanese lady ten inches high, made of bisque, which Saint Nicholas brought one Christmas before the war. It cost an exorbitant eighty-five cents, Hattie later learned.

There were other mementos scattered around: a wagon for the dolls — Ladson had built that too — a homemade slingshot for scaring off rice birds, a hobby horse. One of her favorites was an iron Uncle Tom bank. When you pressed the back of his neck, his eyes rolled in his black face and his tongue shot out to receive a coin. The toys seemed to belong to another person, another time.

Not everyone in Chatham County celebrated Christmas as Hattie's family did. The most conservative still thought it a slave holiday, as the judge had indicated on his visit after Thanksgiving. The Drewgoods clung to the old ways — family gifts exchanged at New Year's, token gifts, if any, given to Negroes a week earlier. Miss Vee had resisted Christmas until Sara convinced her to abandon what Sara called a narrow and old-fashioned attitude.

A passion for celebrating on December 25 had grown rapidly in the 1850s. Fast trains and improved printing presses steadily shrank the nation and enlarged many a provincial mind. Periodicals born in New York editorial rooms found their way by subscription into the more liberal Southern parlors. The magazines depicted Saint Nicholas in his chimney-climbing finery and reprinted Clement Moore's 1822 poem, "A Visit from St. Nicholas." Even children in remote parts of the cotton South could quote stanzas from memory.

The Christmas tree had become an accepted home decoration for all but the most recalcitrant. Magazines such as *Godey's* suggested thrifty ways to ornament a tree: colorful ribbons, strings of beads, angels cut from paper (*"easy-to-follow directions illustrated below"*). Local merchants took no sides in the Christmas–versus–New Year's dispute, briskly advertising and selling "holiday gifts" throughout December. That is, they had until the war emptied their shelves and the new Attila lowered a pall of fear over Christmas 1864.

Hattie packed a few items of clothing in the small trunk Sara brought from the attic. Sara filled a flour sack with some dried root vegetables from her garden, then said to Hattie, "Put two of the small casks of hulled rice into the wagon, can you do that?"

Hattie said yes and dutifully trotted off. The thought of leaving Silverglass, even with so much of it under water, deepened her sadness. She didn't like people who were perpetually in a funk — even at her young age she'd met some — so she chided herself out of it as she struggled to hoist the casks into the wagon bed. What helped most in banishing the cloud of despond was thinking of her pig.

Outside, Hattie leaned on the rail of the pen and observed Amelia, who didn't stir. No doubt about it, of late Amelia had been morose, lying as she was now, adoze with her snout in the sand. Removing her to a new place might improve her spirits. Amelia wouldn't know the flight was caused by the approach of a ruthless enemy.

She hurried back to the house, only to pull up short at the sight of a smoke plume on the far shore of the Ogeechee. The shore itself was hidden by the tall spartina and stunted trees on the intervening islands. A crackle of small-arms fire drifted on the chill air. Hattie ran inside.

"I think they're firing at Fort McAllister again."

"More gunboats?" The earthen fort had already repelled two attacks launched from the Ogeechee.

"Can't tell. Might be coming from shore."

"Either way, Sherman can't open the river as long as the fort holds out. We must go. Are you packed?"

Hattie said she was. Sara slipped a book into an already stuffed carpetbag: a cherished volume of Mr. Wordsworth's poems. Almost apologetically, she said, "It's a small book."

"If you're taking that, I want to take Amelia."

"Young lady, that's very pert. We don't have room for —"

Hattie's curls bobbed vigorously as she broke in: "Yes, we do — the wagon's mostly empty. I'll find a place for Amelia at Miss Vee's. I'll keep her outside and take care of her, don't you worry."

"How will you feed her?"

"I'll give her my rice or anything else I have. I'd starve before I'd leave her for those wicked Yankees to — to —" Words such as *butcher* and *barbecue* refused to form on her tongue.

"All right, bring her. I don't know whether Vee will really approve, but we'll cross that bridge later. Do you think Amelia will consent to the trip?"

"She will if I say so."

Sara laughed and shooed Hattie out the door.

Hattie coaxed and cooed and eventually managed to raise Amelia to all fours. She encircled Amelia's bristly neck with a collar cut from her father's best belt. To this she tied a rope to lead the pig. Amelia backed off, snorting. Hattie waved a scolding finger. "You stop that, it's for your own good. You'll have a grand time in Savannah." Which was a statement she didn't half believe.

She led the reluctant pet into the barn and, with her mother's help, lifted her into the dilapidated wagon. They hitched up their mule, and Sara drove out of the barn. She sent Hattie to the plantation house to lock front and back doors with a large brass key. It struck Hattie as a useless endeavor, but she didn't argue. The pain of leaving was evident on Sara's face.

Amelia squealed forcefully as the wagon lurched away from familiar surroundings. The track leading to the Grove Road had narrowed, lapped at the edges by the flooding. In the water Hattie saw reflections of the smoke rising over the Ogeechee. Cannon crumped with alarming regularity.

The empty slave cabins were flooded, and the mule almost foundered before they emerged onto the Grove Road, which had been churned up and rutted by the passage of many wagons and mounted men. The morning was dark, acrid with blowing smoke; the cries of the marsh wrens and rice birds were stilled. Amelia hid her snout in some straw in the wagon bed.

A half mile down the road they encountered felled pine trees piled up as a barricade; another defense measure, Hattie supposed. It required a detour through soggy bottomland. Several times the wagon was in danger of tipping over. Finally they regained the road, and Sara's color returned.

Hattie pictured all the toys left behind, but

she didn't retain the picture for long. In a wordless but nevertheless real way, she understood that childhood was over. In Savannah she must grow up. She would.

December 12 and 13, 1864
In and Near Statesboro,
Bulloch County

Monday night, Alpheus Winks and his bummers camped in town, within sight of the ashes of the Bulloch County courthouse Uncle Billy had burned. Winks distributed hardtack, now in short supply and selling for a dollar a hunk; he'd obtained his by barter, coercion, and other means.

Winks's scowl discouraged idle conversation. He was riled on several counts. Firstly, he'd been sent to the rear, to comb the countryside for undiscovered stores of fodder for hungry cattle and horses. Food for men and animals would remain scarce until Uncle Billy's troops overcame Fort McAllister and linked up with provision ships anchored offshore. The rebs had thrown defense lines around Savannah, which Uncle Billy was for the moment content to invest and besiege. The city's defenders, alleged to be mostly cradle-and-grave units, still represented a challenge, but Winks had no chance to assess or address that challenge, being, this cold misty night, some fifty miles from the front.

Another reason for Winks's ire was the presence of the colored boy pulled from Ebenezer Creek in a rash moment. The boy, a handsome, bright-eyed sort, had offered his name once, but Winks refused to remember it, nor would he ask. The colored boy had attached himself to Winks's detail and volunteered to drive the forage wagon, as well as perform other tasks. "I cook your food, Captain. I be your servant," the boy said even before he dried out.

"I ain't a captain, I'm a sergeant," Winks informed him. "Go away. Look out for yourself."

"Can't do that. I owe you my life. You're a mighty good man."

No one except Winks's mother had ever called him a good man. "Let me make this real clear to you," he said. "I don't like you or any of your dusky race."

"Then why'd you pull me outa the water?"

"I wonder myself," Winks said. Truth was, he'd been raised to take pity on any endangered human being, of any color, but at that point his humanity stopped.

A certain part of him liked the views of the controversial Gen. Jef C. Davis, especially the general's popular remark that "I didn't come down here to free the slaves." But they had, hadn't they? They were fighting the war to liberate enslaved colored folk, and that rankled especially when Winks thought of Abner and of

Ansel, his beloved brothers. He didn't see any need to explain to the colored boy, however.

After Ebenezer Creek, Davis's XIV Corps had marched on down the Augusta–Savannah road to join the XX Corps of General Williams. Ebenezer Creek had split the army along political lines. The broad-shouldered, usually taciturn Winnebago soldier who wanted to be called Chief Jim revealed Republican leanings by saying loudly and often, "Ought to hang Davis high as Haman." A pie-faced private named Spiker agreed: "He's a tyrant and a fiend." Those on the opposite side, including, it was said, Uncle Billy, scoffed at charges of inhumanity, and rumors that some runaways left behind at the creek had been captured by Wheeler's cavalry, whipped, and sent back to slavery. Uncle Billy dismissed the whole to-do with one word, "Humbug," and announced his intent to ask Grant to promote Davis from brevet major general to full rank.

That night, in Statesboro, Winks sat off by himself, spine against the wagon wheel, gnawing petrified hardtack and brooding. He felt the burden of leadership every waking moment, in nightmares too. A lieutenant usually commanded a forage detail, but Winks's lieutenant had been bushwhacked by a skulking reb not two days out of Atlanta. The reb's ball shattered the lieutenant's knee. He was dumped into a two-wheel ambulance, a regular torture machine. If he survived that, presumably he would be invalided home to Plainfield. The reb vanished in deep pine woods, never caught or identified.

The adjutant of the 81st Indiana, one Captain Gleeson, was an overeducated law clerk from Indianapolis. He'd handed the forage detail to Winks: "We haven't a single officer to spare. Nor any as creatively avaricious as you, frankly."

Winks supposed that was a compliment although he couldn't be sure; his limited schooling in Putnam County hadn't acquainted him with many big words.

Gleeson continued. "Some of those lowlifes in your detail are outright bandits. That's desirable up to a point, but I expect you to keep them from stepping over the line of decency and fairness whilst foraging liberally, as our orders dictate."

Whilst? What was that?

"Any questions, Sergeant?"

"No, sir."

"Good hunting. Dismissed."

Winks left the tent feeling he'd been given a hundred-pound sack of rocks to carry, without permission to lay it down even for five minutes. He was not wrong. Zip's presence added another twenty-five pounds at least. Make that fifty.

By the fire, a night bird's sudden cry roused him; his Deane & Adams .44 was half out of his holster before he knew it. "What the devil's that?"

Strolling in from the dark, the colored boy grinned. "Chuck-will's-widow."

"Didn't see any birds hanging around this town, except turkey buzzards," Professor Marcus said grumpily.

"I know," said the boy. "I done it."

Winks blinked. "What's that? You imitate birds?"

"Yes, sir, all kinds. Care to hear a screech owl? A mourning dove?"

"Definitely not," said one of the enlisted men. "Blasted chuck-will's-widow keeps you awake half the night."

Winks shoved an unlit cigar in his mouth. He circled the fire to confront the boy. "Where'd you learn to do such a thing?"

"Old Cherokee half-breed trader man taught me. Used to pass through Augusta four times a year. It's something I didn't have to pay for, and something I wouldn't get whipped for, so it seemed to me there wasn't no harm in learning."

"Well, I heard a lot of birds back in Indiana, but I never sorted one from another, and I don't propose to start. Why don't you ride shank's mare back to Augusta?"

"Liable to get chained up again if I do that, sir. I go with you, sir — you saved my life."

"Biggest mistake I ever made," Winks said as he stretched out beneath his blanket with his top hat tilted over his eyes. He suspected he couldn't get rid of the colored boy short of shooting him, and he wasn't quite ready to go that far. Yet.

Soon after dawn they waved good-bye to a few bored Union pickets and jeered at some unreconstructed rebels glowering from their houses. The morning remained as dismal as the night before: blowing clouds, chilly temperatures, occasional gusts of rain. Winks thanked his stars for his carpet cape, but foraging had lost its appeal. It bored him, and shortened his temper noticeably.

The land they rode through was alien, not at all like the green hills of central Indiana. It was low lying, flat, cut by creeks and reedy marshes, and it bore the look of wartime: houses dilapidated, barns in ruins, cattle pens empty. Meanwhile, fifty miles away, mighty maneuvers were taking place, Uncle Billy was engulfing Savannah, and Winks wasn't participating. His bummers shared his unease, except for Professor Marcus. In between frequent complaints, the corporal swept his greedy gaze over the landscape with such vigor and concentration that Winks was constantly alert and suspicious.

As they rode along next to a fallow cotton field, a shot surprised and scattered them. The wagon horse reared, but the colored boy kept strong hands on the reins and prevented a runaway. Winks galloped forward, revolver drawn, searching for the marksman at the gray cypress farm house with half its roof shingles knocked in. He waved his men back while turning his horse into the short access road. Someone flew between the back of the house and the barn. Winks raised his revolver and fired at the sky.

"Woman, you better put down that shotgun and come out of there."

She'd taken refuge in the barn. Momentarily, another round from the hayloft hummed by his ear. He spurred into cover behind the house, raising his voice. "If you don't come out, we'll torch that barn." He had no intention of cooking some poor female, but she didn't know that.

A minute passed. Out on the road, Chief Jim let out a victory whoop; he could see the thin white-haired woman emerging from the barn, raising an over-and-under in a position of surrender. Winks rode into the open and saw for himself.

"Lay it down, ma'am." She did. "Step away from it." She did. She was seventy at least — toothless too. He waved his men forward. "Corn, oats, rice — take anything you can find."

The woman crossed her arms on her scrawny bosom. "I hope you all choke on it."

The colored boy reined the wagon in front of the barn while Chief Jim and another soldier hurried inside. Marcus and Spiker invaded the house. Wasn't long before Chief Jim popped back out of the barn.

"Corncrib's a third full."

"Load her up," Winks said, hearing crockery smash and furniture break in the house. He dismounted and walked around the barn to survey their find. The ears of corn looked poor and brown, but the undernourished beeves in the army's herd weren't choosy.

Chief Jim found a shovel and began to shovel corn from the crib to the wagon. The colored boy jumped down from the wagon and volunteered to take over; the Indian gladly let him. The boy wielded the shovel like a demon. Winks shook his head. Why had God given him this burden?

Noise in the dooryard brought Winks around the barn to confront Professor Marcus with a pile of dresses in his arms. Winks cried, "Put those back. I told you before, we don't make war on ladies. I'm all wore out with your thieving ways."

Marcus was oblivious. " 'Who steals my purse steals trash.' That there is Mr. Shakespeare."

" 'Thou shalt not steal.' That's a commandment, though I disremember which one."

"Eight," said the colored boy.

Private Spiker leaned out an open window. "Hey, boy, can you read?"

"No, sir, Bible was taught to me by a preacher man. 'Thou shalt not steal.' Commandment number eight."

Professor Marcus turned on him. "Shut your craw, you uppity nigger." He looked at Winks with more venom than the sergeant had ever seen in his eyes. "You going soft on these people?"

"Oh, I don't expect so. Maybe I've just had

my bellyful of you. Or maybe I rank you, so I don't need to explain an order. I want you to climb into one of those dresses, this minute."

"You're joshing."

"I'm not. Hop to it before I clip your toenails with this." He twirled the Deane & Adams.

The old woman broke her frozen pose and limped toward the porch. "Tell him to wear the purple-dyed one, I was going to rip it up for rags anyway."

"You heard her," Winks said agreeably.

The professor started to argue, saw the set of Winks's jaw, and desisted. Muttering oaths Winks was happy he couldn't hear, Marcus stomped inside. "Spiker, you go and watch him, see he does it," Winks said to the other soldier, who was enjoying the byplay. Spiker vacated the window.

A smile flirted on the woman's thin mouth. "You Yankees ain't so terrible mean after all."

"That is true, and please tell your neighbors. We'll make sure to leave you some corn."

That cracked the old lady's shell. She made a pitcher of ersatz lemonade for them, a few pinches of citric acid powder mixed in well water. She apologized for the weakness of it, saying Florida lemons could no longer be had, not even in their home state. Her daughter, married to a Macon apothecary, had sent her the citric acid. After a turn with the shovel, Winks thought the lemonade tasted fine. The professor refused to try it.

Several hours later the detail departed from the little farm. Professor Marcus wore the purple-dyed dress and a rope around his neck, the other end of the rope tied to the back of the loaded wagon the colored boy drove. The professor carried a scrap of shingle on which Winks had carved the word THIEF.

As they proceeded in the fading daylight, Winks couldn't fully understand why he'd done all that he'd done today, except that Marcus had rubbed him raw with one quotation and one theft too many. When he glanced back at the professor staggering along, eyes maddened with humiliation, Winks figured he'd made another mistake, perhaps one even more serious than pulling the colored boy out of Ebenezer Creek.

Ah, but this new mistake felt so good. He'd worry about consequences tomorrow.

December 13, 1864

Left Wing of the Defense Line

Legrand was afraid. He couldn't recall being so afraid for so long at any other time in his young life. It was the pinnacle, the paradigm, the apotheosis of fear. (Legrand borrowed books from Sara Lester, hence knew plenty of four-dollar words.)

Fear chewed at him during his waking hours and long into the night, when he tried to doze

with chill rain falling on his raggedy tent and the Union sentries shouting insults or firing their weapons to ruin sleep, out there across the flooded rice fields that glowed with reflected moonlight when it wasn't raining, hailing, or otherwise making life more difficult. In return, Confederate artillerists bombarded the enemy day and night, expending a tremendous number of rounds, as many as three hundred in twenty-four hours. Most of the time Legrand was sleep-starved, hungry, sodden, in addition to being terrified.

One of the defenders, a farm boy, expired six hours after his mortar blew up and shot him full of metal fragments. Legrand was both mesmerized and horrified by the death, the first he'd ever witnessed. It sharpened concern for his family. He prayed they were safe at the Pulaski House, likewise Mrs. Lester and Hattie, whose barbs he'd quite forgotten. Hattie would surely think better of him for this service, provided he survived it.

Seaward, nightly signal rockets sparkled and left smoke trails to remind Legrand of the omnipresent blockade ships below the horizon. He liked that word, *omnipresent*. He didn't like what it signified: They were trapped between the jaws of Sherman's vise of wrath. Sherman had four divisions facing Savannah in a broad arc. General Wright's seven-mile defense sector faced Gen. O. O. Howard's entire XV and XVII corps, somewhat to the west southwest of the city. To launch a frontal attack, the Yanks would have to risk exposure on the causeway of the Savannah & Gulf railroad or wade through icy water shoulder-deep. Everyone assumed the attack would come eventually, even though, like Savannah's defenders, the Yanks were rain-soaked and hungry. At night they soldiered mostly in the dark, having learned that campfires and waving lanterns invited return volleys.

Wright's part of the Confederate line was thin: around 2,700 troops and thirty-two coastal siege guns and mortars laboriously hauled from Savannah River emplacements. Rifle pits and a series of hastily built fortifications guarded the flooded land, the Little Ogeechee, and the causeway. The parapet of any fort was the most hazardous position. Grandpa Stubbs was one of those given the dubious honor of standing on a parapet as a spotter for a mortar battery.

Legrand realized he'd slept a while when Savannah church bells woke him. He knuckled his eyes, saw daylight. His lieutenant, a bearded former divinity student, hustled down the line of homemade tents, stopping long enough to kick each sleeper awake. The bells reminded everyone that the defenders were backed up perilously close to town — four or five miles.

At the cook fire, Legrand sleepily greeted comrades. Some were callow, some were half senile, but all were bonded together. Grandpa Stubbs squirted out a stream of tobacco juice and said, "What's fer breakfast? Don't tell me. Rice on toast, without the bread." Never partial to bathing, Grandpa smelled like the inside of a steamer trunk used for storing dead squirrels.

Legrand coughed, stepped back, and allowed as how Grandpa had called it correctly. Legrand's partner appeared, a dry-goods clerk named Buster Buskin. Buster had squinty eyes that were greatly improved when he smiled. Buster chafed his threadbare sleeves and shivered. "Another cold one, huh?"

Legrand glanced at the sullen sky. "But no rain yet, thank the Lord."

Grandpa worked the plug to the other side of his jaw. "Sunny thoughts for sunny times, eh, boys?"

"Yes, sir, absolutely." Legrand refused to express his fear-driven pessimism. "No reason to weep and moan. Distracts from the duty."

"I wouldn't mind being distracted by a minié ball, all the way back to the invalid corps. You boys hear them other guns last night, yonder over the city?"

Buster had but Legrand hadn't: "Sherman isn't attacking from South Carolina too, is he?"

"Nuh-uh, Old Reliable's burnt all the bridges and ferry boats." Legrand thought, *No way to escape?* Grandpa continued. "Those was ours, gunboats on the Savannah at high tide."

Legrand finished his dollop of rice, wiped his mouth and then his tin plate using his sleeve. The lieutenant came by to say the fire had been started at the hot-shot furnace, an ovenlike brick structure well to the rear. He told Buster and Legrand to look sharp and get to their posts. While they double-timed to the furnace, Legrand readjusted his soggy kepi. "What day is this?"

"Fourteenth."

"Can't be, Buster. Yesterday was Monday."

"All right, the thirteenth."

"More than halfway to Christmas." Legrand was surprised and excited; the holiday had been out of mind since he arrived on the line.

"Bet a million they cancel it this year. Everything'll be canceled but the whupping we're gonna take."

"Buster, your attitude's too negatory."

"You blame me? Just look at this pitiful excuse for an army." His gesture swept the line, from rifle pits where waking oldsters scratched at busy vermin and adjusted their porcelain dentures, to the seacoast guns and mortars where General Wright had placed his few experienced men. Some were missing an arm or an eye, or hobbled on crutches. Curiously, these maimed veterans seemed the most feisty and battle-hungry of the lot.

Legrand and Buster serviced a thirty-two-pound seacoast gun at the fort's extreme left flank. For this they employed an iron rod with a shallow ladle in the center. The man in charge of the furnace used tongs to extract the glowing round shot and lower it into the ladle. He and

Legrand and everyone else who worked with hot shot wore thick padded gloves. The shot pulsed bright as a small sun.

Legrand and Buster ran the hot shot forward. Legrand glimpsed Grandpa Stubbs climbing back to the parapet while the mortar crew readied a round. Men at Legrand's thirty-two-pound smoothbore rammed a dry wad, then two wet wads down the barrel, on top of the powder charge. The first time Legrand went through the drill, he wondered aloud why the hot shot didn't instantly detonate the powder. The instructor loftily informed him the shot would cool in the gun before it burned through the wadding. "Read the manual, Johnny." Legrand took the answer on faith, albeit nervously.

They tipped the ladle; the shot slid down the barrel, *clonk*. Legrand and Buster retreated, averted their heads, and poked their fingers in their ears as the corporal fired the long gun. The red-hot shot went blazing over the waters and blew up a geyser of mud not far from some Yankees doing an eccentric dance to stay warm. The spotter peered over the parapet with field glasses.

"Miss."

No surprise — demoralizing rather than damaging, hot shot seldom did more than set fire to wagons or command tents. It was far more terrifying at night, when it flared across the sky like a meteor from Hades.

Yankees sniped at the spotter, who dropped behind the wooden parapet holding his bullet-pierced felt hat. Legrand and Buster hurried back to the furnace. Thus the morning passed, alternating periods of activity and boredom punctuated by spates of rain and the heart-stopping arrival of Yankee shells. Grandpa Stubbs daringly continued to expose himself on the parapet, no doubt awaiting the minié ball that would conclude his service without foreshortening his life. He waved his hat and shouted abuse at the enemy, but no one picked him off. Maybe they deemed him too old, unworthy of a bullet.

A midafternoon lull in the cannonading was followed by a furious renewal of artillery fire across the Ogeechee. Smoke clouds trailed away to the west. "Sounds like they're after the fort again," Buster said.

In the late afternoon the sounds of battle drifting on the salt wind fell off. Sometime after six, Legrand heard distant brass blaring "John Brown's Body." He ran up the ladder, peeked over the parapet, but darkness prevailed. Then star shells showered red lights above the Atlantic. They looked a mite too celebratory.

The band music was soon drowned out by a queer baying sound, rising in the north, toward town. It seemed to sweep toward the Confederate batteries like a huge storm wave. Legrand struggled to identify the sound; when he did, his scalp crawled, and his stomach dropped down to his ankles.

"They're cheering," he informed Buster. "The Yanks are cheering along the whole front." Giddily brave, he leaned over the parapet and put his hands to his mouth, trumpet-fashion. "Hey, Yank, what's that yelling about?"

An unseen picket answered, "McAllister's taken. The cracker line's broken — how do you like that, reb?"

Legrand relayed the news to his friend. Buster said, "We're in the soup kettle for sure." This time Legrand didn't advise him that his attitude was negatory; he feared Buster was right.

Soon thereafter, Union batteries opened up again, lobbing rounds into the defense lines. The brass bands played throughout the bombardment; the hurling of shot and shell kept Legrand and his mates crouching with their heads covered.

Around ten, a mounted courier arrived. He nearly drowned in a sea of clamoring men: "What's happened?" "Tell us." "Is McAllister fallen?"

"It is." Groans greeted the confirmation. "Hazen's division overran it late this afternoon. Whole thing didn't take but about twenty minutes. They say Bill Sherman watched from the roof of Cheeve's rice mill this side of the river."

Someone asked, "Many of our boys killed?"

"Two dozen, give or take, that's the word. 'Bout the same for the Yanks."

"But they got replacements," another weary speaker said. "Sometimes I think they spit 'em out like machine parts."

Officers ordered men back to their posts. A new round sailed in, thunderously raising a dirt cloud way back by the hot shot furnace. Legrand rubbed his hands together, fighting off a new attack of fear for his parents; his crippled brother, Sparks; Mrs. Lester; Hattie; and all the innocent folk now trapped in Savannah. Every man on the line knew the value and significance of Fort McAllister. It was the last river bastion blocking Sherman's path to the sea. Ossabaw Sound lay open; Yankee ships could bring in food, and arms, and more and more men.

As if encouraged by the victory, the Yanks kept up their shelling long into the night. Legrand couldn't sleep. Finally he rolled out of his mothy blanket and crawled from the tent. Buster roused. "You kicked me. Where you going?"

"Just up to the parapet for a peek. I never heard such a good time being had."

"Wouldn't do it. Wouldn't stick my head up."

Legrand disregarded the advice and scampered up the ladder. A picket saw him but didn't bother to challenge him, so deep was the mood of despair on the defense line.

Legrand gripped the splintery edge of the parapet. *Oh, my Lord* — watch fires flickered all along the Ogeechee's southern shore.

Under the white winter stars, a band jauntily played "Camptown Races." He heard a shell whistling in.

Frantically he started down the ladder. He'd gone but halfway when the shell blew up the parapet and knocked it apart in a tornado of dirt and splintered wood.

December 16 to 18, 1864

Savannah, Chatham County

Five days at Miss Vastly Rohrschamp's convinced Hattie that Savannah was in a considerable fix. Sherman's hordes surrounded the city. The vandal-in-chief had established headquarters at an outlying plantation. Bits and pieces of information brought into town by deserters, informers, and a few unfazed scribblers for the local papers told of Sherman's diabolical doings:

Yankee soldiers were lowering the water level in the flooded rice fields to prepare for a land assault. From the garrison at Hilton Head, thirty-pound Parrott rifles were being shipped by water to add firepower to the siege. A long wharf and storage depot were under construction at King's Bridge; supply boats steamed up the Ogeechee from ships anchored off Tybee Island. To supply the Union's left wing, small boats captured from plantations transited the

Ogeechee Canal to the Savannah River. An almighty fix made even worse because Christmas loomed.

Possibly it would be the saddest Christmas ever experienced in Hattie's corner of Georgia. Shops along Bay and Broughton Streets were shuttered or, if open, displayed mostly dust balls in lieu of merchandise. Children awaiting Saint Nicholas might find their chimneys blown away by Union cannon before the jolly old elf had a chance to climb down. Even the weather was out of kilter: balmy with thundershowers threatening.

Before the war, Sara had wryly dismissed Savannah as slow, sleepy, and sedate. Fine homes still enhanced Governor Oglethorpe's charming squares; the finest, owned by a British cotton merchant named Green, had cost over ninety thousand dollars new. In the poor districts, shanties crowded tiny lots; petty crime was rife.

An abundance of mossy oaks still shut out the sun on the main streets, where pride-of-India trees grew untended on promenades down the center. In the midst of war, everything was crowded, dangerous — incessantly noisy. It wasn't the joyful noise of carolers celebrating the season, but the bang and boom of Confederate batteries replying to the attackers, together with the clamor of caissons and carts in the streets, teamsters shouting and swearing, soldiers and sailors roistering on the sidewalks and loudly accosting strangers. From time to time the very sod shook underfoot. Day and night, Miss Vee kept her doors bolted and her windows latched, never mind the temperature.

Savannah's prewar population had been about twenty-three thousand, at least a third of those slaves and freedmen. Now there was no reckoning how many persons the city contained. Army tents overflowed the squares. Forsyth Park, just past the southern city limit at Gaston Street, was a vast campground. Vee said naked soldiers were rumored to bathe in the park's glorious fountain. Her lip trembled in the telling.

Miss Vee's house occupied a lot on the south side of East York Street, number 5, within sight of Wright Square. From the tiny front yard, Hattie could gaze on tents and lean-tos despoiling the square together with a lot of dispirited men, some visibly inebriated well before noon. Surely Legrand hadn't turned into one of those.

The row house resembled many another Savannah dwelling: storerooms on the ground floor and the living area one flight up. This first floor consisted of a parlor and separate dining room in front, two bedrooms and a kitchen behind. The necessary was reached by descending the rear stairs and following a path to the back of the garden.

The house showed many signs of the late Dr. Rohrschamp's profitable practice. The kitchen

99

had a cast-iron stove with a pivoting crane for kettles. The parlor was furnished with good imitation Sheraton chairs, floral wallpaper, and a colorful Currier & Ives depiction of Mount Vernon. Pride of place belonged to a polished upright piano from Chickering & Sons, Boston. Dr. Rohrschamp had bought the piano in 1851, before sectional antagonisms made commerce with Massachusetts questionable. A little snooping showed Hattie that Miss Vee had reinforced her piano bench with iron braces invisible to the casual observer.

Vee moved into the smaller bedroom so Sara could sleep in a large feather bed and Hattie on the trundle rolled out from underneath. Hattie's pet fitted less easily into the household routine. Amelia presented problems of personal hygiene, namely the pungent odors generated by her species. Vee courteously but firmly refused to allow the pet to live in the house. Hattie created a makeshift pallet on the back stoop, tying Amelia there except for the times she walked the pig on a rope. She'd brought a sack of old corn cobs from Silverglass and rationed these sparingly. Amelia did clean up small portions of garbage the humans created but even so, she seemed to grow sadder, thinner too. The once-lively pig spent long hours asleep.

At the dinner table on Friday afternoon, sipping weak tea brewed from Sara's used holly leaves, Sara cleared her throat and discreetly asked, "Are you still taking pupils?" Hattie could have told her; she hadn't seen a single one come or go.

Vee said, "I'm willing, but most quit for lack of money. The last one able to pay left a week ago — Missy VanderPlonk, a promising child."

Hattie said, "You mean she just stopped coming?"

"She and her family chose to escape across the river in a rowboat for which her father paid sixty dollars, gold, she said. I hope they'll be safe, but you know how Sherman hates South Carolina. Oh, dear, I am so hungry."

Vee's deeply felt sigh jiggled her chins. Hattie no longer counted the number of times a day Vee stated her condition, and truthfully, she did look thinner, as did Sara. Why not? — their diet consisted of rice from Silverglass, parched corn, and occasional desiccated vegetables topped off by well water, or a breakfast beverage concocted of okra seeds and chicory mixed with a tiny bit of hoarded coffee.

With the teacups empty, Hattie suggested some music. Sara said, "That's a fine idea. I keep forgetting the season."

Miss Vee dabbed her bow lips with her serviette. "The carols we once enjoyed were written in the North by a lot of radical Unitarian ministers who are also abolitionists. We'll sing some nice English carols." They trooped into the parlor. Miss Vee lowered her bulk onto the bench and they temporarily cheered themselves by warbling "The First Nowell" and "Good King Wenceslas."

Next day, Saturday, Sara sent Hattie to the City Market in Ellis Square. Hattie stayed on the boardwalks because the foot-deep sand in the streets was badly churned by military traffic. Instead of going directly to the market, however, she detoured to Bay Street, where prosperous factors had closed their offices and disappeared into grog shops, there to bemoan their economic loss, Vee said.

A neighbor had told Hattie that curious things were afoot on the river, so Hattie trooped down the steep pedestrian stairs to the wharf forty feet below the bluff. She'd visited it with great pleasure in company with her father. She loved the checkerboard look of the warehouses and retaining walls made of stone ballast from oceangoing ships. If there had been a violent storm upstream, the Savannah might be flowing red, tinted by the unmistakable red dirt of Georgia. Today the river was disappointingly different: greasy yellow, awash with garbage and all manner of waste. Bales of rain-soaked cotton were rotting on the once-busy wharf.

There were activities along the river front that Hattie didn't understand. Negro gangs hammered and sawed and carried lengths of wood out of half-dismantled buildings. A curious construction of skiffs, barges, and rice flats lashed end to end extended from the foot of Broad Street two-thirds of the way to Hutchinson Is-

land. As Hattie watched, men maneuvered another thirty-foot rice flat into place in midstream. Soldiers clambered over it to secure it
with chains and ropes. Hattie marched up to an
elderly Negro resting on a bale.

"Grandfather, what's that?"

The old man smiled a smile that was mostly
gums. "Why, child, General Hardee ha'nt confided in me, but it looks mighty like a bridge,
don't it? Maybe the general's fixin' to sneak off
to Carolina. You'd have to ask him to be sure."

Soldiers planning to abandon the helpless cit-
izenry? Vee would go wild if she heard that;
matter of fact, Hattie was not reassured. She
fled up one of the serpentine wagon roads leading to Bay Street and rushed on to the open-air
market on Ellis Square.

Under a shingle roof resting on brick pillars,
the wartime market typically offered a few
caged chickens, a basket or two of onions or
sweet potatoes, and now and then shrimps and
crabs some brave boatman brought in from
neighboring creeks. Hattie's arrival was well
timed: a burly blue-black shrimperman was just
emptying a sweetgrass basket onto a table.
Hattie hurried to reach it ahead of a paunchy
gentleman with the disdainful air favored by the
well-to-do. She asked the price of the shrimp,
then said, "I'll have half a dozen, if you please,
sir."

"Yes, miss." The shrimperman put the shrimp
into her tin pail while the paunchy gentleman

harrumphed and spoke pointedly to no one about the manners of the younger generation.

"Thank you, sir." Hattie paid and curtseyed. She flashed her sweetest smile at the paunchy gentleman, whose eyebrows flew up while his mouth fell open.

Outside the market she spied pallid and slow-moving Sparks Parmenter. Sparks was twenty, wore a special built-up shoe, and bobbed to the right at every other step. She called his name and caught up with him in Congress Street.

"How are you, Sparks? Is the Pulaski House ever so grand?"

"Pretty grand but pretty expensive. Ten dollars a day for one room. We moved to the City Hotel."

"Have you heard from Legrand?"

"Not a word. Friend of Pa's said Sherman sent a colonel into town under a white flag demanding unconditional surrender. They expect Hardee will say no. You know what that means."

"I don't — tell me."

"Why, we're sitting ducks. Hardee's bottled up." Evidently Sparks knew nothing of the strange boat bridge; Hattie didn't mention it. Sparks continued, "Lee's fighting in Virginia and hasn't any relief troops to send. Sherman's certain to mount a frontal assault across the causeways, torch the town, and turn his men loose to pillage."

"Oh, the beast. When will it happen?"

"If you look out the window and see buildings burning, you'll know."

"My heavens," Hattie exclaimed with a shiver so pronounced, it made her curls bounce. "Can we do anything?"

"No, nothing. Nothing."

"Well, you take care of yourself then, Sparks. Say hello to your folks. We're at Miss Rohrschamp's house near Wright Square. Please come tell us if you get any word from your brother."

"Like him a lot, do you?"

"Why, he" — Hattie practically strangled, finding her excuse — "he's a friend. Just a friend. I'd be as anxious about you, or anyone I knew."

"Sure you would," Sparks answered with a crooked smile that reflected his sour view of life. Hattie stood there with flaming cheeks while he limped away. She ought not be too critical of him. She didn't know how it felt to be unable to run or jump or climb trees.

Back at Miss Vee's, she delivered an edited version of Sparks's unsettling statements but withheld news of the boat bridge. Sara said, "Well, let's not make ourselves miserable waiting for the inevitable, if it is inevitable."

Vee wrung her hands. "There will be outrages — no woman safe, be she eight or eighty. Excuse me while I check the windows." First, however, she checked herself in a hall mirror — patting her hair, smoothing her skirt before hurrying on. Sara put a hand over her mouth to suppress a giggle.

While their benefactor was out of the room, Sara showed Hattie something Vee had discovered in her attic — an old issue of *Godey's*. She opened it to the crafts page. "Isn't this grand? Complete instructions for making a Father Christmas out of pine cones. There are plenty of those lying around town, and we must have some Christmas decorations, Sherman or no Sherman."

Hattie agreed to search the neighborhood. She collected two dozen pinecones, but her heart wasn't in it. She kept reliving Christmas seasons before her father died, when the slaves came up to the house to receive big sacks of pecans, hard candy, and red apples, and Ladson Lester presented them seed for their own garden plots, plus three dollars apiece and a communal fir tree strung with popcorn. One year a married couple sang "Mary Had a Baby" so beautifully, everyone cried. The Lesters, including Hattie, didn't differentiate between black and white, slave and free, not on those faraway, sharply remembered Christmases, anyway. Hattie wished they would come back. Though still a devout rebel, she had read enough, listened enough, to develop an uneasy feeling that slavery was wrong, and finished. She'd never admitted that to anyone except Sara, who agreed.

Saturday night passed with no attack by the minions of the feared Union general. On Sunday morning they tidied up and walked north on Bull Street to Miss Vee's place of worship, Christ Church on the east side of Johnson Square. The church was high Episcopal, presided over by the Bishop of Georgia, the Right Reverend Elliott. Sara didn't know of a Congregational chapel in town, and Hattie supposed she could pray for Legrand in one house of God as effectively as in another.

Holding her mother's hand and marching up one of the two staircases leading to the handsome Ionic portico, she felt her spirits lift, her fear of a sudden bombardment melt away in the mild air. They squeezed into a pew on the right of the aisle near the middle. In the front pew, left, sat Judge Drewgood, his wife, Lulu, and their children. Napoleon was swiveling his head this way and that to observe latecomers jostling into the balcony surrounding three sides of the sanctuary.

Vee attracted sidelong glances when she maneuvered onto the kneeling bench with an excess of gasps and wheezes. Sara, unfamiliar with the ritual, remained seated. Hattie tried to shrink and hide. Napoleon craned around, spied Hattie, and began yanking his mother's sleeve. *We're in for it now,* Hattie thought.

December 18, 1864

Bull Street, Savannah

Miss Vee had informed her guests that Bishop Elliott's stance as a religious leader veered between Confederate zealotry and Christian compassion. He wanted everyone in the parish to do his or her part, whether collecting food for the troops, rolling bandages, or providing nursing care to those who came home wounded or maimed. He no longer prayed for President Lincoln, instead for "Thy servant, the governor of Georgia." Yet he prayed for a swift and merciful end to the debilitating war.

Today the Bishop seemed more healer than warrior; his sermon began with the advent of the Christ child and segued smoothly to forgiveness of enemies as exemplified in the life of the adult Jesus. He quoted the Sermon on the Mount, *Blessed are the peacemakers, for they shall be called the children of God.* He reinforced his argument with Proverbs 24:17, *Rejoice not when thine enemy falleth, and let not thine heart be glad when he stumbleth,* and Proverbs 16:7, *When a man's ways please the Lord, he maketh even his enemies to be at peace with him.*

Many in the packed church reacted with scowls, interpreting the message as acceptance of defeat. Hattie found it all rather murky, as she did most religious discussions. She couldn't picture Jesus sitting down for a chat with General Sherman.

At the conclusion of the service she followed her mother and Miss Vee out of the sanctuary while the shiny-pated organist in the gallery showed off with a noisy Bach chorale. The judge sped down a side aisle ahead of his brood, elbowing male and female parishoners alike; he cornered his quarry outside, at the foot of the steps.

"Ladies, ladies! How delighted I am to see you." He was the picture of Christian rectitude in a suit of sober black. He tipped his beaver hat and bowed so low, Hattie could imagine his nose scraping the sidewalk. "Sara, it's indeed a comfort to know you're in Savannah and not isolated out on the river."

"Very thoughtful of you to say so, Judge. Miss Rohrschamp kindly extended the hospitality of her house."

"And a good thing too," the judge declared. Hattie noticed the Drewgoods' carmine depot wagon parked among carriages and pony carts in front of the church. Old Adam held the reins as usual.

Napoleon slipped an index finger up to his nose, saw Hattie watching, and canceled his explorations; he turned a furious red. Lulu trilled, "Children, say hello to Sara and Miss Rohrschamp. And let's not forget dear Hattie."

"Oh, definitely not," the judge said, managing to sound both pious and insincere.

Merry was quick to offer a greeting, but squinty Cherry only mumbled while gazing elsewhere.

The judge stepped in front of Sara to capture her attention: "I hope you realize the seriousness of our situation. There is no telling when or how Savannah will be attacked. I've written a letter to the *Morning News* announcing that I for one stand foursquare for compromise and conciliation, to prevent our homes from being looted and leveled. But who knows whether Sherman will be in a mood to listen to cooler heads? While that issue is being resolved, Yankee vandals are surely rampaging in the countryside. They say the cavalry of that devil Kilpatrick is raiding south into Liberty County. No doubt the enemy has overrun Silverglass, wouldn't you suppose?"

"It's possible," Sara replied in a guarded way.

"Then all the more reason for you to be receptive to my purchase offer. What would a lady of your gentle disposition do if the Yankees burned the plantation?"

"Why, I'd rebuild it, somehow."

"You have no means, no capital."

"I'd find the means and capital."

That wasn't the answer he craved. His pumpkin-colored eyes drew down to slits. "Being stubborn will only invite tragedy. These are violent times. What if something unpleasant happened to you? Something debilitating — incapacitating?"

"At the hands of the Yankees?"

"Or someone else. We have our own criminal element."

Sara stared him down. "Judge, those are strange words. Should I interpret them as some kind of threat against me?"

"Interpret them how you will." So quick and fierce was his outburst, Lulu whispered orders for Cherry to run to Adam and have him ready the wagon. "I want to buy Silverglass, and I want you to sell it to me."

Sara smiled. "Never. And may I say, Judge, that is the most audacious and presumptuous salesmanship I have ever heard. The matter is closed."

"You think so? You wait." He boomed it in his courtroom voice; the after-church crowd heard him and flowed away from them like the Red Sea parting. He clapped his tall hat back on his head; his little white goatee quivered. He bade them a sharp good morning and propelled Lulu away from the church by wrenching her elbow.

Merry walked more slowly. Hattie darted after her. "Psst, Merry." She crooked a finger. Merry leaned down so Hattie could whisper. "Have you heard from Jo Swett?"

Merry's eyes misted. "No, and I'm so afraid for him. There's no telling what Papa will do if Jo appears. Thank you for caring to ask."

Giving Hattie's hand a squeeze, she answered the judge's peremptory summons and hurried off. Napoleon had already jumped up beside Adam and jerked the reins away from the slave.

"That Drewgood is a viper," Miss Vee declared as she gathered up her hoops to prepare for their walk home. "All he really cares about is property, his and yours. Do you think he's capable of surrendering to Sherman rather than resisting?"

With a doleful expression Sara said, "Alas, I fear he's capable of anything."

At twilight Hattie sat on Vee's front steps, her skirt tucked under her legs, her chin resting on her palm in a pensive way. The military encampment in Wright Square seemed to have settled into an unusual quiet. Maybe all the soldiers were collectively holding their breath, awaiting a Union onslaught.

Distantly, an artillery piece boomed, scaring a spotted hound that went racing past. In the parlor, Miss Vee warmed up with several arpeggios, then launched into "Listen to the Mockingbird," wildly popular a few years ago. Hattie cocked her head, puzzled; Vee was playing the song more slowly than usual. Maybe the whole of Savannah was holding its breath.

Two barefoot Negro girls, eight or nine, paused outside the gate. One smiled at Hattie in a shy way. The other tugged her arm, but the first girl insisted on waving. Hattie returned the wave. The girls passed on into the smoky orange dusk.

Hattie wondered where they lived. She imagined a hovel with no food on the table, pallets of ticking in place of beds, and certainly no toys or other personal belongings. From there it was only a short leap to thoughts of Christmas, a mere seven days away. What kind of celebration would those children enjoy? She suspected it would be poor, for them and all the children of the town. With shortages of everything — including coal — even the stockings of little beasts like Napoleon would be empty. She felt a pressing obligation to do something about it. But what?

At that moment she glanced up. Without making a sound, a soldier had approached along the sandy street. She supposed he was a soldier, although he wore soiled and torn civilian clothes. What prompted her conclusion was a clean white rag tied around his left thigh and a padded crutch under his left arm. Visibility in the dusk was poor, but there was something familiar about —

"Legrand? Sakes alive, is it you?" She dashed down to the street and threw her arms around him.

December 18 to 20, 1864

Savannah

The hug lasted no more than a few seconds; Hattie skittered back, wild with embarrassment.

Her friend was peaked and weary, no longer the "mere boy" of yore. A heady masculine odor surrounded him like a vapor cloud. Bay rum? Or — frightful thought — dressing for his wound? Who had wounded him? What horrors had he seen? "Legrand, where have you been?"

He wasn't offended by her foolish question. "The past two days, I've been at the City Hotel, recuperating. Sparks told me you and your mother were here."

"Come sit down, rest." She tugged him toward the stairs. He gritted his teeth and hobbled up the steps as fast as he could. Hattie dusted the stoop for him. Legrand needed almost half a minute to sit down with the aid of the crutch.

"Were you wounded something awful?" Hattie asked.

"It's a lot more hurtful than dangerous — that was the surgeon's verdict."

"But you saw the elephant, didn't you?"

"And then some."

Hattie thrilled to hear him admit it. She hitched over near him and lowered her voice. "Did you see anyone — you know — pass over?"

"You mean die? I saw plenty, every one of them cold as a wagon tire."

"Ohhh." Hattie shuddered. "How did you get hurt? Tell me everything."

Legrand proceeded to do that, in quick sentences that tumbled one over another. On the night Fort McAllister fell, a Union shell had struck the outer wall of his fort, blown it to pieces, and hurled him backward off a ladder. He landed on his spine and the back of his head, saw a few colored lights, and when he sat up, he discovered a long thick dagger of wood from the rampart sticking out of his left thigh.

"That's when it started to hurt. I passed out for a while. They sent me home the next night."

"Walking?"

"Yes. Wasn't easy, either," he said in a stoic way. He was the complete heroic veteran, grit personified. Excited, Hattie opened the front door.

"Mama, Vee? Come see who's back, safe and sound."

Minutes later, Legrand relaxed at the dinner table, basking in the adulation of three females and shooting rapid answers to questions from the two adults. Night had come; Hardee's rumbling artillery reddened the windowpanes. Sara said, "You've confronted the enemy, Legrand. What's your estimate of our chances of defeating Sherman?"

"Zero. You'll sooner catch a weasel asleep. We're goners unless Hardee opens that pontoon bridge to civilians. There's talk of it, but nothing for sure." He consulted a tarnished pocket watch. "I'd best go now."

"Come again tomorrow," Hattie said. "There's ever so much to discuss."

Legrand hesitated. Then came a twitchy smile

115

— the first smile Hattie had seen since he returned.

"That sounds hugely appealing," he said, and went out.

Next morning, Monday, Legrand returned as promised. He invited Hattie to accompany him to the river, where Hardee's escape bridge was rushing to completion.

The second span was in place between Hutchinson and Pennyworth islands, with a third and final section building to the Carolina shore. The river vista teemed with men, white and black, lashing and anchoring boats, unloading wagons of brush and straw to lay a firm path across Hutchinson Island, piling a carpet of rice straw on the nearest bridge section. "To damp down the sound of horses and men," Legrand said.

A Confederate ram, *Savannah*, smoked and steamed in a circle a short way downstream from the construction. Locally built, she was a queer vessel, her shape reminding Hattie of an iron turtle shell with the addition of a smokestack. Distant artillery banged away, staining the air with smoke and rattling windows along the main streets. Hattie had grown used to the racket. She could sleep soundly through it and in a curious way found its regularity comforting. That would end if the defending army slipped away to Carolina.

On their way back to York Street, a commotion at Hupfeldt's General Merchandise on Bryan Street attracted their notice. Hupfeldt himself, a spiky-tempered Swiss, was hopping up and down in front of a door hanging by one hinge and seizing hold of any person he could force to listen. Hattie and Legrand fell victim.

"Look at this expensive door — ain't it a disgrace? Nobody does nothing. I lost my whole stock of slates and pencils last night. I was going to sell them to bring holiday joy to youngsters. Grown-up thieves broke in, stole everything, and nobody does nothing — they're too busy hammering up those pontoons."

While attempting to disengage, Legrand agreed it was a shame. Hattie smiled at the store owner. "Did those slates and pencils come through the blockade, sir?"

Hupfeldt grabbed Hattie's shoulders. "Are you accusing me? Are you saying I deal in contraband, is that what you're saying, little girl?"

"Here, leave off," Legrand said. He poked his crutch tip at Hupfeldt's chin. Hattie lunged backwards and freed herself. Legrand wasn't exactly speedy, but he kept up a good pace with Hattie leading him.

As they retreated, Hupfeldt was still hopping up and down and shouting: "Tell me that girl's name, I'll put the law on her" — in midsentence he slumped — "if I can find any."

Out of reach of the retailer, Legrand paused to catch his breath. "I didn't know toys were so scarce. Guess I didn't think about it much."

"You were too busy being brave. Yes — I mean to say no, there aren't any toys in the shops. I'll bet that man wanted to sell his slates and pencils for a terrifically gouging price." A memory of the two little girls standing in the gloaming came then. "I'll make some toys. I can sew and whittle. Miss Vee surely has old scrap material on hand — she sews some of her own clothes. Not every child in Savannah will have a toy, but I'll take care of as many as I can."

Legrand leaned on his crutch, regarding his friend in an admiring way. "Tell you what. I don't sew, that's girl's work, but I can whittle. I'll help you if you want. No sense all of Savannah being miserable come Christmas morning."

"Even if Sherman's camped on the doorstep?"

"Even then," Legrand said with another jaw-clenching display of grit.

Throughout the afternoon, Hattie and Legrand ransacked the house for materials to turn into stuffed dogs, cats, and rabbits. A rag bin yielded the makings of dolls. Legrand roamed nearby vacant lots and returned with an armful of stakes from an abandoned garden. Vee surrendered a small hoard of walnuts for doll heads, porcelain heads not to be had at any price.

Hattie and Legrand surveyed the accumulation in a corner of the parlor. They agreed to devote Tuesday to starting their toy manufactory. "When will we deliver them?" he wanted to know.

"Christmas morning. We'll visit houses and ask if Saint Nicholas came during the night."

"For most places you already know the answer."

"Yes, and that's when we'll hand out a present."

"What if the Yankees are here? What if they forbid it?"

"I'll kick their shins if they try."

Legrand left laughing.

After dark, a barrel-bellied sergeant with strong whiskey breath ran along the street knocking at every door. "By order of General Hardee, in the morning the pontoon bridges to Carolina will be open to civilians, up until a deadline at sunset. If you want to escape, it's your chance. Good evening, ladies."

Vee and her guests convened in the dining room, where Vee's best whale-oil lamp threw shadows on the walls. Vee opened the discussion bluntly. "Do we stay or go?"

"How do you vote?" Sara said. "This is your house, after all."

"I'm deathly afraid of the Yankees, but I was born and brought up in Savannah. I've never lived anywhere else. I vote stay."

"I would say that too — I want to see Silverglass again. I particularly want to keep it out of the clutches of Judge Drewgood, and I can't do that if I pole off to another state. You can vote too, Hattie."

Hattie thumped the table. "Stay. I'm going to catch at least one Yankee and thrash the daylights out of him."

Sara didn't laugh at her daughter's militancy. She and Vee clasped hands across the table. Hattie grew bold and laid her smaller hand on theirs. No one stirred or spoke there in the darkened room with three forbidding shadows printed on the walls.

The exodus began Tuesday morning. Wagons and carts rattled up Bull Street, piled perilously high with carpetbags, trunks, pet cages, chicken coops. Entire families rode or walked. Legrand arrived at half past nine to report. "They're crossing by the dozens."

"Well, let's not pay any attention — we have work to do," Hattie said. She told him of the unanimous decision to stay.

"My folks cast their lot the same way, though I think Sparks would go if he could."

Sounds of flight were almost continuous as Hattie plumped herself down cross-legged on the parlor carpet and set to work. Her talent for handicrafts served her well. By noon she'd sewn and stuffed a denim dog, two calico cats, and a paisley pig; Vee's stockpile of sewing scraps was extensive. Sara cheerily joined in, seated in a rocker and gently humming to herself while she snipped apart a coarse sack. From the pieces

120

she stitched mantel stockings. Legrand whittled the garden stakes into passable swords and nailed a short hilt to each.

Miss Vee gave him two small blocks of pine wood; his blade flew. A crude locomotive emerged from the first block. Hattie applauded. Legrand held his creation near the window, inspecting it.

"Needs paint."

"Isn't any," Sara said, sewing without looking up. Passing through on her latest inspection of locks and latches, Vee overheard.

"I suppose I can give up my pen and ink. The ink is my own formulation — extract of magnolia and certain secret ingredients. Will that help?"

"Yes ma'am."

"A lot," Hattie said, showing one of the rag dolls with a gnarled walnut head. "I can put a face on her."

So the afternoon passed, with Hattie taking time only to walk Amelia, then water the pig and feed her some old cabbage leaves. Toys accumulated in a large wooden box previously used to store Vee's collection of sheet music. A clock on an ornamental shelf near the Chickering upright chimed four. From the direction of the river, cannon opened up again. "The ironclad," Legrand declared.

As the daylight faded, louder salvos rumbled and thundered from all points of the compass. Vee brought in a scrawny evergreen cut from the backyard. "I suppose we need a tree, however meager." With Legrand sawing and nailing, a flimsy base was made, strong enough to hold the little tree upright in a basin of water. It didn't look anything like a traditional tree; it was rotund, bushier on one side than the other. Vee brought an engraving from a magazine and pinned it to the top of the tree. "Robert E. Lee," she said, in case they couldn't identify the stern white-bearded person.

The parlor windows continued to shimmer with the ruddy light of artillery fire. Legrand reached for his crutch. "I want to see the bridge."

Hattie ran to him. "I'll go with you."

"Is it safe?" Sara said, leaving off the assembly of another stocking.

Legrand said, "She'd be safe with me, Mrs. Lester. But she can't go without your permission."

Sara relented, and Hattie and Legrand hurried off through the red-lit dark. Shadowy figures filled the streets, rushing every which way. The youngsters stopped a block east of Broad Street and from there watched platoons of ragged men march down to the straw-covered boat bridge. The lines seemed to stretch on and on into the darkness. Legrand waved his crutch.

"I recognize some of those boys. General Wright's men. The left wing's leaving first. What a sad night."

Hattie couldn't hear the tramp of the retreating troops. She understood the reason for the deafening Confederate artillery barrage. "They're all going, aren't they?"

"They are," Legrand agreed.

"We're unprotected."

"Totally."

"What will they do with the cannon, haul them away?"

"Spike them and leave them. I expect they'll burn the turtle ram and a lot of other boats."

"It's too horrible. I think we'd better go back."

"I think so too."

Cold dank fog was settling over Savannah's spires and rooftops. Hattie longed for the comfort of Vee's kitchen hearth. As they turned the corner into Whitaker Street, pistol shots cracked a block to the south. Glass shattered. Legrand seized Hattie's left hand with his right, neither of them quite realizing it was the first time he'd touched her that way.

"Someone's looting a store. Quick, turn around. Go faster," he said over the sudden staccato thumping of his crutch on the plank sidewalk.

December 20 and 21, 1864

Bay Street — York Street

They fled east on Bay Street, then south. On Bull Street they ran into an Irish gang, young toughs rampaging through the fog, tossing stones and nasty epithets at dimly lighted windows. One laid hands on Hattie. "Here's a morsel. Give us a kiss, little girl?"

"Not on your life," Hattie said, giving him instead a sock on the jaw.

This was entirely unexpected from one who looked so tender; his startlement allowed her to separate herself and elude him. She dragged Legrand away while her victim recovered and began reviling her in language to make a stevedore redden.

In Johnson Square, someone had started a bonfire bright enough to reveal the gargoyle faces of other looters battering a town-house door and baying for entry. Hattie and Legrand escaped notice and arrived panting in front of Vee's house.

"Bad night," Legrand said. "I'll stay to protect you and the ladies."

"No, you get back to the hotel, and your family."

"Does Miss Rohrschamp own a gun?"

"I don't expect so. She's an artiste."

"Then find a shovel, a poker — anything. Bar your doors. Lock up your pig. I have a feeling some of these desperadoes were waiting for this chance."

The rising wind dispersed the fog but chilled the skin. Hattie's stomach hurt. "You've changed, Legrand. You're a lot — well, older."

"Guess we all are. *Transmogrified,* that's a

good word for it. You be careful now. Good night." Off he went, hobbling.

Pistol fire and hallooing echoed across the city. Hattie ran up to the stoop. The door refused to open — Vee's handiwork. Hattie beat on the door with both fists. Sara answered. She raised a lamp to light Hattie's face.

"Thank heaven. We've been so worried. I shouldn't have allowed you to go."

"Legrand took care of me, but there are robbers out. The army's gone."

Hattie paused long enough to hug her mother and repeat her friend's advice about weapons of defense, then sped on to untie Amelia. She pulled the pig inside and left her snorting in the kitchen with a chair bracing the door shut. Vee might complain, but Hattie would worry about that later.

She took the kitchen poker to the parlor, where Vee hid the piano bench by sitting on it. Vee's forlorn eyes gleamed in the reflection of Sara's lamp. "What are we to do?"

"Stay awake, all night if need be," Sara said. Her reply was punctuated by doors splintering and looters shouting somewhere nearby.

"Who is out there, Hattie, the colored?" Vee asked.

"Didn't see any. I recognized some Irish, but I expect anyone with empty pockets is running wild tonight." Her eye fell on the box of toys. "I better hide those."

"Under my bed," Vee said. Hattie gave her the

poker, which looked about as useful as sewing thread in the hands of the quivering piano teacher. Hattie hurried the box to Vee's bedroom and slid it out of sight. In the kitchen, Amelia's protests had grown frantic.

"You calm down, Amelia, you'll be all right."

The pig squealed louder to dispute this. In the other bedroom, glass tinkled onto the pegged floor. Someone's heavy boots came over the sill, *ker-thump*. Hattie bolted back to the parlor, closely pursued by a young tough wearing hobnail boots, a checked shirt, and a piratical scarf around his forehead. He was scarcely older than Legrand — a wan, cadaverous specimen of Savannah's poor. His open clasp knife flashed in the light of Sara's lamp.

Vee let the poker drop. She flung up her palms to fend off the intruder. "Get away, get away. You shan't possess me."

"I don't want you, you old bag of blubber. I want your rings. I want your silver. I want your cash. Hop to it."

Sara said, "Hattie, do show the gentleman where everything's hidden."

At first Hattie didn't understand her mother's peculiar request, or the way Sara's eyes darted to the unlit hall. The young tough screwed around on his heel to look that way. Hattie caught on.

"Oh, yes, sir, follow me." She slipped by the felon. Behind his back, Sara quietly set the lamp aside and picked up the poker.

The thief detected a moving shadow. He pivoted again, but not in time. Sara laid the poker across his shoulder. He squealed louder than Hattie's pig.

Both hands on the poker, Sara pounded the robber's wrist. After the second blow, the knife flew into a corner. The thief gaped at the fragile woman with mayhem in her eyes. He ran back into the room where he'd entered and was gone.

Vee shook mightily, not quite sobbing but close to it. Sara handed the poker to Hattie and knelt by her friend. "There, there. No one's hurt. Just a window broken."

"But how many more will come before morning?" Vee's round face glistened despite the night's deepening chill. Hattie collapsed on one of the imitation Sheraton chairs with the poker between her knees. Atop the crude little Christmas tree, Robert E. Lee observed them with manful dignity. Somehow the sight of him made Hattie want to bawl. She resisted.

Sara soothed and calmed her friend. The squeals from the kitchen grew less strident. The night wore on, noisy with running, shouting, shooting — the ravaging of an undefended city by the dispossessed.

Around one o'clock, vandals overturned the backyard necessary and dug in the garden for ten minutes, presumably hunting for buried silver. Finding none, they went away.

The next two hours were comparatively

127

peaceful. About three in the morning, Hattie followed her mother outside to gaze at the red sky to the north. Boats burning on the river? The last desperate act of General Hardee? Could this be but four nights before Christmas Eve? Hattie thought of Christmas as something remote as the moon, never to be enjoyed again.

Only next day did the temporary family hear of events elsewhere, courtesy of some of Vee's neighbors and the *Savannah Republican*, which said in part, "By the fortunes of war we pass today under the authority of the Federal military forces." Around 4 A.M., the mayor, Dr. Richard Arnold, had ridden toward the advancing foe with several of Savannah's aldermen. Arnold carried a white flag.

Unfortunately a half dozen unhorsed stragglers from Joe Wheeler's cavalry caught them on the Augusta road and stole their mounts. The civic delegation met the Union advance on foot. Undaunted by the indignity, the mayor presented his petition. "Strongly influenced by the Christmas season," he said, "we earnestly request protection of the lives and private property of the citizens, especially our women and children."

At Sara's urging, the three left York Street at first light. Sara said that, weary though they were, they should be witness to a significant, if not necessarily shining, moment in Savannah's history: the arrival of the victors. They made their way up toward Bay Street, Sara with the poker in hand.

Hattie's blue eyes were big and round when she saw how the looters had devastated the neighborhood. Glittering chips of broken windows lay everywhere. A torched brougham, overturned, smoldered and reeked of charred wood. A Negro lad hawking papers advised them not to venture down to the wharf: gangs of white and colored were hunting for hidden stores of rice and brawling in the process.

By the imposing granite Custom House, Vee exclaimed, "There's music." Hattie heard it, distant cornets and flutes swelling with the strains of "The Battle Cry of Freedom." Snare drums riffled and thrummed. Stunned citizens watched silently from the walks and Bay Street's central promenade.

The first of Barnum's brigade of Geary's division marched out of Broad and into Bay. Flag-bearers led them, carrying bright divisional banners and the Stars and Stripes to which Lester Ladson and his family had once sworn allegiance. The band appeared, then the first of the conquerors — Westerners, sun-browned men, many with long beards. They kept cadence; some even chanted the obnoxious lyrics of the march — *"The Union forever,"* and *"Down with the traitor, up with the star."* Hattie covered her ears and made a face until Sara ordered her to desist.

"Captured." Miss Vee shuddered. "Humiliated, by rabble."

Sara showed the copy of the paper she'd bought. "Don't fret so. It clearly says our property will be respected by the military rulers."

"Yes, but what about our persons? Our *persons?* I can't believe those men will respect womanhood." Hattie frankly didn't care. She was spent, wanted nothing so much as a handful of rice and a pillow.

The music grew louder. The soldiers passed, looking fit, ill-clad and beaming at the crowds — smiling or smirking, Hattie couldn't decide. Shortly, across the street, the national colors appeared atop the three-story brick front of the Exchange. Hattie nestled against her mother's skirt and took comfort from Sara's hand stealing around her, protective and reassuring.

She yawned. Where was Sherman? When would she lay eyes on the man who had brought so much grief to Georgia? He came like an evil Saint Nicholas sent from the netherworld. He should be treated as such.

December 21, 1864

Pine Woods, Liberty County

Just as dawn light roused the York Street household, Tybee Jo Swett came awake in a forest bordering a country road not far from the city. Without opening his eyes he inventoried his condition:

Belly, empty. Skin, chafed and scratched from skulking through cotton and potato patches, pine woods, and salt marshes, all to avoid main roads. Temperature, definitely on the cold side; farm clothes he'd stolen from a drying line were too thin for December. Taken in total it was discouraging, but in no way turned him from his purpose — a return to Savannah, to hand the pious, sneering Judge Drewgood a memorable surprise.

Jo had lived on his own for more than a decade. His father, the first Tybee Jo, died when he was eleven, leaving him sole heir and possessor of a fishing boat, a handsome, sail-rigged craft with a deep well for fresh catches and thole pins for oars in case the wind fell off.

By spring 1861, Jo had matured into a handsome young man. He supported himself by fishing the offshore banks and reefs. He sold mackerel and red snappers to an agent of the Confederate commissary department and thus justified his failure to enlist right away; he was already doing his part in the war, though he had little taste or sympathy for it. Few Tybee fishermen owned even one slave. Jo paid a burly freedman the sum of twenty cents per day to sail out as his helper. The freedman's former owner, who had manumitted him, had christened him Oglethorpe. Jo called him Ogie.

Ogie lived in a small neat shack within sight and sound of the ocean both of them loved. Ogie and Jo became strong friends, though Jo was footloose and Ogie had settled down with a comely young wife, Marie; together they produced twin boys.

Ogie and Marie often invited Jo to visit and share supper. Marie cooked a delicious she-crab soup, and the two friends watched the pot bubble while Jo dandled one of Ogie's sons on his knee and Ogie dandled the other.

Both men continued to express displeasure over the war and those who had caused it. Georgians generally disliked the South Carolina hotspurs who thought they could leap on their blooded horses, gallop off waving plumed hats and sabers, and be home in time for eggnog at yuletide, having won the independence of a new Southern nation.

Alas, it wasn't that simple, or that short. Union ships appeared off the Georgia coast; they were likened to an anaconda looping its coils around the whole Confederacy, to squeeze the life, and the commerce, out of it. Tybee Jo was one of many driven onshore, the alternative being to keep venturing out and risk loss of his fishing boat and possibly his skin. Jo's boat went into a dry dock yard and Jo went into Savannah, there to pick up work as best he could.

He started as a checker on the river wharf, employed by a wealthy Bay Street factor, the Englishman Mr. Green. Jo tallied outbound cotton shipments, cargo for blockade runners sailing by night for Hamilton, Nassau, or Havana. Jo figured the job was temporary; inevitably he would be pulled into the service, the Confederate navy his preference. This was the situation in the autumn of 1862 when, at age twenty-two, he chanced to meet Merry Drewgood.

Pretty Merry broke the heel of her boot while doing an errand on Bay Street. Jo was sprawled on nearby grass, lunching on two ersatz oysters, which were mostly fried green corn and flour. Coming along at a quick pace, Merry stumbled and would have fallen if Jo hadn't jumped up and caught her; thus he had reason to introduce himself. Merry was a womanly nineteen, educated, and obviously several social cuts above a Tybee fisherman. It made him want her all the more.

Jo was yellow-haired, smiled beautifully if he felt like it, and displayed the bruised knuckles of someone who fought often. Yes, he was a little too eager to right any fancied wrong — he had a temper — but Merry didn't discover that until she was in love and didn't care.

They confined their meetings to trysts in Laurel Grove Cemetery or bowers in Forsyth Park, well away from the multiplying army tents. Merry said it would be best if Jo didn't visit the Drewgood residence. Besides, meeting in secret made their romance all the more heady and thrilling.

One night Merry's squint-eyed and jealous twin sister, Cherry, trailed them to Forsyth Park to spy on them. When Merry arrived home, she was hailed into family court in the Drewgood sitting room. The judge badgered her into tearfully revealing all she knew about Tybee Jo Swett, including the fact that she loved him and would do so until her dying hour.

Jo lived in a little room attached to a livery stable. Sheriff's men broke his door down at night, "discovered" a pistol among his few clothes, and removed him to the imposing County Jail, four stories of yellow Savannah brick. Jo demanded to know the charge against him. Answer: He'd made threats, in person, against the head of the Drewgood family.

Jo protested that he'd never even met the head of the family, or owned a gun. One jail guard shrugged and said the judge had affidavits confirming the threats. Jo angrily denied his guilt. The other guard used a hickory truncheon to cool Jo's temper.

From a cell it was but a short trip to the courtroom of the pumpkin-eyed judge, who waved the so-called affidavits in Jo's face. "You are trash — a nobody, presuming to press your sordid attentions on a refined and innocent young woman."

"Your Honor, I never heard the word *sordid* before, but if it means something bad, something dirty" — the judge began rapping his gavel — "no, sir, my regard for your daughter is of the highest — uh — cleanliness —"

"Silence. I order you to be silent."

But Jo's famous temper was up. "And when it

134

comes to pressing attentions, why, Miss Merry was pressing as hard as I was pressing, the one time I stole a ki—"

"*Stop.* Bailiff, seize him. Milledgeville! Fifteen years!"

The longtime orphan languished in the state prison, there to dream of Merry and think up elaborate, temporarily unworkable schemes for escaping and returning to Savannah to settle up with the man who had separated them. Outwardly Jo was a well-behaved prisoner unless insulted or bullied by guards or another inmate; inwardly he seethed.

In mid-November 1864, all prisoners were abruptly herded into the main yard where they were addressed by Georgia's gaunt and gangly governor, Hon. Joe Brown. Though a Yale-trained lawyer, the governor was known as "the Cherokee County Cow Driver" because of his countrified ways. Plainly fearful of Sherman's army advancing on the poorly protected state capital, Brown offered to commute the sentence of any man who volunteered to fight. Jo was among the first of a hundred or so who stepped forward. Thus, still in his penitentiary stripes, he was enrolled in the governor's "prison militia."

Jo wasn't sophisticated politically, but his quasi-military duty convinced him that the state legislators, and Brown, were a bunch of cowardly charlatans. The convicts loaded so-called state property onto a special train hired by the legislators to run down to the rail junction at Gordon. The "state property" included household furniture, trunks of fancy clothing, hat trees, stuffed bear heads, a harp, a cut-glass chandelier, and other goods that had nothing to do with laws the legislators left half-drafted on their statehouse desks. The governor announced that the special train would go "directly to the front," but how women, children, French brandy, tins of potted meat, or a harp would be put to use in combat, no one explained.

Jo had no intention of sacrificing himself for such chicanery. Wasn't the cause lost anyway? Lee was on the run, Atlanta a scorched ruin. For two days Jo feigned diligence and enthusiasm, but as soon as he was issued a musket, ammunition, and a uniform, he slipped away. In the country he found a likely farm, rid himself of the uniform, and stole less incriminating garments from the clothesline. His purpose remained clear and bright as a flame in his resentful heart.

So here he was, within a few miles of his goal, in heavy underbrush that smelled of pines and the pungent dampness of the low-lying coastal plain. He could hear distant cannonading. In the night he'd been wakened by a large body of Federals moving seaward on the corduroyed road. Jo assumed it would be no more difficult to sneak into a Union-occupied city than one defended by his own side.

He brushed his clothes to remove clinging pine straw and dirt. He picked up the stolen slouch hat crushed into an inadequate pillow. He ignored the grumblings in his middle, crept forward, and parted the palmettos for a peek at the highway.

Deserted. Birds called; random beams of daylight fell from the east. He debated whether he'd be safe using the road, and in that moment of concentration failed to hear stealthy footfalls behind him. Suddenly two Confederate soldiers were on him, one with a stout tree branch for a club, the other showing him a two-barrel revolver. The second reb, ugly as a bad dream and slightly cross-eyed, spoke for both:

"This here piece is a LeMat, which I took off the corpse of one of Joe Wheeler's dead lieutenants. This here barrel" — the lower one — "is loaded with grapeshot. It can tear that pretty face of yours apart if my finger twitches, you got that?"

Jo nodded to assert that he got it.

"All right, then. Turn out your pockets."

"I don't have a penny. Besides, I'm on your side."

The reb spat. "Nobody's on our side no more. We run off from Old Joe's cavalry when my cousin Varner took a Yankee ball in the chest. Right then's when we made our own private peace treaty." The other one, whom Jo assessed as none too bright, giggled.

"Now do like I tell you — turn out your pockets." The soldier poked Jo's stained wool blouse with the gun muzzle.

Jo's eyes flashed. "Don't prod me."

"I'll prod you any dang way I please." He did it a second time.

If Jo hadn't been so chilly and hungry, he might have held his famous temper. Instead, he kicked the soldier with his prison shoe and at the same time boldly grabbed and pushed the gun barrel with both hands. The soldier yelled, "Hey!" His trigger finger jerked. The gun bucked in Jo's grasp, but it was aimed past his hip; the shot merely tore bark from a water oak.

"I didn't come all this way to be robbed," Jo said as he wrenched the gun from the soldier's hand.

"Lord have mercy, he means to kill us," wailed the second reb. He ran like the devil, back the way he'd come. Jo waved the revolver.

"Go on, follow him, before I really get mean about it. I'll count five. One, two —" Between *three* and *four,* the would-be thief disappeared in the dark green gloom. Jo let out a breath, shivering with shock.

Then he recalled where he was, and why. He saw Merry's sweet face; her father sneering down from his judicial dais. He'd make that old man sorry he ever concocted lies to incriminate Tybee Jo Swett.

He hid the LeMat revolver in the waist of his

trousers and tugged the slouch hat lower over his eyes. He set off toward the rising sun, and Savannah, his righteous anger renewed.

Camp of the 81st Indiana, 5:15 P.M.

Toward dark, Alpheus Winks drove the forage wagon into the regimental campsite near the western city limits. His horse plodded behind, tethered to the tailboard. The wagon held a small load: a bushel of sweet potatoes, half a bushel of onions, two pumpkins long past their prime, a dispirited rooster in a cage. Among the acquisitions sat Zip, who'd taken the reins most of the day. He was practicing his blasted birdcalls. Whether brown thrasher, mockingbird, cardinal, or purple martin, to Winks they mostly sounded alike — twitters and wheeps, trills and squawks.

Winks's exasperation with Zip was nearly limitless. Why had he allowed this fellow to attach himself, leechlike, and follow him everywhere? He despised Negroes for what they'd done to his family, though he had a certain reluctant liking for Zip personally; it had sort of crept up on him after Ebenezer Creek, while he was, so to speak, busy elsewhere.

Was it possible to like the person and dislike the race? Winks wasn't sufficiently educated to answer the question. His head hurt when he tried. His head hurt now.

His weary men dismounted and dispersed as Winks reported to the regimental adjutant. After Captain Gleeson listened to Winks's recital of the inventory, he said, "I call that scanty, Sergeant. Scanty in the extreme."

"No help for it, sir. Countryside's stripped clean as a baby after a bath." Winks saw no point in telling the steel-hearted officer that he'd undergone a personal change on the long, slow scour of the country while riding down to the coast. What produced the change was the imminence of the holidays and the increasingly brutal poverty of the hamlets and farms the bummers visited. They had so little, these Georgia people. Nowhere was it more evident than a cropper's shack where Winks found a gray-faced woman digging in the hard clay with a bent table fork. From the saddle, he asked, "What are you doing that for?"

The woman looked at him with exhausted eyes set deep in a worn face. "Trying to find bullets. Hear tell there's a Confederate kitchen in Savannah gives you food if you turn in lead."

"I never heard of it, but if it's so, I expect the kitchen's closed up. Savannah's captured, or soon will be."

"Oh, mercy." She dropped the fork and wept.

Winks waved to forestall the advance of his men waiting on the road. The number had been reduced to four: Chief Jim, Privates Pence and Spiker, and the professor. The sixth soldier, a malingerer, had gored his foot with his own bayonet, possibly on purpose. Regardless, he was dispatched to the invalid corps.

"We've got okra and a little molasses we can leave with you, ma'am," Winks said. The woman began to bless him, weeping harder.

Riding away, he ordered Professor Marcus and the others to go light on what they took from now on, and to take nothing if the civilians appeared to be near starvation. This inevitably displeased certain of the men, most noticeably Professor Marcus.

Captain Gleeson left off scowling, having made his point. "I suppose I owe it to you to say you and your detachment have performed well during most of the campaign. Let it rest there." The captain gestured to dismiss him.

"Beg pardon, sir, but the city's ours, isn't it?"

"It is, utterly. General Geary's charged with setting up the policing — curfews, patrols to arrest drunken or disorderly soldiers — Geary was mayor of San Francisco, you know. He won't have things organized for a day or two, so keep your men reined in."

"Yes, sir. I was wondering, though — is Uncle Billy in Savannah? Never have gotten a close look at him."

"General Sherman to you, soldier. He's up at Port Royal, conferring. I understand he'll arrive tomorrow."

"Well, he's got a mighty nice Christmas present in his stocking anyway."

"I'm sure he's thought of that," Gleeson answered with mordant sarcasm. "Now if you're done quizzing me and sharing your opinions, I have twenty reports to write. And don't let me see that ridiculous hat I know you're hiding behind your back."

"Sir, yes, sir." Winks clicked his run-down heels and snapped a salute.

Outside in the winter dark, Winks fished a stubby cigar from his shirt pocket. The strong-smelling sulfur match barely warmed the insides of his cupped hands. A few snowflakes floated past his nose. The fields of Putnam County, Indiana, often lay white from November until April, but this place, which was supposed to be the sunny southland, was pretty near as cold tonight.

He walked through the camp to the cook fire Zip had laid for roasting sweet potatoes. Winks sat down opposite him.

"Do anything for you, Captain? Shine your boots?"

Crossly, Winks said, "I'm tired of telling you. I'm not a captain."

"It's a term of respeck. I still polish your boots if you wish."

"No."

"Lay down your bedroll? Fill your canteen?"

"Not necessary."

"Anything you want me to do, then?"

"How about joining the pioneers? How about getting out of my sight?"

"Oh, no, sir. I got to pay my debt first. It's a big debt. The biggest."

"Well, I hereby declare it canceled."

"No sir, sorry, I'm the one's got to decide when, as, and if it's canceled. Meaning no disrespeck."

Winks's bad mood cracked and crumbled under an onslaught of weariness. How could you hate such a willing, cheerful darkie, particularly this time of year? Once, several days back, Zip had boldly asked him the reason for his all-too-evident dislike of the colored race.

It was the closest Winks came to snarling out the truth: "White men are dying by the thousands for you and your people. Wouldn't be any war, any vacant chairs, wasn't for slavery." The reference to a popular song eluded Zip, so the conversation lapsed.

"How about a hot tater?" Zip pulled one from the embers, held it out on the point of his stick.

Winks gave in: "Don't mind if I do." He grasped the stick, took a nip of the potato. A few more snowflakes settled among the flowers on the crown of his tall hat. His carpet cape wasn't much protection in this weather, but the warm potato was delicious.

Chief Jim appeared and squatted by the fire. Winks asked, "Where's the rest of the boys?"

The big Indian with the shiny black hair hiding his collar seemed reluctant to answer, but he did. "Moseyed into town — Pence and

Spiker and the professor. Professor said they wanted to get acquainted with the locals. Gauge their mood, now they're whipped. Said they might call on one or two."

"Blast. I know how the professor calls on people. He didn't have permission to leave camp. None of them's got permission."

"Yes, sir," Chief Jim muttered, acknowledging the truth of it.

Winks briefly considered mounting up and riding after Marcus and his confederates. He decided against it; probably couldn't find them and if he could, the way things were going lately, Marcus would likely thumb his nose. He'd hear about their antics tomorrow. It meant a night of worry.

Zip began a series of two-note whistles that sounded like *tee-you, tee-you*. Winks glanced across the fire. Zip interpreted it as sincere curiosity.

"Tufted titmouse."

"Aw sure, I should've known. You can do something for me now."

"Yessir?"

"Go practice somewheres else."

Downcast, Zip tossed his stick in the fire and shuffled away. More snowflakes drifted into the light and melted. Winks suddenly felt lower than a snake. Even Chief Jim had developed a sudden interest in the starless sky, embarrassed.

Miss Vee's, 9 P.M.

The bummers were drawn to the house by golden windows, soft piano music — "Silent Night," slow and sweet — even by the painted siding. "Shows care for the property," Professor Marcus remarked. "Fence isn't falling down neither." Many Savannah fences were; for all the town's mossy charm, there was wartime blight and rot if you looked closely.

Marcus gigged Peter Pence. "Scout the place, Private."

Pence disappeared down York Street. Marcus and Spiker kept to the shadows; behind them, Wright Square was strewn with the detritus of Hardee's men; no doubt the space would be used for a campground again, by a different army. Despite the hour, Union troops, ambulances, wagons, artillery limbers were everywhere, marching or galloping, with many an officer visible. Not one had challenged Marcus and his men. He'd instructed them to stride at a fast pace, as though under orders. In this way they'd arrived in Wright Square after scouting and bypassing five other houses.

Each of Marcus's bummers had a virtue, and a use. Private Spiker's round choirboy face enabled him to worm into places without arousing suspicion. Private Peter Pence's bulk and overhanging brow hinted at a pea-size brain, but he never hesitated to shoot first and think about it later. The professor had played to their avarice, emphasizing the wickedness of secession, the maniacal militarism of Jefferson Davis, and the treachery of Southrons generally. This justified robbing any household. Marcus had done his work successfully, behind Winks's back, once the sergeant had gone soft by banning liberal foraging and tolerating a nigger's presence. Marcus's propaganda worked on all but the Wisconsin Indian, whom Marcus considered a fool.

Marcus and Spiker stamped and slapped their arms in the bitter dark. Wind blew occasional snowflakes in their eyes. Peter Pence returned in ten minutes. "Had to sneak up the kitchen stairs. I spied ladies and a little girl, but nary a man. They's a pig, though. I had to make friends to keep it quiet."

Marcus stroked his chin. "Excellent. I'll bet those females have Christmas presents aplenty for needy fellows like ourselves. Let's not hesitate. 'Glue your courage with the sticking plaster,' as the immortal bard wrote."

Peter Pence said, "How do we go in, bust down the door?"

"Nothing so crude. We combine encirclement and an attack from the rear with a strong frontal assault." The professor laid a comradely hand on Spiker's shoulder. "Frontal assault. That's you. We'll back you up. Forward, march."

Miss Vee continued to play. In the kitchen, where a few sticks of fatwood in the hearth provided a feeble light and a meager heat, Sara sat on a stool in the midst of old newspapers, shredded rags, and a bowl of thin paste made of water and precious flour. She was layering the paper and rags together. When it dried into pasteboard, she would shape it into some sort of crude toy.

Hattie sat across from her at the kitchen table, carefully using the home-brewed ink to create eyebrows on a doll's head made of walnut shell. A clownlike ink smear tipped Hattie's nose. All of them were roused, with varying degrees of alarm, by rapping at the front door.

"It's so late, I wonder who — ?" Sara began.

"We don't want to know," Vee cried, hurtling away from the piano to be sure the bolt was secured. Hattie and Sara dashed into the parlor as Vee peered through the opalescent glass. "Oh, heaven. It's one of those Yankees. You know what he wants."

"We have no idea what he wants, Vee. May I look?"

Vee stepped aside; Sara peered into the winter night. "Why, he's just a boy. Harmless-looking. We should see why he's come."

Vee clucked dubiously but drew back the bolt and opened the door six inches, admitting a rush of cold air that set the lamp flames dancing in their chimneys. The soldier in the soiled blue talma looked only slightly older than Legrand. He touched his cap with his knuckles.

"Howdy, ma'am, sorry to disturb you. My

canteen's empty, could you spare some water for a thirsty soul?"

Vee pondered briefly. "Go around to the backyard, there's a pump if it isn't frozen." She started to shut the door. The boy lunged and rammed the door open with his shoulder. Vee staggered back, falling against Sara while Hattie scrambled to stay away from the tangle.

The young soldier sprang into the room, baring his teeth and whipping an Army Colt from under his cape. "You ladies just stand still, don't cause no trouble, and everything'll be hunky dory."

The back door burst open; two more men ran down the hall and leaped into the parlor. They, too, had sidearms drawn. Vee's sizable legs started to wobble.

Sara jumped to her aid, managed to guide her to the piano bench. Hattie was mesmerized by the mole-spotted face of the corporal to whom the other two deferred. He was stoop-shouldered, homely; she caught a whiff of him and pinched her nose. "Whew."

The corporal seized Hattie's curls and yanked. "What do you mean, 'whew'?"

"I mean you ought to bathe once in a while, you smell worse than — ow, ow!"

The corporal flung Hattie aside. "Boys, I do believe we stepped right into a nest of rebs who need a comeuppance. Search the place. See what they're hiding." He wigwagged his revolver, and the other two, a burly one and the choirboy, ran into the back hall. "You three, sit down."

"Do as he says, dear," Sara whispered. She pulled Hattie to her side on a love seat. "Vee, compose yourself. Possessions aren't worth your life."

"If — if — if possessions are all they want," Vee sobbed, just as a terrific crashing and smashing from the kitchen set Hattie's heart pounding. The burly soldier ran into the parlor with Hattie's box of handmade toys.

"Professor, looky here. These dirty rebs are tryin' to have Christmas."

Marcus peered into the overflowing box, pulled the string of a crude jumping-jack Legrand had helped Hattie whittle and assemble. "We'll put a stop to that."

He gestured three times before the slow-witted soldier caught his meaning and set the box on the floor. Professor Marcus lifted his boot. *Crunch, crack* — "No presents for little traitors, no sir."

One of Hattie's carefully inked walnut heads popped off and rolled. All of her handiwork was rapidly stomped to bits. Hattie would have punched the awful corporal if Sara hadn't restrained her with strong hands and warning looks.

Professor Marcus dusted his hands, surveyed the room. He snatched Bob Lee's engraved portrait from the top of the little Christmas tree. Several quick rips reduced Lee to confetti.

Hattie cried, "How dare you insult a fine soldier that way?"

"We'd do worse than that if we had Old Marse Bob here in person. Boys, where's that porker?"

"Tied outside," said the burly soldier.

"Bring her on in."

"I — uh — turned over an ink bottle back there in the kitchen —"

"Doesn't matter. Get the pig."

Hattie heard Amelia squealing before she saw her. The soldier pulled the pig into the parlor by her tether. "Don't you dare hurt her," Hattie said, this time successfully escaping her mother. She kicked the burly soldier's shin. He shouted for help, and Professor Marcus pointed his revolver at Hattie.

"I never plugged a child before, but you're tempting me. Shut your clapper and quit abusing my men."

Sara caught Hattie's skirt from behind, drew her off. The burly soldier tied Amelia's rope to the leg of a chair. The pig had managed to trample in the spilled ink, thus tracking and staining the carpet. Marcus stroked his chin. "That's a mighty nice pork roast on the hoof. Or pork chops. Or barbecue."

"Say, we'll have a party," the choirboy said. He laid his revolver atop the Chickering, sat down on the bench and began to play clangorous chords, clearly demonstrating he'd never had so much as five minutes of musical education. Marcus pulled out the hem of his uniform blouse like a lady's skirt and performed a series of shuffling dance steps timed to the music.

Egged on by Marcus, the choirboy stepped up on the bench, then the keyboard, then the top of the piano cabinet. At this point Miss Vee collapsed sideways and fainted dead in the middle of the inked carpet. On top of the piano, head bent to clear the pressed tin ceiling, the choirboy danced a step or two, then peered down at his leader.

"Chop this up for kindling?"

"Make a mighty swell bonfire," the burly soldier said. Hattie felt dizzy in the confining crook of Sara's arm. She'd never imagined anything so horrible as this invasion, this desecration —

The choirboy jumped all the way from the piano top to the carpet, rattling the lamps and window lights. "Leave me look around for a hand ax, Professor."

Professor Marcus raised his hand. "Wait. I got a better idea."

They all held still.

"Sometime back, second day out of Atlanta I think it was, there was a piano in the house of some traitors we visited. Winks wouldn't let us take it. Later a lieutenant told me we could've sold it for plenty if we could've moved it. We're going to find a way to haul this instrument out of here, boys."

The end of his speech brought an interruption to swivel every head and fasten every eye on a new arrival stepping in the front door.

"Well, now," said Capt. Stephen Hopewell, not cordially.

Pulaski House, 9:15 P.M.

A bit earlier, Stephen enjoyed an unexpected reunion when he walked into the saloon bar of the four-story hotel on Johnson Square. "Hallo, Davis," he said to the man from *Harper's Weekly*.

"Hopewell. Greetings. What are you doing?" Davis's blank sketch pad lay on the table beside an empty stein.

"Waiting for the first mail boat to arrive."

"So's the whole army. The men are dying to know whether Aunt Maud had to sell the farm or beautiful Nell said ta-ta to her soldier fiancé and found another."

"I haven't heard from my editor in weeks." Not that he was particularly eager to receive more of Plumb's acerbic messages, but he had to earn his wage. "I have dispatches to send."

The room was noisy, smoke-laden, the bar lined with officers congratulating one another on the splendid news of Gen. George Thomas's victory over Hood at Nashville five days earlier. Beyond the dining room archway, an assortment of civilians were swilling at the hotel's public table. Cotton speculators and others

153

eager to take advantage of the misfortunes of war, Stephen suspected.

"Cold night. Mind if I sit?" After a welcoming gesture from Davis, Stephen unfastened the black silk frogs on the front of his cloak coat, doffed it, and took a chair. "What are you doing?"

"Waiting for Sherman. They say he won't arrive until tomorrow." He noticed Stephen's eye on the scarred upright piano in a corner of the room. "Do you play?"

"Some." He didn't know the *Harper's* man well enough to reveal that his last engagement in New York, three nights, 9 P.M. until dawn, was filling in for the ailing colored professor at Madame Celia's Bower of Bliss, a notorious establishment in the Five Points.

The waiter approached. "Order, sir?"

"Do you have real coffee?"

"Indeed we do, sir, genuine Brazilian, though I'm not at liberty to say how or where we got it."

"Fine." The waiter left. "Uncle Billy planning to make the hotel his headquarters, I understand?"

"I was told so. He'll change his mind when someone on his staff checks the tariff. The owner hails from Vermont — a first-rank Yankee penny pincher. I don't expect the hero of the hour to fork up government money for room and board. He'll expect it gratis."

So he wouldn't be able to witness the arrival of General Sherman tonight. Lingering at the

Pulaski House, while pleasant, wouldn't be particularly productive. When he'd drunk his coffee — dark, fragrant, the real article — he thanked Davis for his hospitality, threw on his cloak coat, and set off.

Riding his mule down Bull Street on his way to his temporary bivouac in Forsyth Park, Stephen was on Wright Square's east side when noise and commotion on darkened York Street drew his attention. He turned Ambrose that way and moments later gazed with astonishment at a first-floor window. A soldier appeared to be dancing atop the polished case of an upright piano. There were male voices raised in coarse merriment, and the oinking of a pig.

The man leaped off the piano. Stephen dismounted, certain he'd seen the cavorting soldier before. Soldiers had no business in a civilian house. He tied Ambrose to a picket and slipped through the gate.

He eased his Belgian revolver from under his cloak coat and stole up the stairs. He interrupted the party by bolting through the door suddenly and saying, "Well, now." It wasn't original, but it was spontaneous, expressing his surprise and dismay at the disorderly scene before him.

A pig squealed and yanked on its rope knotted to the leg of a chair. An unlovely little tree, presumably for Christmas, lay overturned. A large, very large, woman reclined on her side, unconscious but breathing like a factory bellows. A pretty but distraught young woman with straw-colored hair hovered near a child with snapping blue eyes and long curls. Ink blotched portions of the carpet, which was further disfigured by a litter of rags, broken sticks, crushed walnut shells and scraps of paper; on one scrap Stephen recognized a mournful eye that might have belonged to R. E. Lee.

Three Union soldiers were ranged about the room in attitudes of confusion (the hulking and angelic ones) or hostility (the homely one). Although the men carried sidearms, they were disinclined to challenge an officer.

"I've met you boys before. Quite a few miles back, wasn't it?" Stephen addressed Marcus. "As I recall, you were wearing earrings. Do you fellows make a habit of abusing those weaker than you?"

It was the choirboy who protested. "Sir, they're nothing but rebel trash."

"They don't look like trash to me. They look like respectable Georgia citizens — harmless members of the fair sex." All but that moppet, Stephen thought; she was gritting her teeth and glaring like a regular little harridan.

The stout woman on the floor was gradually waking with a series of moans and eye-flutters. The pretty woman hurried to her side, helped her sit up as Stephen continued, "We'll find a broom and a bucket of water so you boys can clean up this mess."

"No, no," cried the stout lady, fully awake.

"Don't let them touch a thing with their unclean hands. Make them leave. I was certain they were going to outrage us." The homely corporal snickered.

The pig bolted one way, then another, displacing the chair each time. Stephen said, "Little girl, can you quiet that animal?"

The moppet stuck out her chin. "These men scared her half to death. They threatened to cook her for barbecue."

The pretty woman soothed the child, patting her, speaking gently. "Please try, Hattie. Take Amelia outside. Feed her."

Hattie slitted her eyes at Stephen in an unfriendly way, but she obeyed the older woman whom he guessed to be her mother. Quite a handsome creature, excepting her wartime pallor and general state of disarray. Stephen liked most of the Southern women he'd met — charmingly soft-spoken, with a faintly exhausted air, as though perpetually suffering from the heat. He had no illusions about what lay beneath the facade: iron. Southern women managed to conceal it graciously, in contrast to many New York females who aggressively bashed you over the head with their wants, whims, and opinions.

The young woman blew loose wisps of fair hair away from her eyes. "Go on, please, Hattie." The child untied the pig's rope and drew her into a hall leading to the rear of the house.

"Thank you, ma'am. My name is Captain

Hopewell. May I ask the nature of those broken objects?"

"Toys. My daughter and a friend made toys because the stores are empty. These — gentlemen — smashed them."

Stephen waved his Belgian pin-fire. "Let's have your name and unit. You first, Corporal."

Marcus responded with silence. The others cast uncertain looks at their leader. Stephen cocked his revolver.

"I can't hear you. Speak up."

The homely one cleared his throat. "Marcus O. Marcus, Eighty-first Indiana. Sir."

"Next."

"Private Peter Pence, same."

"And?"

"Private Melancthon Spiker, ditto."

"When we met before, you were part of a detail led by a sergeant wearing a silk hat decorated with flowers." Marcus's sneer showed Stephen that the sergeant had no direct role in this, nor did the ugly perpetrator like him.

"All right, gentlemen, now we can begin to clean up. Private Spiker, straighten that tree and pick up those broken toys. Corporal Marcus, you and Pence sponge the carpet."

Vee intervened: "Oh, no, please just shoo them out of here."

"But we should put the room in order. Then we'll discuss appropriate charges."

"This is my house. I don't want to bring charges. I just want to get shed of them."

Sara stepped forward to wrap the heavy woman with a comforting arm. To Stephen she said, "It has something to do with Christmas, I think."

Stephen addressed the stout woman. "You own this house, is that correct?"

"Yes, I am Miss Rohrschamp."

To Sara: "Are you a relative?"

"A guest. Mrs. Lester is my name." Stephen's heart went plummeting; belatedly he spied the plain gold ring on her left hand.

The girl, Hattie, slipped back into the room. She advised her mother that Amelia was safely tied outside. Stephen said to Marcus, "Corporal, you and your men march out of here before these good ladies have a change of heart. Return to your camp. If you try to run off tonight, I personally guarantee we'll have every spare cavalryman on your trail. We will resolve this tomorrow."

Corporal Marcus slashed the air to signal his comrades to the door. He managed a last muttered thrust. "Ain't anything to resolve. We was only foraging liberally, per Uncle Billy's orders."

The open door brought another rush of December air. The would-be looters talked loudly as they hurried down the steps. One of them, probably the ringleader, laughed. Stephen slid his weapon out of sight. "Should have turned them over to the provost guard. Unfortunately there isn't one just yet."

"You behaved very gallantly, Captain," Sara

said. "I doubt we have anything more to fear from that rabble. Two of them were following orders of the homely chap, and he struck me as a coward, only brave when facing adversaries who are weaker, and outnumbered. We thank you for intervening."

"Oh, yes, we do," Miss Vee agreed. "Allow us to give you a little refreshment. I think there's a tot of peach brandy in the pantry."

Stephen knew he should excuse himself, but the prospect of a warming drink and a chance to converse further with the fair-haired young woman overcame his sense of propriety. Besides, there was that shiny piano — a Chickering, not badly hurt by the marauders except for heel marks and tiny clumps of mud all over the case.

He realized he still wore his black felt hat, remedied that with a swift apology. "Very kind of you, Miss Rohrschamp. You too, Mrs. Lester, but I wouldn't want to intrude on you or, ah, your husband."

"My husband passed away in the service of the Confederacy some time ago."

"My sincere condolences. I'll stay a moment, then. A sip of peach brandy would be welcome."

Miss Vee had recovered her Southern manners. "Take off your coat, won't you? Sit down there — that's the most comfortable chair. We'll clean the carpet in the morning. I'll be right back."

Which left Stephen alone in the parlor with the widow Lester and her daughter.

He couldn't decide which he wanted to get next to faster, the young woman or the Chickering. He certainly didn't want to get next to Hattie, whom he'd classified as a gold-plated brat. She looked on with arms folded, her scowl reminding him of black thunderclouds on the eve of a storm sure to be destructive.

Miss Vee's, 9:45 P.M.

While Vee foraged for brandy in the back of the house, Sara studied their visitor, and not without a certain nervousness. There were two reasons: Hattie's unconcealed dislike of Yankee uniforms and all who wore them, and Sara's own admiring appraisal of their benefactor.

Rather awkwardly, he perched on the edge of the chair Vee had chosen for him. He had swarthy good looks, by no means ideally handsome, but pleasing. His voice was a hundred percent Yankee: nasal to a degree that grated on her ears. He told her that he was one of several news reporters attached to the army at the War Department's insistence. He worked for a paper called the *Eye*, in New York, and she supposed that explained a lot about him.

"You were raised there?"

"No, upstate, but I've been in the city for many years."

"I've never seen New York."

"A pretty fascinating place. Rough some-times. The people are pushy, nervy, because they're crowded together. They knock you down if you're in their way. Still, underneath they're like people everywhere, grumpy or kind, according to the circumstances. New York's the capital of everything — finance, music, theater, social striving, crime, vice — everything."

"I don't believe I've actually met someone from New York before this."

That produced a broad smile; he stretched out his booted legs and relaxed. "Well, contrary to the stories they're dispensing in Richmond, those of us above Mason and Dixon's line don't have horns and forked tails. We do have strong disagreements with you Southern folk about the unbreakable union and your, ah, peculiar insti-tution — isn't that what you call it?"

Sara quickly moved Hattie from her stool and pointed her toward the kitchen. "Do see whether Vee is finding that brandy, dear. Our guest is thirsty."

Hattie gave Stephen a look and departed. Sara said, "I'm sorry she's not sociable. She's quite the little rebel."

"So I have deduced." Stephen's careful reply was designed to acknowledge the truth of the statement but without giving offense. Not only was the captain reasonably good-looking in a Mediterranean sort of way, but he was also in-telligent — Sara didn't know any men who slipped words like *deduced* into conversation. Polite, too — he and his army were the new masters of Savannah, but you would hardly know it from his behavior.

Sara sat down opposite him. "I should imagine it's lonely for any soldier, being away from his family this time of year."

"True. It's melancholy even when you don't have someone at home. In Canandaigua, that's a pretty little town up near Lake Ontario, my only relatives are two cousins and a maiden aunt. I don't see them often."

No wife, no children; she'd gone fishing just as he had a while ago. She changed the subject. "Those men you drove off — will they be disciplined?"

"Mrs. Lester, I'd be less than honest if I said it's a certainty. I'll do everything I can, but there are a good many in the Union army who feel that Southerners are the only ones needing punishment. Then there is the necessity to move forward with this campaign. It takes precedence over everything. General Sherman badly wants to invade South Carolina and reduce it. Misbehavior of the kind we saw may be swept under the carp—" With a sheepish smile, he finished it by saying, "Overlooked."

Vee, with Hattie right behind, sailed into the parlor carrying a teacup and a stoneware bottle. "Here we are, here we are." Vee uncorked the bottle ceremoniously. "I hope you care for the taste of peaches?"

"Oh, absolutely." Stephen accepted the tea-cup and took a generous sip. "Delicious."

Having decided the officer had no designs on her, Vee warmed to him. "Captain, until tonight, we wouldn't have believed a man on your side of this war would come to our rescue."

While Stephen modestly basked in the compliment, Sara added, "I only wish we could offer a more tangible reward for your kindness."

A pointed silence ensued. Sara didn't understand it until she noticed his dark eyes fixed on the Chickering upright. "Permitting me to sit and play would be a more than ample reward."

Vee said, "Oh, do you play professionally?"

"Wish I could claim that. I fill in occasionally for others."

Enthralled, Sara exclaimed, "Fill in? Where?"

"Oh, ah, various venues. Social clubs where gentlemen congregate. I wanted to train for the concert stage, but my parents were too poor for lessons. Also, I found out at a young age that I wasn't really suited. I'm too easily diverted by life's pleasures. I may be a trifle lazy — I've been accused of it by my editor." His grin banished any possibility that he thought it a serious fault. "How would you feel about it, Miss Rohrschamp? May I?"

"You may, you may," she trilled. Grinning, Stephen took his place on the bench.

He flexed his fingers. He folded the music

rack down, then raised it. He shifted slightly to the left. He pushed up the cuffs of his clean but unadorned sack coat of army blue.

"Allow me to play an anthem for you. This terrible schism that's taken so many lives on both sides will soon be over, and we'll all be saluting the same flag again."

Before Hattie could blurt that he'd better not include her in his predictions, Sara laid an index finger across her lips. Stephen launched into "The Star-Spangled Banner," played loudly, with many a flamboyant shake of his curly black hair. At the end of the piece, the ladies applauded, more politely than enthusiastically.

"All right, here's something perhaps more to your liking. A man named Dan D. Emmett wrote this for his minstrel troupe. Four years ago, the Lincoln Republicans picked it up as their marching song. Somehow it migrated down this way." While Sara was still sorting out those facts, Stephen struck the first notes. To the piano he added a pleasant baritone. *"Oh, I wish I was in the land of cotton —"*

Sara joined in. *"Old times there are not forgotten."*

Vee pressed one fist to her bosom and with her other hand saluted the heavens while making it a trio: *"Look away, look away, look away, Dixie's land."*

They sang all the verses, Sara clapping with the beat, Vee raising her hems high enough to allow her to march to and fro. When the song ended, even Hattie clapped.

Momentarily downcast, Vee said, "Is that really a Northern Republican song?"

"Really" — he nodded — "though like so many other parts of history, I expect that'll be forgotten."

Her throat curiously dry, Sara asked Vee for a sip of the peach brandy. Vee was surprised but sent Hattie to fetch another cup. For the first time in many a month, Sara felt deliciously secure and happy, due to the presence of this intriguing man from New York. Stephen took a deep breath.

"What a treat to play again. I thank you sincerely. I must be moving along, but I can't leave without a song of the season. How about this one?"

He played the opening bars of "Jingle Bells." Miss Vee pounced. "Wasn't that written in Boston?"

"Yes, by a Reverend Pierpont, a Unitarian, I believe. He composed the song in 1856. We were still one country then," he added with a trace of testiness. "Is the geographic origin of a song important to you, ma'am?"

"Of course it isn't," Sara said before her friend could mention her boycott of compositions by abolitionist clerics. "This is the season of forgiveness. Play, Captain. Play and we'll all sing."

Sing they did, softly at first, then with more

fervor and volume. By the second stanza even Vee seemed to enjoy herself. The exception was Hattie, who sat on her stool with her arms crossed, refusing to join in despite piercing looks from her mother.

Shortly afterwards, Stephen bade them good night. What lingered in his mind as he rode south through the occupied city were the broken toys, the visions of empty Christmas stockings they conjured.

Sara also had things on her mind. The captain's merry smile. The joy he found in his music, poured out for all to share. Her own surprise at liking a Northerner even a little . . .

Mysteriously, Wordsworth intruded: favorite lines from an 1807 poem about a wood dove's plaintive cooing.

> *He sang of love, with quiet blending,*
> *Slow to begin, and never ending;*
> *Of serious faith, and inward glee;*
> *That was the song — the song for me!*

The house lay still; turmoil in the city had died away. Hattie breathed lightly in the trundle bed below. All at once Sara felt guilty and foolish. She mustn't betray her dear dead husband. She'd have no more truck with the enemy, no matter how charming.

December 22, 1864

Camp of the 81st Indiana

Stephen rode his mule through the city next morning. The air remained cold, the wind less like the expected Southern breeze than like a December bone-chiller blowing across the Hudson palisades.

Conquered Georgians — women, youngsters, grandfathers, veterans with bandaged heads or padded crutches — filled the sidewalks, going about their business as if no army of invaders had come to town. It contrasted with Atlanta, where Stephen had composed dispatches about scenes of fire, riot, misery — thousands abandoning the city on Sherman's order, dragging their belongings through muddy streets, fighting or bribing their way into wagon convoys bound south to the railway depot at Rough and Ready.

Despite the morning's activity, in every street and square he saw signs of suffering. Artillery had demolished the roof of a small doctor's building, rendering the surgery unusable. Nothing remained of a stable but black timbers fallen like jackstraws on a carpet of ash. A cracked window in a cottage displayed a thin wreath of evergreen; a scarlet ribbon added a touch of faded color. As Stephen jogged by, an old man carrying firewood raised a free hand, not friendly so much as to acknowledge Stephen's presence, the army's presence, without a visible demonstration of wrath.

Christmas, Stephen thought. *Whipped as they are, starved as they are, they're catching the spirit.* He wished he could.

The season and temporary respite from the march affected the occupying troops. They joshed and sang "John Brown's Body" off-key as they marched or rode in the sandy streets. The encampment at Forsyth Square, where he'd spent the night in a wall tent with Davis of *Harper's* and two temporarily unemployed telegraphers, buzzed with anticipation of arriving mail, newspapers, back pay, passes for sightseeing: this was a city, after all, a quaint one that looked nothing like the prairie hamlets of Illinois and Iowa. Already Stephen had been invited to a scheduled horse race, a Christian fellowship meeting, a high-stakes card game, a boating excursion on the Savannah. Sherman's army was in fine spirits; it had won through to the sea with minimal losses and showed determination to reward itself with a festive yuletide.

At headquarters of the 81st Indiana, he was directed to the adjutant, Captain Gleeson. The captain was discovered in his blue trousers with his galluses down on his hips; he was about to start his morning toilette with a razor and scrap of soap. Stephen inquired about men answering the description of Marcus and his cohorts. The captain told him where they could be found: Sergeant Winks's forage detail.

"Winks? I have a feeling I've met him. Tall skinny fellow? Wears peculiar clothes?"

"A great many of our foragers array themselves like peacocks. It's tolerated. Winks is a Putnam County rustic — you can't expect good taste. At least in Indianapolis we have a modicum of civilization. Winks was an exceptional forager until recently. As we drew closer to Savannah, he brought back less from each venture into the countryside. Why do you want him?"

"I happened along when his men invaded a private house on York Street last night. They did a goodly amount of damage before I drove them out. Winks must hear about it."

"Their commanding officer too."

"Let Winks take care of that. May I ask, sir — do you happen to know when General Sherman arrives?"

"This morning, later." Gleeson waved his razor in lieu of returning Stephen's salute, then turned to address his whiskers in the small mirror hung on a nail. The mirror was a triangle broken from a larger silvered glass; Stephen didn't want to know how Gleeson got it.

Following the captain's directions, he passed between tents laid out in the usual soldierly grid. At the junction of two aisles he nearly collided with Private Pence. The looter gaped, whooped, and ran.

He soon found Winks's wedge tent, two halves laced together over a ridge pole and staked at the sides. The front flap was up. Stephen overheard a colloquy between a handsome young Negro in old clothes and the long-haired sergeant who carried on conversation while patching a dingy suit of underwear with a square of red flannel. He used a needle and thread from a little leather housewife lying beside his camp stool.

Stephen remained outside the tent, unnoticed, while Winks said, "I never swallowed an oyster and don't suppose I'll start now."

"Captain, you ain't never tasted a truthfully rich an' delicious oyster pie like I can bake up for Christmas dinner."

"First you'd need oysters, wouldn't you?"

"Yessir, but —"

"And to get them you'd need a rowboat, I assume?"

"That's gospel truth, but —"

"And before any of that you'd need a pass permitting a darky to roam freely, so —" Stephen stamped his feet as though to restore circulation.

The sergeant saw Stephen, and his shoulder straps. "Sir!" He threw aside his sewing, tried to stand and salute at the same time; he had to stoop to avoid the ridgepole. "Beg your pardon, we didn't notice you there."

Stephen ducked to enter the tent. "At ease, Sergeant. I'm here about some of your men who stepped seriously out of line last night."

"Zip, this here's a private talk." The dismissal

sent the colored boy scuttling. Winks swiped a hand across his forehead, though how anyone could sweat in this cold, Stephen couldn't imagine. Winks stood two or three inches taller than Stephen, and looked down at him, but with due deference. "Um, which men might those be, sir?"

"Their names are Marcus, Pence, and Spiker."

"Oh, Jehoshaphat. My rotten apples. I been fixing to ask the colonel to get rid of them and sign me up a new crew if we're to forage over in Carolina."

"You may do more than replace them when you hear about their treatment of helpless women. Sit down, I'll tell you the story. Then you can decide who else hears it, and what punishment those men deserve."

Winks hunkered in the center of the tent; his gesture invited Stephen to take the stool, which he did. "I seen all three of those boys in camp this morning."

"I should hope so. Last night I sent them back with strict orders to stay put. I promised they'd be pursued and driven to ground if they ran. I encountered Pence a few minutes ago. Evidently they believed me."

"Or they figured what they did wasn't all that serious?" Winks fished in the pocket of his blouse, found an unsmoked cigar, which he offered to the visitor.

Stephen took it. "Thanks."

Winks struck a wooden match on his boot

172

and lit the cigar, then a stub for himself. The two men sat in the midst of turgid blue smoke. The wind had died; the calm sharpened the constant noise of the camp.

"You decide whether it's serious," Stephen said in a way that clearly indicated he'd already rendered his verdict. Beginning with his arrival outside Miss Rohrschamp's, he described subsequent events. Winks's wind-reddened face showed attentiveness, then astonishment, and lastly anger.

"Those blasted rotten no-goods."

"It seems to me that you were tolerating that sort of behavior the first time our paths crossed, Sergeant."

"I admit it, sir. I've changed some since then. You meet an' talk with enough starving folks, things look different. I'll take care of those boys, Marcus first — he's the ringleader."

"Don't you want to turn it over to your commanding officer?"

"Not till I take steps on my own."

"Then I leave it in your hands."

Winks bit down hard on his cigar. "You didn't say much about them ladies you rescued."

"There were three, starting with a piano teacher, Miss Rohrschamp. She owns the house. Her guests are a widow named Lester and the widow's daughter, eleven or twelve. I don't mind saying I was quite taken with the widow."

"That so?"

"Lot of good it did me. The widow's husband died in the war, which would account for her reaction to this uniform. Also, I'm from New York."

"I thought you talked funny — no offense meant."

"Nor taken. The widow lady was cool as the polar ice cap. A mighty disappointment."

"Daughter feel the same?"

"If anything, more so. At least the widow was polite. The child, Kitty or Letty or Hattie or something like that, was distinctly unfriendly."

When Stephen pressed a bit, Winks was evasive about the exact steps he'd take to discipline his men, probably because he was still working it out. Stephen rose to go.

"Who's the colored boy wanting to bake an oyster pie?"

"A pest name of Zip. I pulled him out of Ebenezer Creek 'cause he couldn't swim. I should've thrown him right back. He trails after me like a pet dog. Drives me out of my mind practicing fancy birdcalls all the time."

"Well, whatever his faults, don't be too quick to reject his offer. Oyster pie can be tasty. You might find you like it."

"I might," Winks said, clearly meaning *I won't.*

Stephen returned Winks's salute and left.

Pulaski House — Charles Green Manse — Pulaski House — Miss Vee's, 10:30 A.M. to 4 P.M.

Stephen rode back to town on faithful Ambrose. Although the morning was scarcely half gone, much had changed since he left his bivouac in search of the looters. Armed pickets patrolled the streets. In the squares, soldiers with mauls were nailing up shanties and pegging down tents in scenes reminiscent of the Confederate occupation. General Geary had taken charge; a nightly curfew, 9 P.M., was already posted.

Outside the Pulaski House he expected to see horses with regulation army saddles. He saw none. The desk clerk said the general and his retinue had arrived earlier, having boated up the Ogeechee to King's Bridge and then traveled overland on horseback. The prophecy of Mr. Davis of *Harper's* had been fulfilled: The landlord of Savannah's best hotel wanted payment for room and board. Sherman curtly refused. While the general and his staff withdrew to ponder their options, a colored boy brought a letter of invitation from the English cotton factor, Mr. Green.

"He offered his house to Sherman, no charge, and the whole party rode off. You all should find Union headquarters down there."

So Stephen mounted up again and jogged south to Madison Square, where Charles Green's opulent home graced the northwest corner, facing West Macon Street. The mansion was a two-story masterpiece of tawny yellow stucco with elaborate cast-iron filigree ornamenting the veranda and fancy oriel windows jutting from the second floor.

Outside the new headquarters Stephen found the usual to-and-fro of officers passing in and out, as well as an unexpected throng of black men, women, and children craning for a glimpse of their liberator. A woman with a bright head scarf stopped Stephen. "Sir, will you be seeing Mr. Sherman?"

"I certainly hope so."

"When you come out, will you tell us what he's like?"

He promised he would, and they let him through.

His credentials got him past the two guards whose bayonets barred interlopers. His boots clattered on the fine foyer tiles. Within Mr. Green's house he discovered crystal chandeliers, marble fireplaces, a lavish display of fine art — luxury and ornamentation worthy of Fifth Avenue. Field desks filled a spacious parlor where Stephen observed heavy double doors that evidently closed off a second, similar room. A lieutenant directed him to the rear veranda overlooking the paths and plantings of a parterre garden. There, Major Hitchcock sat busily sifting through voluminous paperwork. As Stephen presented himself, bells rang in the steeple of a handsome church adjoining the garden.

"Ah, Hopewell. What brings you here?"

"Requesting permission to interview the general, sir."

"Sorry, it's impossible. General Sherman's closeted in the inner parlor with Mr. Green and his partner, Mr. Low."

"Later this afternoon, perhaps?"

"No, a delegation of colored pastors is scheduled to call, then relatives of Generals Hardee and Gustavus Smith seeking special protection. We also expect some schoolchildren — the general's door is always open to youngsters. Enemy or no, he's a famous person. As soon as he's finished here, he'll inspect the city."

"What about tomorrow?"

"I wouldn't stake my life on it. You know how he feels about you fellows from the press."

Stephen stifled his annoyance; it wasn't Hitchcock's fault, after all. He saluted and, outside again, told the disappointed Negroes that he'd been unable to see their hero in person. He then rejoined Ambrose, who was tied to Mr. Green's cast-iron fence. He stroked the mule's warm muzzle.

"Turned me down."

Ambrose peeled back his lip and brayed to express sympathy.

"I overstepped. I transgressed. In a word, I erred, profoundly."

The speaker was a gregarious and portly Treasury agent who'd introduced himself as A. G. Browne. A half dozen listeners pressed around him, Stephen among them. He was trying to ease his frustration in the Pulaski House saloon bar at four in the afternoon. Officers were permitted to drink when and where they pleased; typically they sought private establishments and avoided the whiskey sold by the commissary, when available, for thirty cents a gallon.

A cavalry colonel with Burnside whiskers finished a drink and whacked his glass down to command the barkeep's attention. "Phew, what's in that jug, laddie? Tar water? Turpentine? Lamp oil?"

The barkeep stuck out his chin. "The best whiskey we can get through your blockade."

"Pour me another and let's hope I survive till sunset." He addressed the civilian. "Pray continue, sir."

"Thank you, sir. To say that the general lost his temper would be understatement. He erupted like Vesuvius."

Stephen said, "You're referring to Uncle Billy."

"None other. It was not pleasant to experience."

Stephen had difficulty understanding Browne's

good humor in the wake of Sherman's wrath. "Why did he go up the spout?"

"Because I informed him that I'd come here from the garrison at Hilton Head to take possession of all the rebel cotton on behalf of the Department of the Treasury. He insisted it belonged to the army and he, not I, would dispose of it. Well, sir, I could tell from his face — red as his hair, it was — not to mention his numerous expletives, that I couldn't win the argument. Assuming I might need favors later, I knew I must get back in his good graces. I recalled President Lincoln's dark moods after long years with incompetent generals who brought our side little success, and I thought, Here's a monumental success worth reporting, in the spirit of the season. I suggested that General Sherman send a telegraph to Washington. In fact I suggested the exact wording. He responded favorably."

"He sent it?" someone else asked.

"He will by this evening, on a fast packet up to Fortress Monroe, then over the wires to the War Department."

"The words, laddie, the words," the colonel demanded.

Browne cleared his throat, poised a finger in the air. " 'I beg to present you as a Christmas gift, the city of Savannah, with one hundred fifty heavy guns and plenty of ammunition, and also about twenty-five thousand bales of cotton.' "

He paused for the expected applause, received it, then continued. "The general edited my original figure on the cotton. I think you'll find something like forty thousand bales when you total what's on the river front and in warehouses."

Stephen whipped out pad and pencil. "I wonder if I might have a few more details, for a dispatch to the *New York Eye*? Let's retire to that corner table. Quieter."

The flattered civilian went where directed.

Stephen left the Pulaski House thirty minutes later in a buzzy-headed state of inebriation. He had material for his dispatch, though he didn't feel good after three big slugs of the hotel's private stock. Ardent spirits were no solution to a man's frustrations, of which he seemed to have plenty.

A curious array of pictures and sounds mingled in his head. Sara Lester's fetching smile blended with the robust and thrilling notes of "Rock of Ages" as he imagined them played on Miss Rohrschamp's upright, which of course he couldn't get near, any more than he could get near Gen. W. T. Sherman.

Hattie felt fretful and hostile. She didn't like herself for it but couldn't banish the feeling.

Although she'd always been outspoken — Sara encouraged independence, more liberally after Ladson Lester's passing — Hattie's pertness seldom erupted into anger. She was close to it now. Amelia had received a tongue-lashing for tracking mud into Vee's kitchen. Sara tartly observed that Hattie was ten times more exercised than the owner of the house.

Perhaps she felt angry because that awful Sherman's capture of Savannah brought home the final, inevitable end of the Confederacy. Perhaps it was all those blue uniforms, all the racket from soldiers once again despoiling Wright Square with their hammering and singing and reeling about.

Perhaps it was Christmas too — rather, the lack of anything resembling Christmas. Hattie was too old to crave presents for herself, especially in current circumstances. She no longer believed in a jolly fat man who squeezed down every chimney in the world in a single night. She missed the festivity of Christmas; the carols, the kindness. She missed amply laid tables and brimming punch bowls.

To feel she was accomplishing something, however little, she'd gone that morning to the City Hotel and fetched Legrand for a session of refurbishing any toys that could be salvaged. Now, Thursday afternoon, the winter light outside was dimming. In the parlor, the scrawny Christmas tree had been righted, sans General Lee's portrait. All but a single deep scratch on the Chickering's case had been obliterated by Vee's vigorous attentions. Hattie and Legrand sat cross-legged with scissors and another bowl of thin flour paste, some rusty tacks and a few walnuts that had escaped the looters. They gamely pushed ahead with their repair of dolls and jumping jacks, saying little except when one or the other needed something passed. Sara had gone to the public market alone despite warnings from Miss Vee, who was pottering in the kitchen. At that moment an apparition tapped at the front door.

Or Hattie thought it was an apparition until she spied the visitor's blue sack coat partially hidden by a cape made of carpet. Instead of a forage cap, the young man wore an old silk hat ornamented with drooping artificial flowers. He peered in and knocked again. Hattie noted a young Negro out beyond the gate holding the bridle of a swaybacked horse. She ran to fetch Vee.

"Someone's at the door. A soldier."

"Heaven protect us from his base appetites." Hattie offered to tell the stranger to go away. "No, no, I will do it. You and Legrand get ready to run." Hattie couldn't understand why, if Vee was so frightened, she rushed to the parlor with her cheeks aglow.

Vee unbolted the door, opened it five inches, and leaned her considerable self against it to prevent further progress. "Who are you? What do you want?"

"Sergeant Alpheus Winks, ma'am. Eighty-first Indiana Mounted Rifles. Some of my men disturbed you last night."

"Disturbed hardly covers it, sir."

"Yes, I know they did bad things. I come to apologize. Would you let me step in?"

Vee darted looks at the children; Legrand was already armed with the poker. Vee stepped back. The Yankee entered and removed his peculiar hat. He exuded a powerful odor of tobacco.

"Ma'am, are you Mrs. Lester or the lady of the house?"

"The latter. Miss Rohrschamp."

Winks indicated the toys under repair. "Those the things my men busted?"

"That's not all," Hattie said. "They threatened to barbecue my pig. One of them danced on top of the piano. See the mark?"

"I'm mighty sorry."

Vee's face was purple with excitement. For someone in mortal fear, she stood rather close to the newcomer. "I trust the vandals have been arrested and punished."

"Uh, not quite yet. I figure to speak to the leader of the pack before the day's over, but the matter of punishment's — well, you might say it's loose. One man causes trouble, he gets a few days of confinement or extra guard duty. Another man, same offense, he may be bucked and gagged."

"I have no idea what that means, but it sounds revolting."

The sergeant did his best to explain the technique of rendering a prisoner extremely uncomfortable with ropes and a stick. "Wouldn't expect my men to get a dishonorable discharge

— they'd probably be grateful for it. The colonel will sort it out soon as he can. Meantime, I do offer apologies. Even if it takes a while, we'll settle the hash of those boys."

"And — that's all that prompted your visit?"

"Yes, ma'am, though I'm pleased to make your acquaintance. This is a fine house. Is this handsome child Letty or Kitty?"

"Hattie," said the child in question. "Who's that colored boy outside, your slave?"

"We don't practice slavery in Indiana. He's just some boy I fished out of a creek, name of Zip. He follows me around and I wish he wouldn't. He wants to be a regular soldier but Uncle Billy has different ideas. Zip's situation is, you might say, holding. Like the punishments. Christmas and all."

Vee huffed. "It's hardly Christmas for us. We are a conquered people, lying supine and submissive before the ravening hordes."

Round and round in his rough hands he turned the brim of his tall hat. "I suppose that's true, though I don't know how many of us is ravening just now. There's lots of boys who wish this blasted war was over and done with. Wish we'd never fought it."

Legrand spoke for the first time. "You aren't aching to burn Savannah or Charleston to the ground?"

"Mebbe Uncle Billy is. Not me."

Vee said, "You don't blame the South for all the carnage?"

"Well, sure, you folks put all those nigra men and women in a state of servitude and tolerated it too long. But the way I look at it, if we didn't have the colored on these shores in the first place, wouldn't have been any argument, or any war. It's the black folks caused all the trouble. It's them who took Abner and Ansel away."

"Relatives?"

"My dear departed brothers. Both volunteers, like myself."

"My sincere condolences. Did they die bravely, in battle?"

"No, ma'am, they did not. Ansel perished at Shiloh Church with a ball in his back. His regiment was in retreat. Abner was serving in Kentucky. He — I'm not sure I should say."

"Of course you should. What caused his passing?"

"An attack of — pshaw, I can't. Just say he drank some bad water and nature took its course. Both were fine upstanding boys. Mama grieved something fierce, I was informed."

The odd byplay between the piano teacher and the Yankee puzzled Hattie. Vee seemed to be running toward and away from the sergeant at the same time. Hattie sidled close to Legrand. "Time to exercise Amelia."

A large lace handkerchief popped into Vee's hand from somewhere, like a magician's prop. She waved and waved it, trilling, "Go on, children, go on. Hattie, be sure to put on your shawl. Don't forget Amelia's muffler, the temperature is dropping. Go on, enjoy yourselves, I'm perfectly safe."

Hattie suspected Vee was right. Whatever else Sergeant Winks might be, he probably wasn't one to commit those frequently mentioned outrages. He didn't have horns.

A serious disappointment.

Bull Street, 4:40 P.M.

If there had been no laughter, the story would end differently. It fell out this way:

Hattie and Legrand left Vee's house, Hattie wearing her old plaid shawl for warmth. Legrand's leg was healing nicely, but he found it less strenuous to move along with the aid of his crutch. Amelia trotted at the end of her rope; wound around her neck was the woolen muffler Hattie had sewn two years ago, when cloth was less scarce. Amelia didn't like the muffler but had given up resisting it.

The winter sun was already sinking; pale amber light tinted the city. Town houses and live oak trees, passing horsemen and creaking conveyances threw long shadows. Legrand said, "First time I ever met a hoozer."

"Hoosier, it's *hoosier."*

"You ever been to Indiana?"

"I should hope not."

"What's it mean, then?"

186

"I don't know and I don't care. I suppose it's an Indian word for 'peasant.' "

They wandered north in the direction of Miss Vee's church. Amelia stopped to snuffle on someone's lawn. Hattie pulled her rope crossly. Legrand said, "That Yankee didn't seem like a bad sort. I was ready to brain him if he so much as looked cross-eyed, but he didn't. He took responsibility."

"I know."

"I always say it takes a big man to admit a wrong."

"I know."

"Can't believe I was shooting at fellows like that out on the lines."

Their peregrination took them to Johnson Square, around through the chilly shadows of Christ Church and the Bank of Georgia and back down Bull toward Wright Square. As they reached the corner of York Street, Hattie noticed that the Yankee and his Negro had gone. Before she could remark on it, a party of five Union officers of varying ages emerged from the haze hanging over the new tents and shanties in the square. The officers seemed in a light mood, chatting and joking as they approached a large open carriage driven by a corporal. The youngest of the officers, a lieutenant with long blond mustaches, caught the attention of a companion. He pointed at Amelia, who was oinking joyously, sensing the warm sanctuary of Miss Vee's not far off.

The officers laughed, though not the oldest, at the center of the group. He was the queerest, shabbiest soldier Hattie had ever seen, tall and lanky, with a face reddened by the winter air. His beard, closely cut, was rust-colored. The shoulders of his stained blue coat bore no straps indicating rank. He wore ill-fitting brown trousers and an old black slouch hat disreputable as the rest of him. Largely ignoring the merriment of his companions, he peered at the ground, hands locked behind his back, as though thinking furiously while chewing his fuming cigar. All this Hattie absorbed in a single glance, before the mustachioed officer called out, "Little girl, you have a handsome baby. What's its name?"

Hattie thrust Amelia's tether into Legrand's hand. "Wait, don't," he exclaimed, "I saw a picture of that —" She didn't hear the rest, charging across the rutted sand to confront the officers.

"I demand an apology. That was a rude remark. I suppose it's typical of Yankees who strut and swagger because they've beaten a lot of old men and boys."

The unkempt man, fortyish, stepped to the fore; the others made room. "See here, child," he said, not unkindly, "Lieutenant Dunn meant no offense."

"But he gave it and I won't stand for it. Your lieutenant had better apologize to my pig. Some

188

of your soldiers wanted to roast her on a spit last night."

"Truly?" The lanky man scratched his beard.

"Yes, they broke into our house and deliberately destroyed the toys my friend and I were making because the stores are empty. That's my friend over there, holding my pig."

"Hmm." The man wasn't able to pursue the thought because uncontrollable laughter seized the mustachioed lieutenant. Hattie's restraint gave way. She lowered her head, her curls dancing, and sailed into the lieutenant. She gave him two sockdologers, right fist, left fist, in the midriff. "See here, stop that," the lanky man said. Hattie spun about.

"You keep out of this. You don't even look like a soldier."

"Be that as it may —"

"Get away, little girl," barked another officer, seizing Hattie from behind. She blew like a barrel of dynamite then, kicking and writhing free. The lanky man grabbed her to forestall further violence.

"Oh, no, you don't," Hattie cried, delivering a powerful kick to his shin. The man yelped, seized his right ankle with his left hand, and hopped about like a stork.

His minions were goggle-eyed. Hattie tossed her curls and marched back across the street to Legrand, whose mouth hung open.

"I guess I showed them they can't mistreat the innocent people of Georgia." She snatched

Amelia's rope and, chin high, continued marching straight along to Miss Vee's gate. There she turned in.

Legrand chased her and caught her at the stoop. "For heaven's sake, do you know who you attacked?"

"That brute with the yellow mustache."

"No, no, the other one, the one you kicked."

Hattie saw the officers heatedly arguing, no doubt trying to agree on a strategy of retaliation. All, that is, except the lanky man. He grasped a convenient shoulder while standing on one leg and massaging the other. Hattie couldn't hear what he said, but she had no doubt he was exercised.

"That dirty old wreck? I don't care who he is. I wouldn't care if it was Sherman himself."

"Well, you should, because it is."

Hattie didn't incriminate herself; Legrand's stricken look gave them away. Sara pressed for an explanation. Ladson Lester had taught his daughter always to be truthful. Admittedly she thought of lying, but the idea didn't last long. She told all.

Sara said, "I don't condone your behavior for one minute, but I understand it."

Vee said, "I have an idea. Claim it was an accident."

"Nuh-uh, not the way she lit into him," said Legrand.

"Claim it was mistaken identity."

He perked up. "That's what it was, mistaken identity."

Sara shook her head. "Whatever the excuse, we must be ready for the inevitable."

"Do they arrest children?" Vee said.

Sara said, "We'll surely find out."

Camp of the 81st Indiana, 5 P.M.

When Winks finally left his tent to search for the miscreants, Zip materialized like an ebony ectoplasm. He wanted to perform his perfected imitation of the catbird. Winks sent him away, and not politely. The report by Captain Hopewell had ruined his day and disposition; he was obliged to buck the incriminating facts up the ladder to the colonel, but not until he personally confronted the wrongdoers.

He followed the *cling-clang* of horseshoes and coarse laughter and easily found Corporal Marcus and Private Spiker. They were outdoors, near their tents, at a newly dug horseshoe pitch. Both were in fine spirits, as though their misdeeds had never happened. This only confirmed Winks's belief that most law-breakers were numskulls.

A damp winter dusk was settling; Spiker and the professor didn't see their sergeant until he stepped forward and kicked Spiker's ringer away from the peg.

"No more skylarking. Stand at attention when I talk to you."

Marcus responded with a slovenly representation of military posture. Spiker, more literal-minded, snapped his shoulders back and puffed out his chest. Winks stomped up and down the horseshoe pitch, angrier than he'd expected to be.

"A captain name of Hopewell looked me up today. I believe you boys ran into him last night. I guess he broke up your little party. I'm informed that you terrorized a bunch of innocent women, damaged their property, and threatened to roast their livestock."

"What of it?" Marcus retorted. "They're just rebs."

"That's true, but Uncle Billy said there was to be no more of that sort of behavior while we're enjoying Savannah hospitality."

Spiker said, "Wasn't my idea, I only —"

Marcus kicked Spiker, then jutted his jaw: "So what are you going to do, ask for a court-martial? Bet there isn't a man jack in this army would censor us for ragging those rebs."

"I think you mean *censure*," Spiker said. Marcus kicked him again. With a stentorian "Oww," Spiker reeled away and fell, almost knocking down a tent before he landed on his rump.

"The colonel's got to hear a full report," Winks said. "How he punishes you, that's up to him. I came here for a different reason. I came to say I don't want you in my detail from now on, and if you show your faces within half a mile of me, I'll whale the tar out of you."

Marcus sneered. "So it doesn't matter how good a job we done, you're throwing us out like old junk?"

"You went too far. Threatening to cook a little girl's pig — dancing on a lady's piano — what kind of behavior's that?"

The stricken choirboy betrayed his cohort by exclaiming, "He put me up to it, I swear."

Professor Marcus threw a handful of dirt in Spiker's face. Winks leaped forward, clamped the professor's wrist, and shouted, "As you were," which brought a few heads popping from tents roundabout.

He took a fistful of the professor's soiled blouse and shook him. "I hope the colonel fries your gizzards, but if he don't, I better not catch you hurting any more women and children." He shook the professor once again and released him. "Do we have an understanding here?"

"Sure, and glad of it." The professor dusted himself off with exaggerated gestures implying injury. "Ask me, we'll be a whole lot better off foraging on our own. 'A wise man makes more opportunities than he finds.' "

"You just think that up, did you?"

The professor sneered again, more richly. "For your information, you dumb country boob" — outraged, Winks was in motion — "it was the outstanding English philosopher Frank Bacon."

Winks blasted the professor's jaw with his right hand, lifting and sailing him into the iron peg, which impacted the back of his skull. Spiker looked faint.

Marcus felt his pate, peered at a tincture of red on his finger. "Shouldn't've done that. Sergeant or no sergeant, shouldn't've done that."

"Threatening me?"

"Take it how you want."

Winks wheeled about and stalked away down the dusky lane between tents now lit by lanterns. A few chilly raindrops splashed his face. He felt foolish. To lose his temper with Professor Marcus only ripened the enmity between them.

Winks proceeded to regimental headquarters, the domain of Col. Herman Jolley. The colonel, an apothecary in better times, loved military pomp, and the war itself. He loathed rebs of every description, almost as much as he loathed his ill-tempered wife and disobedient children. He dreaded the day he'd be mustered out, forced to return to his savage brood in sleepy Crawfordsville. Of late he'd contemplated slipping away anonymously to California, the Isthmus of Panama, or even Europe.

Winks waited nearly an hour before Captain Gleeson granted him entree to the presence of the large ruddy-faced Colonel Jolley. Winks felt

like a tattling schoolboy as he related Hopewell's charges, which the colonel wrote down
while his lips twitched in a curious fashion. The
colonel promised appropriate action.

After Winks left, Jolley broke into a fit of
chuckling and filed his notes in a lard bucket
holding trash.

Winks was a good man, if inclined to senti-
mentality. Of course he didn't have to serve with
the men he'd disciplined if that was his choice,
but the colonel had no intention of punishing
them. He heartily wished they'd go right on and
do more damage to the secesh.

December 23, 1864

Savannah Riverfront, 9 A.M.

The gentleman was as unhandsome as his
name, Isaiah Fleeg.

To begin with, he was short, which often in-
duces a certain pugnacity. His protuberant eyes
were the color of white grapes. His nose, though
not nearly as large as an eggplant, had acquired
some eggplant coloration from long hours in
taprooms. He slouched rather than strode, a
habit developed during frequent escapes from
the scene of this or that felonious misdeed.

Approaching forty, Isaiah had long ago recognized the truth told to him by any looking glass.
He compensated by arraying himself in the

latest, most colorful male fashions, often acquired from vendors who dealt in stolen goods. He saw himself as a vivid cardinal in a drab aviary of male sparrows and cowbirds.

Isaiah was a fifth-generation scion of the New Jersey Fleegs, people who persevered despite repeated negative encounters with sheriffs, constables, jailers, and hanging judges. His forebears were arrested and prosecuted for everything from drugging unsuspecting tourists who woke up on outbound cargo ships captained by lascars, to the furious driving of chaises and gigs in crowded thoroughfares with total disregard for laws of courtesy and personal survival. New Jerseyites were famous for bad driving, and Isaiah was not one to besmirch the record.

Isaiah had been fortunate to find a wife uglier than himself. She bore him fourteen children before she died of exhaustion. He had a strong appetite for profit and had been feeding it for six months in one of the many dives on Robber's Row at Hilton Head. Self-exiled, he fleeced Union soldiers at cards while avoiding a Weehawken arrest warrant for arson.

His experience as a cheat outmatched the innocence of the boys in blue whom he lured to his table. He projected a strong aura of patriotism, reflected in his marked decks. Their red and blue suits were American eagles, national flags, five-pointed stars and Federal shields. The face cards were Union generals: Grant,

Sherman, Halleck, Meade, McClellan. (The decks were old.)

The Hilton Head garrison, extant since Admiral DuPont captured Port Royal Sound in November 1861, had attracted several thousand civilians: sharps, saloon keepers, military outfitters, fish house proprietors, souvenir sellers, hard-faced ladies of dubious reputation, even a few parsons striving to save souls. Recently Sherman had arrived by water to confer with the garrison's poorly regarded Gen. John Foster. Afterwards Sherman set out for the return trip to Savannah on the steamer *Harvest Moon*. The steamer ran aground about the time Dr. Arnold was surrendering the city.

Sherman's delayed arrival was unknown to Isaiah as he prepared to inspect the captured city. Weeks ago, a letter from his son Freddi, already criminally adept at thirteen, had informed him that the arson matter had largely faded. Freddi reminded him that draft substitutes were still in demand, at a going price of three hundred dollars per head. Since the War Department endorsed the suitability of Negroes for the military, a substitute's color was not an issue.

Thus, on a chill gray morning two days before Christmas, Isaiah loitered on the open deck of the steam packet *Princess Poweshiek*. On leaving the Hilton Head pier, Isaiah had asked the gruff German supercargo who Princess Poweshiek might be. The supercargo guessed she was some unlettered Indian from the barbaric tribes living on the Iowa plain — assuming there was an Iowa plain, the supercargo really didn't know or care.

The manifest listed Isaiah's occupation as "authorized recruiting agent." The person who had authorized him was himself. He was, as always, regally attired. His overcoat, green checked wool, matched his green silk cravat; collar and cuffs of dyed rabbit fur ornamented the coat. His trousers, top hat, and ankle boots were black, his leather gloves lemon yellow.

The packet negotiated the curves of the Savannah River on a favorable tide, carefully avoiding red-and-white pennons bobbing on floats; the Federal navy had set these out to mark rebel torpedo sites. Isaiah found the December air pretty deuced cold but comforted himself with the thought that a dozen contrabands trussed up and shipped north would outweigh temporary discomfort.

Bells rang, the packet's whistle blew. Isaiah made certain that his hideout pistol, a Colt's .31 caliber, was secure in a special deep pocket of his waistcoat. It was a popular and dependable traveler's gun; several rash gentlemen had confronted Isaiah's piece with much grieving afterwards on the part of widows and common-law companions.

He stepped ashore amid bales of moldering cotton dripping water through gunny cloth. Stevedores swarmed on Savannah's main wharf, every one an able-bodied colored man.

He spoke to the first one he found catching a breath: "Boy, are you someone's property?"

"No sir, not no more. Mr. Linkum 'mancipated me. Gen'ral Shermung's come to make it for sure."

"Delighted to hear it, congratulations to you," Isaiah said with false bonhomie.

An Army captain, smelling of rum this early in the morning, was yet able to offer a select list of hotels. He informed Isaiah of General Geary's curfew and warned that Fleeg was subject to arrest if abroad after 9 P.M., unless on official business, with appropriate documentation.

Carpetbag in hand, Isaiah slouched up the steep pedestrian stairs to Bay Street. He thrilled to the sight of so many young bucks running about in perfect freedom. Hurrah! — he would have no trouble filling his anticipated quota.

Camp of the 81st Indiana, 10:15 A.M.

A poor night's sleep plus dissatisfaction with the colonel put the notion into the head of Alpheus Winks. He decided the idea was brilliant, or as close to brilliance as he could get with his limited book learning, because it successfully addressed one problem and at the same time temporarily rid him of a pest.

He found Zip not far from the tent, seated on a log and wrapped in an old horse blanket to keep off the damp. Head tilted back, Zip was uttering a series of sharp barks.

Winks usually stifled his limited curiosity about Zip's peculiar hobby, but this vocalizing was so strange, he blurted, "What kind of bird is that, a dying crow?"

"No siree, something new. Gray squirrel. Lots of 'em around here, notice? I'm trying it out. How you like it?"

Winks sidestepped. "I have a task for you."

"Yessir!" Squirrels forgotten, Zip jumped up as though he'd heard Saint Peter announce his admittance to Heaven. "What you need done?"

"I want some of the boys in this regiment watched, but not watched so they know they're being watched."

"Which boys'd those be, Captain?"

Winks had long ago abandoned hope of clarifying his rank for the pesky youth. "Professor Marcus and his chums, Spiker and Pence. I threw them off the forage squad last night. They abused some innocent civilians here in town. Would have robbed 'em but for a shoulder straps that happened along. Colonel Jolley don't seem too interested in giving them a dose of army discipline, and something's telling me those boys won't mend their ways."

When Zip repeated "Yessir" with less enthusiasm than before, it testified to the bad character of those Winks had named. "Where I find them sojers at, you suppose?"

"The new horseshoe pitch, or close by. Loiter

201

around there. If you hear anything suspicious the next day or so, let me know."

"I'll see what I can find out. Can't do it past nine o'clock. Provost guard's mighty hard on anybody they catch after curfew."

"Don't worry your nappy head about that. I'll write you an iron-clad, brass-bound, guaranteed, foolproof pass. Follow me."

The last instruction was wholly unnecessary.

York Street —

Charles Green Manse, 11:30 A.M.

Hattie's heart pounded when she saw the carriage whose clatter drew her to the window. It was the carriage that had awaited Sherman and his officers before Hattie's fateful kick; its top had been raised against the morning showers. Black lacquer on the carriage body collected raindrops that gleamed like opals before they broke and trickled away.

A Union officer alighted with an umbrella. Hattie ran through the gloomy hallway to the kitchen, where Sara and Vee sat with mugs of ersatz tea.

"Mama, there's another Yankee coming to the door."

Sara turned pale as milk. "You stay here, I'll see to this."

She disappeared. Vee clasped Hattie's hand in

an anguished way. Hattie listened for the knock, the sound of the door unbolted, the indistinct voices. The Yankee spoke softly, making it all the more ominous.

Sara returned. "His name is Captain Coker. He asked your name, Hattie. I felt obliged to tell him. He's not here to arrest you, but General Sherman saw you dash into this house yesterday. He wants to speak to you at his headquarters."

Hattie's eyes grew large and round. "What for?"

"The captain won't say. At very least I think you can anticipate a reprimand." She grasped Hattie's shoulders gently; spoke without recrimination. "Are you up to that?"

"That and more," Hattie exclaimed, feeling a rush of courage. Old Sherman was just an ordinary man, wasn't he? He'd turned his vandals loose to pillage Georgia, hadn't he? She was glad she'd barked his shin. She wished she'd done it twice.

"You should go with her, Sara," Vee said.

"He only asked for Hattie. He promised she wouldn't be harmed."

"They probably say that to every prisoner before they bring out the firing squad."

"Vee, don't alarm the child."

"I'm not alarmed, and I can go by myself," Hattie said. Perhaps if she were lucky, she could give old Sherman the sockdolager he deserved. "Mama, have you seen my shawl?"

Vee had a last advisory: "They've hung their flags all over town. If you come upon one, don't respect it by walking under it. Walk around — that's what my friends are doing."

But Hattie had left the kitchen and didn't hear.

On the ride through the rain, Hattie kept her mind off the coming inquisition by asking questions of the captain. Did the general intend to march into South Carolina and punish that state as he'd punished Georgia?

"He has no animus toward Georgia" — Hattie sniffed to show her opinion of that assertion — "but South Carolina is another bucket of fish. General Sherman believes the Palmetto State forced the war. He's awaiting General Grant's permission to resume the march."

Was the general some sort of savage, then?

"Not at all. He thinks strategically. He's also very — ah — unbuttoned, one might say. Not strong on ceremony."

"Does he have a family?"

"Yes, his wife, Ellen, is back in Ohio. She's the daughter of Senator Ewing, the general's foster father. You know also that his brother is a United States Senator?" *Oh, worse and worse,* Hattie thought, though she merely shook her head.

"The general and Mrs. Sherman have children, but that's a subject I would avoid. After Vicksburg, he brought the family down to celebrate. His oldest, Willy, contracted typhoid and died. Willy was nine — the general's favorite."

Hattie was somewhat annoyed to feel a pang of sympathy. "That's too bad," she said, almost inaudibly.

"That isn't the end of it. When the general arrived in Savannah, he learned that his youngest child, a baby boy, had succumbed to illness during the march. He's taken the loss hard, though I'm sure he won't let on to you."

"You can be sure I won't ask. What does he want with me?"

"He's curious about you. How old are you?"

"Twelve."

"That was his guess. He said you're as audacious as many an adult."

"Is he going to tan my hide for kicking him?"

With a tilt of his head and a glint in his eye, Captain Coker said, "If you take that tone, it's a distinct possibility."

"Right up the stairs, miss. First door to your left. The general ordered some luncheon. Would you care to join him?"

"I would not." Hattie was so agog over the sumptuous furnishings of the Green residence — the large oil paintings, the sculpture on pedestals — she nearly forgot her manners. "Thank you."

The orderly showed Hattie to a spacious front bedroom with a large dining alcove. Under a flickering chandelier, the feared Union general took up the whole of a large round table with his paraphernalia: maps; orders and reports inked by various hands; cigars, both unlit and residing as smelly stubs in an inverted jar lid; several dinner plates. William Tecumseh Sherman put aside his knife and fork and pulled his crumb-laden napkin from his throat, revealing a soiled dickey. He nodded to the orderly.

"That will be all. You may close the door."

Hard rain splashed the room's oriel windows. The general cleared his throat, rose to offer his hand. He was taller than she remembered. "Miss Lester, I believe."

"Yes, sir, that is right." Although good manners prompted her to shake his hand, she didn't. His seamed face reddened a little more, but he concealed any anger he felt.

"Won't you sit down, then?" Sherman pulled out a chair. "I've looked forward to making your acquaintance." Hattie doubted that. With a ladylike rearrangement of her petticoat and overskirt, she took the offered seat.

Peculiarly, she wasn't overly awed by the famous general who smiled at her while he raised his napkin to dab a few last crumbs from his lips. Seldom had she seen a military man so untidy, not even in the ragged ranks of the Confederacy. His rust-colored hair seemed to grow in several directions; his barber might have been a blind man wielding an ax. His baggy brown trousers didn't match his unbuttoned blue blouse, still with no emblems of rank on it.

"As a rule, I like children. They like me. After you whacked me yesterday, I realized you look a lot like my second daughter, Elizabeth — Lizzie. She's about your age. You kicked me good and hard, you know." He rubbed his right ankle after he crossed it over his left knee. Instead of proper boots, he wore low-cut shoes, badly scuffed and scratched, like a common laborer's. Instead of two spurs, he wore just one, tarnished. "I won't ask for an apology, but I won't ask for another kick, either. Are you sure you wouldn't like some lunch? Leg of lamb? Yams? Corn bread?"

"No, thank you."

In the litter on the table he found a small paper bag. "A peppermint, then? Good for digestion."

"No, sir. May I ask why you brought me here?"

"You may, Miss Lester" — he stuck a partially smoked cigar in the left side of his mouth, lit it — "I wanted to meet the little girl who had the nerve to march up and deliver a swift kick. I've met a number of Savannah children but none like you."

"I'm not little — I'm twelve, like your daughter. And all of the children in Savannah aren't spineless jellies, either." She felt dangerously rash. "I want you to know something. My father died serving our side, because you Yankees went to war against us."

"My sincere regrets, Hattie — may I call you Hattie?"

"I prefer Miss Lester. I don't know you very well."

"Yes, well — Miss Lester, then. I want you to know something too. Your side, not mine, fired on Fort Sumter and commenced the bloodletting. I hold those Charleston hotheads principally responsible. However, despite the differences that have divided us, you and I remain Americans. I earnestly wish you could find it in your heart not to hate me."

"After all you've done to Georgia? And my family?" Generals weren't talked to like this, she supposed. Well, she had even more to say. She shook her index finger under his nose. "We may have lost our rice plantation because of you."

His eyebrows shot up. "Is that so? Again, my sincere regrets, but —"

"You didn't have to march across the whole state, did you? Shooting, thieving, burning?"

"There have been excesses, I'll not deny it. I deem them the unavoidable, if unfortunate, effects of our broader plan."

He didn't seem to be an ogre, just a hard-eyed, determined man arguing his point, as if with his own daughter. Hattie refused to surrender; she stuck out her chin. "What plan? To bring Georgia to its knees?"

His eyes danced and shone; a slight jerk of his head suggested ire. "Yes, that was my intention. It occurred to me that the quickest and most humane way to end this sorrowful war was to destroy the South's capability to wage it. To make the lot of ordinary citizens so miserable, for a short time, that they would plead for — demand — peace. I want this country to be whole again. I have great respect and admiration for Southern people."

"Excuse me, but you have a queer way of showing it."

Sherman threw back his head and laughed. "I have never, ever met anyone as outspoken as you — well, not under the age of twenty. You aren't persuaded by my explanation of why I undertook to march all the way from Atlanta?"

"No, sir."

"Hmm." He rummaged among the inked field orders, produced a copy of the *New York Eye*. A steel engraving on its front page depicted a merry fat man shouldering a pack of toys beside a snowy chimney. He tapped the picture.

"Might you reconsider? This is the season of forgiveness, you know."

"Also of plundering."

"What do you mean?"

"Some of your brutes broke into our house the other night, drunk as coots."

For the first time the general looked genuinely stern. "Did they abuse anyone in your household?"

"They would have. They wanted to barbecue Amelia, my pig, but a captain came along to stop them."

"A captain from the Union army?"

"Yes. I think his name was Hopewell."

"I commend him. I will look into the matter."

Sherman licked the tip of a pencil stub, scribbled a note on his soiled shirt cuff. He stretched out his lanky frame and gave a mournful sigh. "I admit to a measure of guilt, Miss Lester. Perhaps I haven't enforced my special order on foraging as vigorously as I might have. In Savannah I want to exercise more restraint, tolerance — respect for the spirit of the season. I have ordered my men to rest and enjoy the charms of this attractive city. I believe your mayor, Dr. Arnold, and his aldermen, have no objection to Union soldiers sharing Christmas with you."

Hattie held her hands tightly clasped in her lap. The rain pattered the glass. Sherman subjected her to a long, calculating look. "One last question. Is it remotely possible that you and I could be friends?"

At that moment Hattie couldn't help liking him just a little. He seemed thoughtful, genuine — fatherly. She remembered his losses.

She had to put them out of her mind to answer: "No, sir, I don't think so."

"But we needn't be enemies."

Hattie fidgeted. "Am I to be arrested for kicking you?"

"Arrest a child? Never." He shook a finger over the table, a deliberate reprise of her earlier reproof. "Just don't do it again. Thank you for allowing this meeting."

"All right, sir." Hattie slid sideways from her chair, stood. So did General Sherman. He held out his hand. Again she refused it, taking refuge in a curtsy.

"You are a damned little rebel, excuse my language," he said with an exasperated smile. "But you do bear an uncanny resemblance to my Lizzie. Here, take these, no argument." He twisted the top of the bag of peppermints to close it, tossed it to her. He bit down on his sparking cigar. "Merry Christmas."

Hattie opened the door so fast, she surprised the orderly dozing on a chair tilted against the wall. She ran down the stairs with the precious candy, buffeted by conflicting emotions. At one point she'd almost wanted to jump on the general's knee and fold his arm around her, like a proper father's.

Miss Vee's, 12:15 P.M.

Sara wore a path between the Chickering and the front window, each time lifting the lace curtain, then dropping it while sighing anxiously. So occupied was she with thoughts of Hattie, she scarcely heard Vee's invitation to a special meeting of some kind at four o'clock.

She missed the sponsor's name, forcing Vee to repeat: "The meeting's at the home of my friend Miss M. G. Parsley, formerly of Jackson, Mississippi. Mayo is a minister's daughter and a fiery secesh. A stick of dynamite, compared to which, one might say, Jefferson Davis is a damp squib.

Mayo's had many beaux" — this was said rather wistfully — "but she's dismissed every one as deficient in patriotism. One disappointed suitor threw himself in front of a rifled cannon at Fredericksburg."

"Enemy cannon?"

"Ours. Mayo has that effect on boys."

"What's the purpose of this meeting?"

"To allow us to abuse and rail against the Yankees behind closed doors. There will be singing, and speechifying, to protest the brutal occupation."

"So far it hasn't seemed all that brutal."

"Sara, have you forgotten those beasts who broke into this very house?"

"But that good-looking captain — what was his name? Hopewell. He prevented a tragedy."

"When it comes to the enemy, you certainly have a keen memory."

Sara blushed. "Fiddlesticks. He did us a good turn. I liked his music. That's hardly a crime. Now about this meeting. Is it possible you could get arrested for attending?"

"I can't imagine the Yankees hearing of it. Should the worst happen, however, I pity the jailer who tries to close a cell door on M. G. Parsley. He'll find he's trying to cage a little wildcat."

"And you? Can you emulate that?"

"Well" — Vee retreated into determination — "no, but I'm going anyway."

Sara was frankly weary of the endless rhetorical drum-beating. The notion that the South could yet wrest victory from defeat was nonsense. The Confederacy and the Richmond politicians who dominated it were whipped. Perhaps the inevitable outcome was wrong (in regard to the peculiar institution, Sara didn't think so), as well as sad, but the loss of her husband, the threat to Silverglass posed by the Drewgoods, and of late the gentle spirit of the yuletide enfolded her in a mantle of resignation, even forgiveness. She remembered part of Wordsworth's "Farewell Lines."

> *But, surely, if severe afflictions borne*
> *With patience merit the reward of peace,*
> *Peace ye deserve.*

It was apt for Georgia; it was apt for the nation.

Vee repeated her invitation. Sara shook her head. "I'm in no mood to protest. You go along, but do be careful."

Noise in the street announced the return of the carriage that had borne Hattie away. Sara rushed to the door and nearly collided with her excited daughter. Hattie showed her a paper sack.

"The general gave me this, Mama. Peppermint candy, can you imagine?"

Vee exclaimed, "Lord preserve us. There's been no candy in the shops for months."

"Here, have one." Hattie pressed the sack on her. Vee peered inside, as though Sherman's peppermints might be poisoned. Vee declined the candy, but Sara popped a piece into her mouth and savored it. She'd almost forgotten how peppermint tasted.

Hattie threw off her shawl and shook her blond curls to rid them of a few drops of rain. Vee peered outside. "The driver's waiting for you to signal you're safe and sound."

Hattie opened the door, stepped on the stoop and waved. The Union soldier tipped his forage cap and drove off. Vee said, "I didn't know Yankees were capable of such courtesies."

Having swallowed the last dissolving bit of peppermint, Sara said, "We mustn't noise it about." Vee missed her friend's irony.

Sara turned to her daughter. "Do I understand correctly? You got a present instead of a tongue lashing?"

"Yes, can you feature it? The general even offered me luncheon. He was polite. He wanted to be friends." Hattie seated herself close to the sorry Christmas tree, now decorated with two strands of popcorn, mostly burnt, and a trio of tiny unlit candles. She described her visit with W. T. Sherman down to the last crumb on his dickey and the last smudge on his shirt cuff.

An hour later, Legrand came by. Hattie shared the peppermints and again suggested they exercise Amelia. With the pig trundling at the end of her tether, the friends set out.

Candle-lighting time failed to blunt the sharpness of the air, although the blue shadows of impending night lent a picturesque quality to the tents and hovels in the square. Hattie could almost imagine poor but honest mudsills living there, not the invaders.

Legrand turned up the collar of his wool coat and remarked on spits of rain in the air. Hattie agreed that the weather didn't look auspicious for Christmas. "So we have a duty to brighten it as best we can."

"Those Yanks who busted the toys pretty well cooked that goose, wouldn't you say?"

"We should make more."

"Yes, but time's short. The fixings, too."

"Still, don't you think we should try?"

Legrand sighed and nodded, his surrender.

During this conversation the friends walked south along Bull Street, in the direction of Chippewa Square. Had Hattie been thinking about it, she might have chosen another route, for down this way dwelt the Drewgoods — East Perry Street, closer to the Old Cemetery than any Drewgood liked to admit. On the square's north side, two brisk walkers approached from West Hull Street. Hattie recognized Napoleon and his squinty sister.

"Hello, hello, we didn't see you there," cried the unbeautiful twin, causing Hattie to suspicion that Cherry Drewgood was pleased to encounter them for some reason as yet unknown.

Legrand tipped his kepi. Hattie said, "Hello yourself. Out for a stroll?"

"Errands, but we must hurry home, we've extra special company coming for dinner."

"A big frog in the pond," Napoleon said.

"One of the biggest," said his sister. "The judge is entertaining a Union general, second or third to Sherman himself."

Hattie recoiled. "You invited a Yankee to your table?"

Napoleon said, "Yes, and he's one of those nigger-loving abolitionists, too. Phooey."

"Father believes we must meet and greet our enemies in the spirit of the season," Cherry said. "Like Sherman, the general's from Ohio. Well connected in Washington. We're fortunate to get acquainted with someone so important, don't you think?"

Not waiting for Hattie's opinion, Cherry yanked her brother's hand, and the Drewgoods melted away in the direction of home. Hattie frowned. "Mama will have conniptions. Did you see the airs they put on?"

"Yes I did. Sounds like the old judge turned his coat. Mighty fast, too."

"You can bet he's not doing it because the Christmas elves filled his bosom with kindliness. I wonder what he's up to?"

Judge Drewgood's, Early Evening

The Hon. Cincinnatus Drewgood rehearsed his household as thoroughly as Hamlet rehearsed the players, although his soliloquy was considerably less elegant. Elegance not being the judge's forte, he simply drilled home his demands in his intimidating voice:

"Lulu, change your clothes. Powder your cheeks. Stay out of the kitchen and do not for an instant let on that you prepared the meal. Merry, smile and look happy for our guest. Cherry, rouge your cheeks. Slick up. Don't act as though you're attending a wake. Napoleon, keep your fingers away from your face. Adam, pretend a cook is handing you each dish as you bring it out." The white listeners were grouped around the dining table while Adam remained in his customary corner. "Get cracking — our guest is due at seven."

They scattered to other parts of the house. Slow-moving Adam inadvertently stumbled over a chair on his way to the kitchen. No one took notice.

The judge remained seated at the head of the table. What an evening it promised to be. He had introduced himself to the imposing and obviously important officer at the Exchange that morning. With much fawning and flattery he lured the brigadier to Perry Street, having suggested that he'd never truly endorsed the war which fired his neighbors to such foolish extremes. If he comported himself properly to-night, directed the conversation in the desired direction, Sara and Silverglass would be parted forever. He planned a slantindicular version of what he referred to in the courtroom as "the true facts."

The Drewgood house was old, dusty, and poorly maintained. The judge insisted that lamps be trimmed low to conceal its impoverished condition. One sniff revealed the pervasive mold smell of the seacoast, a second sniff the family's abrupt conversion to the celebration of Christmas instead of New Year's — odor of pine. Boughs and wreaths were abundant downstairs. On returning from the Exchange, the judge had dispatched Napoleon with a small saw wrapped in valuable but expendable wallpaper. The boy's destination was a house eight blocks distant, where the judge had previously noticed many pines in the yard. The house belonged to an elderly lady confined to bed. Napoleon cut and stole an armful of boughs without detection. His father patted him on the head when he returned. A skimpy Christmas tree had been moved into the house the day Savannah surrendered.

The brigadier's carriage arrived at the stipulated hour. His orderly preceded him to the door with an umbrella — light rain fell again — and used the tarnished door knocker. The judge had donned his evening finery: a single-breasted burgundy tailcoat with black trousers, white silk waistcoat, and tie. Keeping the lamps low would help hide the fraying of his cuffs, the raveling of his seldom-worn cravat.

His family waited in a line at one side of the hall. Cherry did her best to simper. Merry's expression varied from blank to disapproving. The judge threw the door open and greeted the guest in a voice that nearly blew the orderly off the porch. "General Sensenbrenner, welcome to our humble abode. Felicitations of the season."

"Thank you, sir, we are pleased to be here in a spirit of cordiality and reconciliation." The general turned sideways to squeeze through the opening.

To say Brevet Brigadier H. H. (Hiram Hugo) Sensenbrenner of Columbus was fleshy was akin to saying the falls of Niagara were damp. He was a behemoth, a rolling jiggling mountain of blubber. He stood four inches over six feet. The judge wondered if he had to be hoisted to the saddle in a sling, as old Winfield Scott had in his latter days.

The general shrugged out of his coat cloak; the judge signaled Napoleon forward. General Sensenbrenner dropped the cloak without noticing who received it. Napoleon almost collapsed under the weight. He lurched off while the general waved his orderly back to the carriage and closed the door.

For an officer in the middle of a wartime campaign, the brigadier was amazingly clean and trig. His long thick fan beard, tawny brown with white streaks, was neatly clipped. Single stars on his shoulder straps gleamed, as did eight paired buttons on his double-breasted frock coat and the bullion fringing of his sash. Napoleon reappeared. General Sensenbrenner handed him his chapeau de bras. Napoleon left.

"Our festive table is ready," said the judge. "First, however, I must introduce my dear family." He began with Lulu and ended with Napoleon, who returned gasping for breath. As they filed into the dining room, the judge kept chattering.

"All the Drewgoods are delighted you're here, sir. The sanguinary war will soon end — never much supported in this household, I assure you again. Please take the seat of honor — the head of our humble table."

General Sensenbrenner creaked the floor prodigiously as he circled to his place. Adam stood in his corner. The general pointed to him. "Is your nigger aware that he's free?"

"Oh yes, he knows all about Abe Lincoln's proclamation, don't you, Adam?" The judge smiled; his oddly colored eyes warned Adam not to speak.

"That's excellent. We don't tolerate your peculiar institution further than I can throw an elephant. If you have any friends who are still thumping the tub for the South's outmoded and outrageous economic system, we suggest you not associate with them."

"Noted, noted." The judge waved to shoo Adam to the kitchen. The twins and Napoleon seated themselves along the sides of the table; Lulu took the chair at the judge's right. "Alas, we not only have friends of that persuasion, but a relative, namely Lulu's sister-in-law."

Adam returned with a plate of cornmeal muffins and a decanter of French claret imported illegally on a Fernandina blockade runner. While Adam poured wine, the general stuffed a lukewarm muffin into the center of his beard. "We must hear of that in due course. Who is returning grace?"

"I shall," the judge said. All bowed their heads. The judge proceeded to pray for seven minutes, ending with a stentorian, "Amen." General Sensenbrenner emptied his wine glass and reached for another muffin.

"Savannah has suffered cruel shortages, General, but I can assure you that everything set before you tonight will be pure and wholesome. No frog or mule meat on this table, hah-hah."

"No rat, neither," said Napoleon. The judge glared.

He rang a small silver hand bell. Adam brought in a barely hot casserole of shrimp, followed by the fowl course, a broiler awash in its own congealing juices. The judge had commandeered the bird from a bail bondsman who owed him a favor.

"Salt, General?" Lulu waved the cellar. "Butter? Sugar?"

"Not at the moment. We must say, Mrs. Drewgood, for a wartime feast, this is more than adequate — though of course not as lavish as the table which feeds that poltroon Jef Davis. We hear he sits down to gumbo, chicken, olives, salad, jelly cake, and chocolate ice cream nearly every day."

"Scandalous," the judge said, eyes heavenward.

"As soon as Richmond falls, we'll curb his appetite with a hang rope. Now" — the general continued between bites — "about this unreconstructed relative you mentioned."

"Her name is Sara Lester. She owns three hundred acres of prime rice land on the Little Ogeechee River. Her deceased husband exercised a measure of restraint with his slaves, but the widow is unbelievably harsh."

Brows furrowing, the general said, "We don't like hearing such charges."

"Nor do I relish repeating them. Unfortunately the woman is without a conscience. She beats her niggers mercilessly, and when that won't avail, starves 'em. Frankly, she doesn't deserve to reap the profits of her plantation."

Cherry said, "No, definitely not." Napoleon cried, "I'll say." Lulu agreed by bobbing her head. Merry pressed her serviette to her lips, silently appalled.

"As you know, Judge, I serve on the general staff, with access to the highest echelons of authority. We have ways of dealing with unreconstructed rebels. For example, land may be confiscated and offered at public sale."

The judge's eyes flashed, the conversation having arrived at the desired destination. He feigned an expression of piety. "For a very modest price, I would hope, sir. Darkies can't afford to pay huge sums."

This generated a belch and a shrug, in that order. "We sell not only to colored persons but to anyone who cares to bid on the property. What is the name of said plantation again?"

"Silverglass."

"On the Little Ogeechee, you say?"

"Precisely." The judge provided the approximate location. General Sensenbrenner promised that the Federal authorities would delve into the matter and take action.

"Thank you, General. You will be serving humanity and Christianity, isn't that right, children?" Cherry and Lulu offered amens. Napoleon bounced up and down on his chair and applauded. Merry continued to look appalled. The judge reached for the decanter.

"More wine? For dessert Lulu has prepared her special fruitcake."

"We shall enjoy that," said Gen. H. H. Sensenbrenner while the others at the table, except for Merry, exchanged sly looks. Adam observed this from his corner, darkly handsome as always and, as always, invisible.

Perry Street, Near Midnight

Union troops were camped in the brick vaults of the Old Cemetery, which they'd emptied of the original residents, building fires inside. The infernal glare lit up Perry Street halfway to Chippewa Square. So long as men didn't venture outside the area after curfew, they were free to search for valuables rumored to be buried among the tombstones. Mounded earth, flying shovels, looters silhouetted under dripping trees created a bizarre midnight mosaic. To this was added the fretful neighing of army horses penned in a corner of the property.

Tybee Jo Swett, he of the choleric disposition, avoided this brighter end of Perry Street and skulked in the lee of a porch across from Judge Drewgood's. Jo busily scratched his leg. He needed a bath, if not delousing, before he executed his plan. He also needed to fill his aching middle. On reaching Savannah he'd sneaked over to the mansion of his former employer, Mr. Green, only to find it aglow with lanterns and aswarm with Billy Yanks. No chance of cadging a few morsels from the Green kitchen.

In three days Jo hadn't digested anything more solid than berries and bark. Just like the war, this state of unwashed starvation would end soon, and his personal crusade would be completed as planned. This he vowed several times a day.

Darkness cloaked the Drewgood residence. They were all slumbering in there, his darling Merry and her vicious father who had jobbed him to Milledgeville to dispose of him. That gentleman was in for a big surprise. People didn't tread on Jo Swett with impunity.

He studied the ground-floor windows, selected one he thought promising, over there past the fence pickets and flower beds on the east side of the house.

A trio of soldiers in calf-length overcoats approached from the direction of the square. Jo assumed they belonged to the curfew patrol. One bellowed "Just before the Battle, Mother." Jo eased the LeMat from his waistband. He'd plug all three rather than be captured when he was so close to success.

The soldiers straggled to the cemetery, never suspecting a jailbird nearby. The young men became indistinct figures in a garish mural of firelight and earth. Horses continued to bemoan the rain. Jo eased the LeMat back into his waistband. Nothing more to be accomplished on Perry Street tonight. He addressed the dark house through gritted teeth.

"Sleep well, Merry dear. And you, you old devil — I'll wake you up pretty soon, count on it."

December 24, 1864

Miss Vee's, 10 A.M.

Hattie and Legrand left the house on York Street with a dozen lumpish dolls pieced together before last night's curfew sent Legrand home. The youngsters had decided to distribute the toys a day early, in a poor, largely Negro neighborhood. Amelia remained behind, snuffling in her loneliness. Sara didn't have the heart to turn the pig out in a chill drizzle.

Vee, meantime, was out of sorts — had been since she huffed into the house after the gathering at M. G. Parsley's. She'd gone to bed immediately, without commenting on what had transpired. Attempts to learn more this morning had proved fruitless.

At ten, Sara decided her friend had been moody long enough. She went to the parlor where Vee was playing G. F. Handel's "Joy to the World" at a tempo appropriate for a funeral. Sara seated herself, folded her hands. When the music stopped, she began. "Vee, it isn't my business to pry, but you've been grumpy ever since you came home from that rebel caucus. What went wrong?"

Vee drew a breath; her sizable self seemed to inflate even more. Sara waited. Suddenly Vee banged the keys with both hands, a noise so discordant, Sara started. She saw tears on Vee's cheeks.

"Christmas. That's what did it, Christmas."

"It is the season," Sara agreed. "Do you care to explain further?"

Vee dabbed her eyes with a kerchief. "It all went swimmingly at first. One of M. G. Parsley's guests vilified Abe Lincoln for ten minutes — 'upright ape' and 'prevaricating snollygoster' were the kindest terms used. Another guest attacked Generals Grant and Sherman. M.G. produced her pitch pipe — she chopped up her piano for her fireplace, poor thing — and we sang 'The Bonnie Blue Flag' a capella. We'd hardly begun the second stanza when a guest dashed to the window, hearing voices."

"Carolers?"

"Yes, five of the dearest children you ever saw. Four white, one colored, standing in the rain chirruping 'Joy to the World' as if the sky were blue and cloudless. We all fell silent to listen. M. G. Parsley herself burst into tears. How could we celebrate with thousands of boys in graves far from home? How could there be joy with thousands more lying in filthy hospitals, maimed, all hope of a decent future dashed?"

"And how can there be peace and justice when men and women can be sold like so many cattle?"

Sara's gentle question brought a look of deep concentration to Vee's round face. "Yes, I suppose we must think of them. I admit I haven't done so before." She collected herself, resumed. "A lady found twenty Confederate dollars in her reticule and gave them to the children. The money's worthless now, but the children thanked everyone and ran away in the dark. When someone suggested we end the meeting, no one disagreed. I heard M. G. Parsley still weeping as we raised our umbrellas and left."

Vee gulped, brought her own tears under control. "It must be Christmas, Sara. I found I couldn't hate Mr. Lincoln very much, I was too busy thinking of the sweetness of that carol, and the starved faces of the little ones braving the rain to sing. I woke up this morning realizing the suffering of this war had touched me in a way I never expected. I yearn for peace. I even thought kindly of that Yankee sergeant."

"Winks?"

Vee fluttered her tear-dampened kerchief. "Oh, I don't remember his name." Sara knew she did of course remember. "I just recalled how courteous he was, and how angered by those men who threatened us. He's not a well-educated person, but he's handsome — striking, in his own way." Vee fanned herself rapidly.

"I understand." Sara did feel tenderly sympathetic, yet at the same time was seized with an urge to giggle. Miss Vastly Rohrschamp was love-struck, or the next thing to. Vee flung herself around to the keyboard and played "Joy to the World," this time with gusto, at peak volume.

Twenty minutes later it was Sara's turn to blush and burn hot as a June afternoon. Stephen Hopewell presented himself at the front door. If Saint Nick's sleigh had plummeted through the roof, she couldn't have been more surprised.

Vee answered the knock. Stephen jammed his black felt hat under his arm and, ignoring rain dribbling off his eyebrows, asked cheerily, "Beg pardon, ma'am, is Mrs. Lester at home?"

"Why, she is, do come in." Vee stepped back to admit him. Upon arising Sara had washed and combed her hair, but she was otherwise unrouged and pale, a condition of which she was uncomfortably aware.

"Sara, here's a visitor. You'll excuse me if I tend to matters in the kitchen. Come, Amelia, let these two chat in private."

Vee's discipline had relaxed since the invasion of the house by Marcus and company; Amelia was prone on the parlor rug and saw no need to respond, except to grunt. Vee extended her foot and nudged Amelia's ribs, not hard, but with sufficient energy to send the pig trundling from the room. Sara felt tongue-tied, idiotic — suffused with warmth like that of an airless summer afternoon at Silverglass.

Stephen turned his hat in his hands. This seemed to go on a long time, until Sara remembered herself. "Won't you please sit down, Captain?"

"Thank you, Mrs. Lester." He took a chair. Sara took another across the room, as far from him as the size of the parlor allowed. She hardly dared admit that she liked the rakishly attractive New Yorker, so different from her shy, slow-spoken Ladson.

He cleared his throat. "The fellows who crossed your threshold with bad intentions have been reported to their commanding officer."

"That's good to know."

"However, it isn't the primary reason I called. General Sherman has ordered a review of the troops for late today. It's sure to be a grand event. Journalists aren't obliged to march or otherwise participate. I wondered if you'd care to accompany me to view it?"

Sara wanted to leap to her feet and cry, *Yes, yes!* She pressed her lips together. The pink in her cheeks faded. "Thank you for the kind invitation, but I can't accept."

"Not even on Christmas Eve?"

"Not even then. You are a gentleman, Captain, and this is not against you personally."

"That's your final word?"

"Final, yes."

"Because we're still at war."

"Yes."

"And I'm a Yankee."

"Yes."

"That attitude won't be currency forever, Mrs. Lester. Not if you want to get on with your life. I'm sorry that you refuse, but of course I'll honor your decision." He jammed his black felt hat on his head, not the most polite gesture inside a house; she detected color in his cheeks.

He spoke with strain: "In any case, it's a distinct pleasure to see you again. Let me be among the first to wish you a merry Christmas."

"Merry Christmas to you, Captain Hopewell."

He went out. Rain brushed the parlor windows. Misery overwhelmed Sara.

Why, why had she rejected him, when she wanted so badly to let him squire her to the grand review? Then she wondered why she felt attracted to him at all. He was a Northern newspaper scribbler, most certainly holding abolitionist views. He hailed from that den of cupidity and sin, New York, and no doubt freely participated in illicit revels there. How could she possibly be interested?

No, she didn't understand, there was nothing in her experience to explain the strange yearning, the stranger sense of loss in her breast. She flung herself into a chair and pressed her hands to her face, confused and heartsick as any adolescent.

Winks's Tent, 4 P.M.

Thunder bumped; he heard it through a veil of darkness. Someone pulled his foot. Coming awake was like swimming to the surface of a glue pot.

Bugling followed the last reverberations in the sky. Winks fuzzily recognized the notes of assembly, remembered the review; he'd nodded off. Shouldn't have wrapped up in his blanket.

Someone pulled his foot a second time, this time removing his left bootee, one of the low-cut square-toed shoes he wore when he wasn't in the saddle.

"Oops, sorry. I got your gunboat right here, Captain. Looky, it's me."

Winks grunted, eyes still shut. "It's who?"

"Me, Zip. I got news. I heard something at the horseshoe pitch."

Winks sat up so suddenly, he wrenched his neck. "You mean to say they were playing horseshoes in this weather?"

"No, sir, they was inside a tent near the pitch. Two of them, that professor man and the one looks so innocent."

"Spiker."

"Yessir. I happen to spy him when he was answerin' nature's call at the sink."

Details of Winks's surroundings came into focus, especially his dark-skinned shadow kneeling in the tent entrance. Winks took back his scuffed black bootee, disgusted to note a new hole in the sole. Like most of the army's contractor-made goods, the shoddy shoes lasted about thirty days. He stretched to put on the shoe. "Go on."

"Those two was laughin' and carryin' on. I could smell their cee-gars an' the whiskey they was tossin' down like it was cider. Where do you 'spose they got it?"

"Not important. Tell me what you heard."

The regimental bugler repeated his call. Men scrambled in the muddy camp streets, their gear rattling as they readied for the review. "They tole each other how much money they'd get for the pianner they gonna steal."

"Piano?" It hit him like a slap.

"Yessir. They figure to take it tonight, after the review, when folks be thinkin' of everything in the world except thieving."

"Soulless devils. Did they catch sight of you?"

" 'Fraid they did. Must've made noise. They tore out of their tent pretty wrathy. Called me nigger and a lot worse."

"Were you recognized?"

"Not sure. They had the staggers from swallowin' all that chain lightning, and I was runnin' on canteen water. I got away pretty easy. You think they really mean to steal a pianner?"

"Yes, and I bet I know which one. Christmas Eve. Feature that. Somebody besides Saint Nicholas needs to greet those boys. Change your shirt — review's at five."

"Huh? Me?"

"You're part of my detail, aren't you?"

"Guess I am." Zip's smile gleamed. "Guess I am now. Oh, wait. I got no other shirt."

"I have one extra. Guess you can wear that."

"Lord have mercy," Zip said, clasping his hands in wonderment.

Judge Drewgood's, 5 P.M.

Old Adam delivered the summons while Sara busied in the bedroom, combing tangles out of Hattie's hair so she'd be presentable for supper with the Parmenter family. Adam handed the folded square of wrapping paper to Vee and left before Sara knew he'd called. She was distressed not to have thanked him.

Dear Cousin, the note began. The salutation was an effrontery, inaccurate as well as implying a specious familial warmth. The message, opaque in the extreme, nevertheless inspired a serious case of nerves this dreary evening:

Kindly present yourself at my home at the hour of five, to receive important information about the status of your property. With felicitations of the Season,

> *I remain*
> *Yr. humble & obd't. etc.,*
> *The Hon. C. Drewgood,*
> *Juris Doctor*

"I must go," Sara said after puzzling over the threatening words.

"But what does it mean?"

"I don't know, Vee. That's why I must go. To find out."

Hattie looked up from brushing Amelia with the same bristles used on her curls. Sara was too distracted to reprove her. "Vee and I will go to church at seven, Hattie. Then Adam and I will call for you at the City Hotel, and I'll visit with the Parmenters for a bit. When we're home, we'll have a small exchange of gifts. Legrand's coming to escort you to supper, is he not?"

"Yes, Mama." Hattie sensed something wrong, kissed her mother's cheek, felt its unfamiliar coolness. "I'll be fine — don't fret." Sara moved away, as though she hadn't heard.

As Sara stepped out of the house, a distant cannon boomed to signal the start of the grand review. While Sherman's regiments marched along Bay Street, she marched in the other direction. Band music — "When Johnny Comes Marching Home" — followed her a few blocks, then faded.

No rain fell at the moment, though the stars hid behind a cloud layer. Savannah's streets remained a sea of mire. Small clods of mud clung to Sara's shoes. She stomped on the Drewgood stoop to get rid of them.

Adam answered her knock. A smile spoke of his pleasure at greeting her. "Step right in, Miz Lester, a merry Christmas to you."

"And to you, Adam. I'm here to see the judge."

"Waiting for you in the parlor. I take your bonnet, ma'am." She undid the ties; Adam carried the bonnet to the hall tree and hung it.

A strong scent of wood smoke issued from the parlor arch. The judge sat to the left of the blazing fire. From the mantel hung four stockings of various sizes and quality; Sara wondered if Merry's might be the one missing.

"Good evening, Judge."

"Come in, cousin. Warm yourself." The judge waved her into the parlor without bothering to rise.

A noise on the stairs signaled Napoleon's arrival. Adam was slow to step aside; Napoleon caromed into the black man, angering the boy. He crashed his fist into Adam's hip. "Clumsy old nigger. Stay out of my way."

Adam rubbed his left hip. "Didn't see you coming."

The judge slapped the arm of his chair. "Don't sass your master. There's your place." He indicated a corner near the Christmas tree lit by small white candles. Adam shuffled to the corner. Napoleon approached his father.

"Can I go downtown and watch the Yankees parade?"

"I suppose, but don't attract attention to yourself, or speak to any of them."

"I wouldn't spit on them, but I like soldiering. Guns and bugles and all."

"Watch for cutpurses and riffraff. Be home in time for church." He patted Napoleon's head and scooted him along with a gesture. Exiting to the hall, Napoleon stuck out his tongue at Adam. The old slave remained stoic, although the glowing candles reflected in angry eyes. Sara seated herself to the right of the fireplace.

"Will you take a cup of holiday cheer, cousin? Eggnog, or a flip?"

Sara was past feeling more than a twitch of righteous anger because he had ingredients for such libations. "Neither, thank you. I'm not here to celebrate." She produced the folded brown scrap. "I would appreciate knowing the meaning of this message."

The judge clearly enjoyed her discomfort. He prolonged it by snapping his fingers. "A flip, right away." Adam limped out. "I'm partial to flips this time of year, though the beer we're forced to use is poor stuff. The rum and sugar are good. Both from Barbados."

"Will you please tell me what this means?"

The judge tented his fingertips in front of his nose. "There is no gentle way to convey the essence of my message, cousin."

"Don't call me that." His false piety infuriated her.

"All right, here is the long and short of it. You may own Silverglass tonight, and tomorrow, but that ownership will only remain for a few days."

Sara's heartbeat quickened. "I remind you, Judge — I'm the rightful deed holder."

"Not for long. The army is confiscating the plantation. It will be sold at auction."

The nature and enormity of his scheme fell on her like a blow. "With you bidding for it, I suppose?"

Adam shuffled into the parlor with a pewter tankard on a tray. This he set on a small taboret at the judge's elbow. He retreated to his corner while the judge tasted his flip, smacked his lips. "You are correct. Happily, my credit with certain local lenders is still excellent. I have every hope of entering the winning bid."

Sara lost all restraint. "You miserable old cheat. Who connived with you?"

"Connived? What an uncharitable word, especially this time of year. My new friend Brigadier Sensenbrenner, of Sherman's general staff, began the process when he learned you were an unfit landlord."

"Unfit? Why on earth — ?"

"Routine and excessive abuse of your slaves."

Sara was quivering, sputtering, aflame with wrath. "All our slaves have run off. When Ladson was alive, he never raised his hand to a single one."

"Oh, it isn't your poor dead husband under scrutiny. Did you not hear me before? You're the culprit."

"I've never injured a black person, at Silverglass or elsewhere."

"Deny it all you want, my dear, Brigadier Sensenbrenner believes differently. Your cause is lost. Your acreage, too."

A log fell in the grate. Cascading sparks

snapped and died. Sara bowed her head. The judge had won.

"He believes different 'cause you told him lies."

The voice stunned both white people. The judge's head snapped around. Adam stepped from his corner, taller than he'd seemed before. The judge cried, "What did you say?"

Adam spoke over his master's head, addressing Sara. "They had that Yankee sojer to supper the other night. The judge told big stories about how cruel and mean you was to your black folks. I heard every word in the dining room. I was in the corner — in my *place*."

The judge leaped out of his chair, waving his pale hands. "I'll have you locked up, boy."

"Ain't no boy," Adam said. "I be sixty-one years old next January second, and sick and tired of the way you and your kin treat me."

"This is treachery. Rank betrayal."

Someone trooped down the stairs; Lulu's round eyes and rouged mouth appeared in the arch as Adam boldly met the judge's stare. "Possible you could see it like that, Judge. 'M too old to fight you any other way."

Lulu edged into the room. "Cincinnatus, what is all this commotion?"

"Your husband just got a Christmas present he didn't expect," Sara said. "Adam, are you willing to repeat your statement about the judge telling lies to the Union general? Repeat it in a courtroom, under oath?"

The judge snorted. "Ridiculous. Niggers have no legal standing. Their word counts for nothing."

Adam's gnarled brown hand rubbed at his hip. "Think it will now that Gen'al Sherman's took over, and Mist' Linkum's giving the orders up in Washington City. Miz Lester, I'll swear to the lying on a Bible, but I got to get out of this house, for good."

"Come with me. I'll protect you."

The judge struck a commanding pose. "Stand there. Don't move."

Adam shook his head.

"I order it. *Order* it. You're my property."

"Not no more. And you can tell that no-good son of yours I hope he chokes."

Lulu's eyes rolled up in her head. She sagged sideways and would have collapsed on the rug had not an ottoman been conveniently beneath her backside. As she draped over it, swooning, Sara offered her arm to Adam.

"Shall we go?"

He hesitated. Her eyes gave him leave. He grinned.

"Yes'm. Be delighted."

She slipped her hand through the crook of his elbow. They walked out arm in arm.

Christ Church, 7:00 P.M.

Sara, Vee, and Adam arrived at Christ Church at ten before seven. As they climbed the outside stairs, Sara whispered, "Have you ever attended a white church?"

Adam turned an old soft hat in his gnarled hands. "No'm. The Judge didn't 'low it. I go to the First Africal Baptist now and again."

"I'm sorry to say that you must sit in the gallery."

"The section for colored people. I heard about it."

Hesitating at the entrance, Sara touched Adam's hand. "I wish there were another way."

"It don't trouble me, Miz Lester. I'm free to come here, or not, thanks to you. I meet you after the service."

Candles poured light into the sanctuary. Christ Church had anticipated a crush of Christmas Eve worshippers; stools and crates jammed the side aisles to deal with the overflow. Every downstairs pew was filled, as were the improvised seats. Sara murmured, "Well, it's the gallery for us too. Please, Adam, go ahead."

Giving a little nod, he began to climb the stairs slowly; bent as he was, he was a picture of dignity and strength. Sara and Vee followed.

Some seats for white worshipers remained in the pews on the south side of the gallery. Vee excused herself rather loudly as she squeezed past annoyed parishioners in order to sit down and thus reserve two vacant places; she easily filled both. Adam slipped off to the segregated seats beyond the organ, which was located at the center rear of the gallery.

To make room for Sara, Vee scooted sideways; a frail gentleman on her right, temporarily crushed, expostulated. His wife hushed him. Sara took her seat after counting heads in the first row downstairs. All the Drewgoods were present, except Merry. A strange calm enveloped Sara as the organist began the prelude, a transcription of the overture to Handel's *Messiah*. She didn't for a moment regret her behavior at the judge's house.

Vee tapped her wrist. "Look at the organist."

Sara turned toward the rear of the gallery but could see little more than a mass of wavy black hair above a dark clerical robe. "What's wrong with him?"

"He isn't bald. Our organist is bald as an egg. Either he's wearing a wig or it's someone else. I can't place the shape of the head, although he looks fam—" A gasp. "Oh, heavens. It's that Yankee."

"Playing here?"

"It would seem so." Vee giggled in a way that didn't fit the solemnity of the occasion.

A senior member of the vestry sat in the high-backed chair usually reserved for the Right Reverend Elliott; the bishop had departed Savannah with General Hardee's army, no doubt fearing some sort of reprisal from the Union invaders. The organist finished the prelude. Sara was atingle, and not a little off-center. Vee had correctly identified Captain Hopewell.

★ ★ ★

The service proceeded on familiar lines — kneeling to pray, rising with hymn books in hand to sing "O Come, All Ye Faithful," listening to a soprano beautifully render "Lo, How a Rose E'er Blooming," and then the small choir offering *"Stille Nacht"* in the original German. During the prayers, led by the vestryman, Sara eagerly bowed her head and sent her gratitude winging away: thanks for her sprightly daughter, for steadfast Vee — old Adam too. With the long, sad war ending, the rights of former slaves expanding, Adam's testimony could foil the judge's Machiavellian perfidy. She and Hattie could go home to Silverglass without fear. Adam would have a home there as long as he wanted.

Another vestryman stepped forward, Bible in hand; he read the timeless Christmas story from St. Luke. Sara's eye kept straying to the wavy black hair of the organist. A rush of guilt prompted her to improvise a little prayer during the Scripture. Wherever Ladson might be, she implored him to understand and forgive the emotions of a woman too long alone.

The odors of tallow, feminine powders, male hair pomades, and close-packed bodies grew stronger as the minutes marched by. The service lasted less than an hour. When the postlude, *"In Dulce Jubilo,"* reverberated thrillingly, and worshippers readied themselves to go, Sara was among the first on her feet.

"I must speak to him. Wish him merry Christmas."

"Must? Really?" Vee said with arched brows. By then Sara was struggling against the outflowing tide of Georgians refreshed and temporarily lifted from wartime despond by the Nativity's message of peace on earth and goodwill to men regardless of whether they lived above or below Mason and Dixon's line.

Nervous and fearful of stumbling, she reached the rear of the gallery. In front of the splendid pipe organ, Stephen Hopewell was gathering up his music. "Why, Mrs. Lester. What an unexpected pleasure."

"I — you — that is — we were tremendously surprised to see you playing, Captain."

"The regular organist fell ill. Someone got my name, and members of the vestry contacted me. I was happy to fill in. I love sacred music."

"We — they — that is — you play beautifully."

"Thank you indeed." He gave her that broad smile that jellied her knees and intensified her tingling. "Not all of my amateur performances take place in Bowery deadfalls."

"Did you miss the review?"

"Yes, I came here to rehearse. No loss — I had no companion to enjoy it with me, after all." He gazed at her so warmly, she almost fainted. "Do you by chance need company for the walk home?"

Once again she wanted to cry *Yes, yes!* Then

the old reaction repeated itself: a negative bob of her head, a flustered, "Kind of you, but my friend Miss Rohrschamp is with me." She saw a reprise of earlier disappointment.

"Perhaps another time, before the army moves on."

"I hope so, yes, I do hope so," Sara exclaimed. "A merry Christmas to you, Captain."

She fled downstairs. There she confronted the Drewgoods coming out by the center aisle. The judge, with Lulu in hand, fixed Sara with a malevolent stare. As he brushed by, he muttered words that had no place in a church.

Cherry followed her parents, squinty-eyed and dutifully hostile. Napoleon would have kicked Sara had she not showed her fist to forestall it. The boy's attention switched to the gallery stairs, where old Adam had just come down with a number of others of his race. Napoleon yanked the tail of his father's coat as the family marched out the main door into the December dark.

More than a little dazed, Sara started when Vee tapped her arm. "Are you feeling well?"

"Yes, perfectly," Sara answered with a forced smile. Her vision was misted, blurry. Trying to clear it, she fixed on the sanctuary candles slowly dripping wax on their silver stands. Like them, she was burning. Burning and melting from the memory of the captain's face.

Oh, dear. What was she to do?

Outside Judge Drewgood's, 8:20 P.M.

The air, heavy with moisture, congealed into fog. It suited Jo Swett's strategy of concealment followed by a surprise assault on Fortress Drewgood.

The day's activity had wearied him, but inner excitement kept him from succumbing. Early that morning he'd set out for his old haunts on Tybee Island. After trudging a quarter mile on a sandy track overhung with dripping live oaks, he'd been lucky and hitched a ride in a parson's shay. He found Ogie seated on the beach near his shack, mending a shrimp net. Ogie regarded him with a laconic eye.

"Shrimp season's been bad, but I got to feed my family. I thought you was put away in Milledgeville penitentiary."

"Looks like I'm not. Looks like I'm back."

"Mighty dangerous, I'd think," Ogie said.

Jo waved to Ogie's twin boys romping barefoot in the surf, seemingly unaffected by the cold. Ever-hungry gulls cruised above the gray rollers that dissolved in white froth on shore. A brown pelican streaked down, plunged into the shallows, and took off again, stealing a meal from under the beaks of jabbering gulls.

"That's true," Tybee Jo agreed, "but the judge jobbed me into jail, and he isn't going to get away with it. Does Marie's brother still own a pony cart?"

247

"Coleman got the cart, yes."

"And a horse?"

"That old nag, he's on the road to the glue works an' it's a short road. Figure him to drop dead any time."

"I need the cart and the horse tonight. I need them for, oh, maybe a week."

"Why?"

"Tell you afterwards."

"I got to trust you?"

"When we sailed out to fish, you always did."

Ogie considered that. "Guess you right. We go over and see Coleman."

"I need one more favor. I need a note delivered in town. Does Marie still trek to Savannah to do laundry for white folks?"

"Every day 'cept Christmas. She's already gone. You sendin' something to the judge?"

"To someone in his house, and only that person. I can't go myself, not in the daylight."

Ogie felt the weight of friendship; he expressed it with a rueful sigh. He tossed the net on the sand and called to the barefoot twins laughing and kicking cold spray at each other. "You boys watch this here net. I be right back."

He tramped off over the dune. Jo followed. Ogie's shack was snug and tidy as ever. From a high shelf Ogie took a rusting tin can without a label; coins rattled.

"I loan you this ten-cent piece, I 'spect to see it again, jus' like Coleman's cart."

Tybee Jo pinched the coin between thumb

and forefinger. "What am I supposed to do with this?"

"Hire a colored boy off the street to make your delivery. Plenty of hungry boys in Savannah. This'll buy one of 'em a bit of rice if it can be found."

Both friends peered at the coin. Guilt overcame Ogie. "Oh, here" — he plucked a second dime from the can — "it's Christmas."

"You're a fine friend, Ogie." Ogie didn't disagree. "You'll get everything back."

"I better," Ogie said. "Le's go wake up Coleman."

Tybee Jo hid Coleman's cart and horse in an alley near Chippewa Square. He prayed the old plug would neither neigh and attract attention nor fall down and expire with much the same result before he finished his night's work. Jo had seldom been afraid of any man or any thing, but the deed he planned to carry out was new, utterly foreign.

He wouldn't turn back; still, he knew nothing of the real consequences of the step he contemplated. He did believe that much satisfaction lay in store if his nerve held out.

He stole along Perry Street in the coiling fog. He settled down to wait under an old magnolia, nervously watching soldiers passing in front of fires in the cemetery. A few minutes after eight, all the Drewgoods save for Merry returned from church in their depot wagon. One by one lamps were lit in various rooms. Soon all were dimmed to black except for two that were taken upstairs.

Tybee Jo crept into the front yard carrying a short stepladder. The ladder had been burgled from Bettelheim's hardware store. Regrettably, he'd had to break the cheap hasp on the back door, but he had no intention of being jailed on a false charge a second time. After he found the ladder, he wrote on a blank page torn from an account book.

I PROMIS TO PAY THIS STORE FOR ONE (1) STEP-LADDER WHICH I MUST HAVE TO-NIGHT. THIS IS NO JOKE, YOU WILL GET YOUR MONY. I WISH YOU ALL VERY HAPPY HOLIDAYS, SINCERLY YRS JO. SWETT ESQ.

He dated the promissory note and left it in plain view.

Jo hoped all was quiet inside the Drewgood residence, but he had no way to knowing. Hiring a waterfront waif to deliver his note had been easy, although he couldn't be sure of reaction to the note or whether his intentions and instructions were fully understood. He could only hope.

He owned no watch, thus had no clear sense of time, but he knew that after 9 P.M. the streets would be patrolled by Geary's provost guard. He was therefore inclined to haste. Hurrying, he tripped in wet weeds at the corner of the house. He lurched against the cypress siding, held his breath, waiting for a lamp — an alarm raised.

The moment of danger passed.

He crept along the side of the house to the chosen window. There he unfolded his ladder. Again his excitement betrayed him: The ladder slipped from his perspiring hand and fell against the house, this time making a noise that must have carried for blocks.

Actually it didn't, but it carried as far as the two-person necessary in the backyard. Napoleon emerged shoeless from the rude little structure just as the ladder banged.

Napoleon smoothed the front of the flannel nightshirt that reached to his ankles. No one would dare break into the home of a man as influential as his father. He suspected a stray animal, or some drunken Yankee wandering in search of his camp. Napoleon squared his shoulders and marched to the rear of the house and down the grassy strip separating the Drewgoods' from the neighbors. Fog hampered vision, but Napoleon had no trouble spying the silhouette of a man with his foot on a stepladder.

"Halt there."

"Oh, perdition. Who's that?"

Napoleon recognized the voice.

"Pa, Ma, anybody, wake up, help, Jo Swett's trying to break in, we'll all be murdered."

Tybee Jo raised his fists. "Will you shut your clapper? I'm not going to murder —"

"— *help, help, help,*" Napoleon wailed, not hearing a syllable of the denial. In a mysterious fashion, the window a foot above the stepladder slid upward. A valise came flying out. Tybee Jo shouted, "Oh, blast blast blast," sounding less angry than grief-stricken.

A door crashed open; another nightshirted figure appeared at the front of the house, leveling the pitted muzzle of a .36-caliber Leech & Rigdon, a revolver from a reliable Confederate armorer in North Carolina. The judge seldom fired it and never oiled it, so it tended to jam, which didn't occur to him just then.

"Identify yourself or I'll shoot." The judge held his weapon in both hands without appreciably steadying it. A feminine head appeared in the window a foot above the ladder.

"Papa, don't point that at Jo, it might go off."

The judge's barrel drooped. "I thought you were confined to bed with the vapors."

Merry flung a leg over the sill, affording Jo a glimpse of clocked white stocking which he found impossibly titillating despite his high state of nerves.

"I had to fib or you'd have forced me to attend church. Napoleon, stop bellowing like a heifer." With one foot on the ladder Merry struggled to wriggle out of the window backwards. She

swayed, flailed in the air. Tybee Jo leaped forward.

"Hang on, I'm coming."

"Stay away from my child," the judge cried.

"Why should I when we're going to be hitched?"

"Hitched?" the judge repeated. *"Hitched?"* The barrel drooped all the way down to his spindly shank. "You and my — ? You can't be serious. I thought you came to do murder."

"Sure, you'd think the worst of me, wouldn't you?" Tybee Jo gingerly grasped Merry's waist, feeling electric thrills from the mere touch. "You'd be sure to think that's why I ran all the way back from Milledgeville, to get even for being put away by your pack of lies. It makes me mad as hornets, you old buzzard, but I care more about Merry than I do about getting even. I came back to make this lovely person my bride. I sneaked a note to her stating my intentions."

"You mean to *elope* with her?"

An upstairs window opened; Lulu's head popped into the fog, thickly masked by a white cosmetic paste. She echoed her husband with an even louder, *"Elope?"* and then swooned over the sill.

Jo clasped Merry's hand — her other clung to her little straw bonnet — and picked up her valise. He nearly threw his back out doing that. What had she packed, a cast-iron trousseau? "Come on, darlin', we can make it," he panted.

Together they ran past the judge, who uttered a plaintive, "Merry, why are you doing this? Why are you abandoning your family?"

"Because you're not fit to be called family anymore, you're a pack of greedy grasping cheats, and I'm in love. In love, in love," Merry sang as Jo careened to the front gate, Merry clutching his hand and her little straw hat too. They ran into the fog, toward the hidden pony cart, their destination a justice of the peace Tybee Jo knew slightly, down near a defunct cotton gin at Pembroke.

The judge leaned against the house. He listened for sounds of the retreat of Jo Swett and his daughter. He could hear nothing over Napoleon's blubbering. Then came a new sound from a previously opened window upstairs. The judge flourished his Leech & Rigdon in a paroxysm of rage.

"Cherry, stop snoring."

The revolver went off.

Thus the lovers made their successful escape.

Miss Vee's, 9:30 P.M.

The raiding party consisted of Professor Marcus, Melancthon Spiker, Peter Pence, and a listless horse named General Longstreet.

As their open wagon creaked through Savannah's fogbound alleys, Spiker complained: "What if it was Winks's nigger who spied on us?"

Reins in hand, the professor replied grumpily, "You aren't sure, are you?"

"No, I ain't sure, but —"

"Because you were too obfuscated by drink. So we don't know. So shut your face."

Spiker wasn't easily deterred. "It's past nine o'clock."

"Couldn't get the wagon sooner. Things slow way down on Christmas Eve. Now look sharp, we turn here. We go in the back, haul the piano out the same way. Take some doing on those stairs but they's three of us, we can manage."

Hunkered in the dark on York Street opposite Miss Vee's, Winks and Zip suffered and shivered, waiting. "Curfew rung ten minutes ago, Captain. S'pose they don't come."

Winks picked another pest out of his beard and bundled his carpet cape tighter around him. "They'll come. Before I signed my enlistment in Indianapolis city, I didn't know a thing about the criminal classes. This army's been a real education. The professor definitely belongs to the criminal classes, and the criminal classes are long on greed but short on smarts. Just keep watching."

General Longstreet responded to a tug on the reins, stopped, and gratefully hung his head. Professor Marcus climbed down the wheel, looped the reins and snugged them around the brake lever. The heavy air bore the none-too-

256

pleasant scent of Dr. Rohrschamp's necessary a few feet away. Peter Pence asked, "How do we unload the pianner once we take it?"

"I found a buyer already. Trawler captain beached here with a busted ankle. Lives up at Georgetown, wherever that is. His wife wants a piano pretty bad — she's refined, he told me. He's givin' her a late Christmas present."

"How'd you find him?"

"Worked the docks. We deliver the piano to him, he takes it the rest of the way when, as, and if he can. He pays seventy dollars, gold, we don't accept Confederate."

Pence scratched his head. "That don't work out three ways even."

"Why, yes it does. I get forty, you and Spiker get fifteen apiece. Who's the brains here? If we're all done with the quizzing, let's get to it before the provost guard wonders why we're havin' a tea party in this alley. All ready, Spiker?"

Spiker showed his stolen Allen pepperbox pistol. "Ready."

"Pence, you got the straps for the pianner?"

Pence showed the rubber articles in question.

Marcus slid a well-maintained Army Colt from the holster attached to his belt. He swivelled 180 degrees, watching until he was satisfied. Over in the square, men sang "O Come, All Ye Faithful" in a manner that would never threaten a trained choir.

"Tempest fidget," Marcus said. "Here we go."

Professor Marcus's plan didn't call for sub-
tlety. He smashed the kitchen door with his boot
and tore the latch out of the jamb. He leaped
into the kitchen palely washed by parlor light
from the other end of the hall. Amelia sprang up
as though launched by a catapult. She ran
round and round, oinking. "Capture that
porker," Marcus cried. "This time we'll have
some barbecue."

Peter Pence advanced, dangling the rubber
straps. "Here pig, pig, pig."

A shadow of more than usual size blocked the
hall. Still dressed and awaiting the return of her
boarders, Vee put her hand on her brow Indian
fashion and peered. "Amelia? Why are you carrying on?"

"I have a pistol aimed at you, woman,"
Marcus said. "Step back. Me and my boys are
comin' through."

The professor advanced down the hall, then
Spiker. Amelia shot between Pence's feet, under
the chopping block, and out the kitchen door.
Pence uttered an oath and followed the others.

Four scented candles placed in saucers
around the parlor cast a gentle umber glow. The
tree with several small, crudely wrapped pack-
ages lying beneath it appeared less skimpy in the
muted light. Bosom heaving, Vee raised her
hands submissively.

"I accept my fate. Please remember I am a
gentlewoman."

"Oh, shut up, you old hippopotamus, we ain't got time to mess with you." Marcus waved his Colt at the Chickering upright. "There she is, boys, let's get her out of here."

"I see 'em in there, Zip. Here we go."

Winks dashed across the street, his companion close on his heels. Winks's top hat sailed off, but he didn't stop or wait to test for a lock on the front door. He entered as Marcus had, using his boot.

He dived into the room, Deane & Adams .44 preceding him. The rapid intercession didn't permit a lot of original thought; Winks exclaimed, "Caught in the act. Find some clothesline, Zip. Tie them up while I cover them."

Marcus wasn't about to be penned. "Don't stand for it, boys. If we do, we'll get a cell or a walk to the gallows." He fired his Colt.

Winks's right arm throbbed above the elbow. The sudden shock discharged his revolver as he dropped it; his bullet hit Spiker's thigh. Spiker realized he was shot and collapsed on the carpet.

Winks glanced down at the blood soaking his sleeve. Anger more than dismay animated his face. He couldn't stay upright, fell sideways into a chair. Miss Vee, meanwhile, pressed palms to her round face and screamed like a steam bellows.

Waves of pain rose in Winks, blurring his vision. Professor Marcus screwed up his mole-dotted face and sighted on Winks's breastbone. Calmly, Winks thought, *I am a dead man*. It might have been so if Zip hadn't hurled himself across the parlor, both hands flying to Marcus's windpipe.

Marcus's gun hand was knocked askew by Zip throwing him to the floor. The Colt roared; the lead ball tore a cup-size hole in the wallpaper. Vee screamed louder.

Zip crawled all over Marcus, knees in his belly, fists crashing against his ears, jaw, forehead. Marcus managed to shove Zip off, roll away. He jumped on top of his black adversary, reversed the Colt, and began to pound Zip's skull. While this took place, Winks grabbed his bloody sleeve and gritted at Miss Vee, "Quit yammering and help that boy."

Miss Vee responded. She gazed from chair to chair, deciding which one to ruin; that gave Marcus a chance to whack Zip's head again. Far from defeated, Zip in turn had his fingers clamped on Marcus's throat. "You nasty man," Vee cried as she broke her least favorite chair over the professor's skull.

"Oh," he moaned, eyes crossing, and again, "Oh."

At the front door, a rectangle of foggy darkness, Sara appeared suddenly with Hattie in hand and Adam right behind.

Supper at the City Hotel had lasted longer than expected; until after curfew. Mrs.

Parmenter served a large casserole of rice and okra perked up with little chunks of tough chicken. Sparks served small tumblers of ale from an unknown source and seemed almost jovial. The meal finished, Mrs. Parmenter presented Sara with a small vial of Paris perfume saved since before the war. Sara had anticipated something like this and reciprocated with a lace-edged sachet filled with English lavender. She grew the shrub at Silverglass and had brought the dried leaves to town in a small pottery jar.

More than once, Legrand sidled toward a mistletoe sprig fixed to the mantel. Each time Hattie smiled charmingly and skipped to the other side of the room. When they left the City Hotel, Sara encouraged speed from her companions, realizing the lateness of the hour.

"My goodness" was all she could say at the sight of Vee's parlor: Winks barely awake in a chair, his right sleeve leaking blood onto the bosom of his uniform; Spiker unconscious and bleeding on the carpet from his injured leg; Professor Marcus supine, plucking at his blouse and moaning while Vee sat on his legs to ensure his submission; Zip raising his head to peer at the new arrivals through eyelids already puffy from punishment. Pence had previously sneaked out the back way. Bitter smoke was dissipating slowly.

Hattie wrinkled her nose. "Phew. Papa used to smell like that when he fired his rifle."

"Gunpowder," Adam said with a nod.

Sara knelt by Winks. "This poor man needs a surgeon."

Vee adjusted her bulk on the professor's legs. "This one needs to be tied up before he does more damage."

"What did they want here?" Hattie asked.

"The piano. They came to steal the piano."

"On Christmas Eve," Sara said, struck with sadness at the thought of human beings sinking so low. Amelia trotted into the room and gazed at the carnage, comprehending none of it.

Adam was more composed than the others. "I find some tools. Put this door back on its hinges." Without waiting for permission, he disappeared down the hall.

Zip sat up, massaging his head. His lower lip was cut and puffy, his right lid purpled and swollen shut. A racket on the stair announced three members of the provost guard, one a corporal. They burst into the parlor, rifle bayonets twinkling and flashing.

"Who fired shots? Who wounded these men? Who owns this house? Give us your names. Ladies first. Everyone is under arrest."

"Ain't this a howdy-do," Zip said, which just about summed it up.

Miss Vee's, 10:20 P.M.

The ladies and Hattie ignored the corporal and his minions while making Alpheus Winks as comfortable as they could in his chair; Sara refused to move him. Winks drifted in and out of consciousness, obviously hurting. Sara slit his sleeve using scissors. The ball seemed to have passed through the fleshy part of his upper arm. Whether there was bone damage, she wasn't qualified to decide.

Carefully, she bound his arm with a long strip torn from her petticoat and knotted it. Winks roused and cried out, but the tourniquet slowed the blood flow.

Sara confronted the nonplussed corporal of the guard. "This man urgently requires medical attention. Send one of your soldiers to fetch a surgeon, without delay."

"Do you know his regiment?"

"I believe he mentioned the Eighty-first Indiana."

"Yes, ma'am. Brewster, you heard the lady. Run."

Out the door went Brewster, just as Geary's adjutant galloped up. Gunshots had been heard in the neighborhood. The adjutant demanded to know what had transpired.

Vee and Sara obliged with a graphic account. The adjutant ordered Marcus and Spiker removed by ambulance to temporary confinement in the Chatham County Jail. Sara mentioned the arrest order. The adjutant immediately countermanded it. The corporal of the guard slunk out.

"Let me be correct about the number of persons residing here," the adjutant said. "Do both Negroes belong to the household?"

Vee, bless her, promptly said, "The older one does, his name's Adam. The other came here with the sergeant. He helped rescue us."

The adjutant leaned down. "Sergeant? Can you hear me? Are you able to speak?"

Winks muttered.

"I understand the young nigra belongs to you."

Winks groaned, which might have been a denial.

"We'll place him with other African refugees from outlying plantations. They're camped all over town."

Winks roused sufficiently to say, "No, sir. He stays. Wasn't for Zip, I'd be dead."

"Body servants are not condoned or permitted in the army."

"He's not a servant, he's — my friend."

The adjutant turned to Zip. "He said you're a friend, not his bondsman. True?"

Overjoyed, Zip said, "Yessir."

"Well, since you're a free man of color, you can stay or go, as you choose."

"I stay right here, Captain."

Winks overheard, turned his cheek to the chair back, and shut his eyes.

The exchange of gifts forgotten, everyone welcomed the long-bearded regimental surgeon and his orderly when they arrived shortly after the adjutant departed. The surgeon conducted a brief examination; then he and the orderly carried the limp sergeant to Vee's bedroom and shut the door.

Vee paced the parlor carpet, now permanently ruined by ink, grime, and gore. Sara held Hattie's hand tightly. Zip stared at his shoes with his one useful eye. Adam whistled a one-note melody in the kitchen.

Presently the surgeon came out of the bedroom, untying the strings of his bloodied apron. A pungent odor of chloroform followed him.

"Looks worse than it is, I'm pleased to say. The ball tore a nasty hole in his flesh, but there's no injury to the humerus or condyles, else we might have been faced with amputation." Vee swayed dangerously and supported herself by leaning on the Chickering.

"I dressed the wound and administered an opiate. He should sleep through the night. The sergeant won't be able to tote a pail of water or fire his pistol, let alone rejoin his regiment, for some time. Otherwise, rest and recuperation should heal him up nicely. I'll arrange to have him transferred to a local hospital, though I must say I've inspected one such and found it sadly lacking. Medicines can't be had, sanitation is questionable — most able-bodied doctors are serving in the war zones."

"He can stay here, with us, if you allow it." Vee's enthusiasm startled everyone, not least the surgeon. "He'll be much more comfortable, and we owe him so much."

"A generous offer, Miss Roarlock."

"Rohrschamp."

"Sorry, sorry. I'd agree at once, but I'm reluctant to have a soldier quartered in a household with livestock."

Hattie marched up to him. "My pig's neat and clean, Mr. Doctor. And she's not livestock — she's a pet."

"Is that correct, ladies?" Sara and Vee confirmed it. "Very well. I will write orders for the sergeant's care. Spoonfuls of the opiate, which I'll leave with you, must be administered per my schedule. His wound must be inspected and cleaned at regular intervals. His cold-water dressing must be changed frequently."

Vee blanched. "Certainly, I — I can do that."

Sara knew she couldn't. She slipped an arm around her friend's waist. "I'll help."

The surgeon clapped his hat on his head, summoned his orderly who carried the medical bag, extended greetings of the season, and left them.

Christmas Day

Miss Vee's and Elsewhere

What a dreary Christmas it promised to be: rain in the offing at daybreak, supplemented with lightning bolts and thunderclaps. The impending storm woke Hattie on her pallet in the parlor; Sara had insisted Vee share her bed. Zip and Adam slept on blankets in the kitchen, disturbing Amelia until she got used to them.

No sooner had Hattie washed her face with cold water and brushed her teeth with a twig than another Yankee officer presented himself at the front door. Sara and Vee were already dressed and busying with pots of rice for breakfast.

"Ladies, I am Major Hitchcock." The visitor swept off his black campaign hat and stepped out of the rain. "I serve General Sherman. I am here at his express instruction."

Even though he represented the enemy, Vee remembered the day and responded politely. "Won't you please sit down?"

"No, thank you, I prefer to stand. The general deeply and personally regrets the incident of last evening. We have had reports of petty thievery and alcohol-induced rowdyism among our troops, but nothing so violent or crassly premeditated as the attempted robbery at this house. Marcus and Spiker will be brought up on charges, which I personally will draft. In civilian life, I am an attorney. The other malefactor, Pence, is the object of a wide search, but we fear he has deserted. He is not the first," Hitchcock added with a weary air. "So many of our young men are eager for this war to end."

Sara said, "They aren't alone. Thank the general for us, please."

"Are you ladies fully supplied with victuals? The general and his staff will enjoy a traditional Christmas dinner later today, and he would very much like to send a chef to prepare a similar meal for you."

Hattie was agog. Vee's answer was a spirited, "We'd be most grateful."

"Consider it done. Good morning, ladies, and a merry Christmas to you all."

The belated exchange of gifts took place soon after Major Hitchcock left. The gifts were small and, as it turned out, handmade by each of the givers.

To Sara and Hattie, Vee gave wooden picture frames, obviously antiques. Under the glass she'd mounted illustrations from *Godey's*: two slender, rather anemic females, one per frame, stylishly dressed with gloves and hat. Vee had tinted portions of both pictures with water-colors — light green, pale blue, mauve.

Sara's gifts were identical sweetgrass baskets for holding small objects on a lady's bureau. Hattie had sewn two pincushions of scrap calico stuffed with Spanish moss. They were wartime gifts, created with a certain desperation, and perhaps the more valuable for all that. All three recipients expressed great delight over their presents.

Around noon the thunderstorms abated; white clouds appeared, with intervening patches of blue. South of the city, a raft poling from Coffee Bluff into the Little Ogeechee's tidal current carried four young soldiers from the 85th Illinois. The soldiers enjoyed sightseeing amid the river islands and rice canals until the white clouds darkened and the blue patches vanished. Slanting rain began with hardly a warning.

One of the soldiers spied a head bobbing in midstream. "Boys, that fella's drowning."

Moments later, they hauled a soggy and terrified man onto the raft. He lay belly down, gasping and retching. They knelt around him. One asked, "You with the army?" His sodden clothes didn't reveal it.

"Y-yes."

"Where were you going in this weather?"

"Trying to swim to the other side of the river."

"Not much of a swimmer, are you? What's your name?"

"I don't guess I should tell —" An unlovely stream of water erupted from the nether parts of his stomach. He rolled onto his back, looking green.

"Pence. My name is Pence. Save me, boys, I never felt so sick in all my born days."

Stephen spent Christmas afternoon mooning over Sara Lester. He'd conquered many a maiden's heart, but in regard to the widow, he was, so to speak, butting his head against granite without leaving a mark.

He daydreamed of New York at holiday time: the cheerful crowds, the enchanting lights decorating the department stores, the sparkle of fresh snow hiding the dirt and ordure of Fifth Avenue. He longed to rent a sleigh and dash along the wooded roads of the new Central Park, his companion sharing a lap robe and marveling at all the sights so amazing and new to her. . . .

Instead, he sat in Georgia. In the rain. Rebuffed.

Admittedly, the mood in Savannah, if not precisely happy, was far different than he'd anticipated when the army marched from Atlanta. His notebook bulged with remarks copied down from Sherman's soldiers:

"Less malignancy toward Yankees than we have seen elsewhere."

"People seem glad we have come."

"There is a delightful entente cordiale *between officers and ladies."*

He should show that one to Sara.

Stephen had the use of a desk in a corner of the editorial rooms of the *Savannah Herald,* née the *Morning News,* until the army turned out its staff of aging secesh and replaced them with members of its journalist corps, abetted by a few literate volunteers from the ranks. A nearby window afforded a melancholy view of rain-drenched Bay Street. Stephen had labored for two hours phrasing a dispatch critical of Gen. Jef C. Davis and his actions at Ebenezer Creek.

The piece lacked snap. Further, his editor, Plumb, was such a hard-headed Unionist, he no doubt would spike any copy questioning the performance of senior commanders.

Giving up, Stephen found the other Davis, of *Harper's*, with his feet on another desk and his pad on his knee. Davis had decorated the pad with squiggles and arabesques. Stephen recognized ennui when he saw it.

"What time's the mess for the ink-stained wretches?" he asked the sketch artist.

"Four. Bet you already know the bill of fare."

"Let me guess. Rice, followed by rice, then more rice. A slab or two of Georgia beef from the herd. Coffee. Canned milk if we're lucky."

"Also a surprise."

"Ah. Rice pudding?"

"Mince pie. I have it on good authority."

Stephen nudged Davis's shoulder to direct his attention to Bay Street below the rain-speckled window. "Will you look at that?" He referred to an Army wagon with SANTA'S SLEIGH painted on the side. Crude antlers made of sticks were roped to the heads of two mules pulling the wagon through the wet and rutted sand. The driver wore long red underwear buttoned over his blue tunic and a cotton beard tied to his ears. Soldiers in ponchos sat in the wagon, amidst gunnysacks.

A Negro child ran up beside the slow-turning wheels. A soldier reached in a gunnysack and handed down a rag doll. The child hugged it.

The soldier grinned. The ersatz Santa guided the wagon around the corner.

"Merciful heaven," Stephen said. "Volunteers?"

"I would guess so. Good for them." He offered Stephen one of his pale green cigars.

They lit up and puffed. Both men felt better. Now if he could only forget the widow Lester. . . .

At the Charles Green mansion, a party of twenty senior staff dined in General Sherman's second-floor rooms. The general's mess caterer, Captain Nichols, served up roast turkey with stuffing, accompaniments of vegetables, and excellent clarets and sparkling wines supplied by local merchants who wished to remain anonymous. Charles Green's crystal, plate, and silver graced the table.

Conversation was jolly and spirited. With much wine consumed and toasts drunk to the holiday, peace on earth, the Union, and other good causes, there were no expressions of guilt anywhere around the table.

To Sara fell the task of cleaning the sergeant's wound and applying new dressing. It was odious work, but she understood that her friend wasn't up to it; if Vee undertook even part of the duty, Sara would have a second patient on her hands.

Vee took over the relatively less challenging

job of rousing Winks every few hours, measuring out his medicine, and spooning it down his gullet. In midafternoon she woke the Union soldier on schedule. He smiled at her. His eyes seemed clearer, more focused. Vee withdrew the spoon and said, "Might I ask you one or two personal questions?"

"Why, I expect I can stay awake. Go ahead."

"Is there a Mrs. Winks at home?"

"Yes, indeed there is."

"Oh. Do you — ah — have children?"

"I don't. She did. My brothers and me."

"I see, I see. Thank you so much."

"That all?"

"Permit me to ask — in your wartime encounters, did you — I hope you won't think me indelicate — did you ever —" She seized the moment, fearing it would never come again: "— commit dishonorable acts upon the person of a civilian female?"

"Say, you can believe I didn't," he exclaimed with surprising vehemence. "Neither did any of my men while I had charge of 'em. I wouldn't allow it."

"We heard stories about the licentious behavior of Yankees."

"I don't doubt Jef Davis would like you Southrons to believe everything you hear, and maybe some of ours acted that way, but none that rode with me. They was just greedy stinking thieves. You've had experience with those." He yawned.

Vee tiptoed out, vaguely let down, yet excited by pleasing new thoughts. He liked her; she was sure of it. And he wasn't a monster.

Possibilities for the future were all at once boundless.

At half past four, a United States commissary wagon rolled up to the cottage. A portly German chef and two colored stewards carried in food hampers. The stewards began setting the table with Vee's china and silver. The chef fed kindling into the stove — he brought his own supply — and informed the ladies that the twenty-pound turkey had been roasting throughout the afternoon; now it must be finished. Adam stepped in to assist the stewards without being asked.

The house filled with delicious aromas, so pervasive and mouthwatering, Hattie grew dizzy with anticipation. She tried to find the treachery in all this Sherman generosity and couldn't.

At half past five, the chef said dinner would be served in an hour. With darkness lowering and the rain in abeyance again, Hattie decided Amelia needed a walk. Sara asked Zip to go along and look after her. Hattie didn't object; she'd taken a liking to the runaway.

Strolling north on Bull Street, Zip began to utter a series of strange wheeps and whistles. Amelia shied and grunted at the end of her tether. Hattie said, "What on earth's that?"

274

Zip explained his fondness for imitating local bird life.

"Is it hard?"

"Not so hard long's you practice."

"Could I learn?"

"Some of the calls is pretty tricky, but there are one or two that's easier. Salt crow's easy, but it grates on the ear. Here's one I like." Despite his puffy lip, he delivered a whistle that slid upward cleanly on the scale. This he repeated, following it with a series of staccato whistles on a single note. "Can you get your tongue around that?"

"What is it?"

"Red cardinal."

Hattie whistled. Zip grimaced and offered corrections. Hattie tried again. Zip granted that it was better. Hattie practiced the cardinal call all the way back to York Street, delighted by her newfound skill.

The two returned to Vee's in the dark, another rain shower imminent. Over by the military camp in the square, Hattie saw a man she'd noticed before, loitering near the double stairway leading up to the doors of Christ Church. She hadn't seen him following them and perhaps he wasn't, but things about him made her uneasy: his ugly face, his purplish nose, his gaudy checked overcoat with fur collar and cuffs. The man picked his teeth with a silver pick and stared. Hattie gave him a glare as they hurried on.

Inside again, comforted by the lamps and

candles and Miss Vee at the Chickering playing "O Little Town of Bethlehem," Hattie forgot the stranger.

At twenty past six, Sara drew Vee aside with a proposal. They discussed the idea and agreed on a course of action. They repaired to the steamy kitchen, where the colored stewards were busily filling bowls with fried oysters, sugared yams, butter beans, mashed cranberries, and hot corn bread. The golden bird sat in its roasting pan on top of the stove, exuding aromas of oysters and sage.

The chef bowed. "*Ja,* madam, what may I do for you?"

Sara screwed up her courage and began. "We're ever so grateful for all these fine dishes —"

"*Ja,* you will enjoy, I am sure."

"But there are so many starving people in town — refugees camping in abandoned buildings, feed lots, boxcars at the rail yards — surely they'd welcome a hot meal. Would you think terribly of us if we asked you and your men to pack everything into your wagon and find people more in need than we are?"

The chef considered. "To remove all this — deliver it elsewhere — that is not so hard. What is hard is understanding your request."

"Christmas," Vee said. "It's the time to remember the poor and needy. Have you read Mr. Dickens's tale of Ebenezer Scrooge?"

"I don't read no *Englischer* books." The chef's severe expression melted into a smile. "But you are good ladies. We pack up and find the hungry ones."

"And don't tell General Sherman," Sara said.

Thus Sara, Hattie, Vee, Zip, and Adam dined on plates of soggy rice and cups of imitation tea. Vee then suggested more carols. They repaired to the parlor, where Vee launched into one of Hattie's favorites, "Jingle Bells." Sara heard a faint call from the bedroom and hurried to respond.

Awake in the dark, Alpheus Winks said, "I'd be grateful if you left the door open so I could listen."

"Happily, Sergeant. In a little while I plan to read the Christmas story from my Bible."

"Haven't heard that since I left Putnam County," he said with a drowsy smile. "This is a mighty good evening."

In a cramped but satisfactorily cheap room in the garret of the Pavilion Hotel, the same sentiment occurred to Isaiah Fleeg, though not for the same reason. Out trolling the local population between rainstorms, he'd spied a handsome buck perfect for his collection.

December 27, 1864

Miss Vee's — "Under the Bluff"

Military and commercial activity that stopped for the Sunday observance of Christmas accelerated as the new week began. Sherman issued a special order to make sure the local population was treated with "civility." A second order allowed disaffected residents to travel under a flag of truce to Charleston or rebel-occupied Augusta; a third granted his regiments permission to add Savannah to the list of battles sewn on their colors. Captain Poe, in charge of the Union engineer corps, sent crews to survey Hardee's defenses and rebuild them where necessary. A steamer docked and offloaded crates bearing an unexpected legend.

FROM THE CITY OF NEW YORK
— TO —
THE CITY OF SAVANNAH
RELIEF SUPPLIES (FOODSTUFFS)

A mate on the steamer said a similar relief ship was loading in Boston despite opposition from Secretary of War Stanton.

Incoming papers described President Lincoln's delight at receiving Sherman's telegraph message in the White House on Christmas eve. The text had flashed across the North. In a *New York Eye* column, Stephen read that the moderate stance of municipal officials and the behavior of Savannah's war-weary citizens combined to give the city a more favored status than that of despised Charleston. The charity of Northerners was not so difficult to understand.

Even so, Sara and Vee saw evidence of misery. Homes both modest and elegant showed ugly signs of vandalism: fences ripped out, siding torn off for firewood. Dead horses lay in the streets. Vee pointed out a former Latin teacher hawking corn dodgers amid the huts in Wright Square. No doubt the teacher's wife had baked the little cakes, and she and her husband had gone hungry to supply the ingredients.

A canvasser knocked at the door Tuesday afternoon. Hattie answered. The man handed her a long foolscap sheet.

"Military food mart opens tomorrow. All are welcome, regardless of income. Have the lady of the house write down her needs — flour, beans, bacon, pork, sugar, molasses, coffee — then present the ticket for admittance." He tipped his palm leaf hat and bustled on.

Zip and Adam spelled each other standing guard outside the house. Zip wore an old coat sweater that had belonged to Dr. Rohrschamp; heavy as it was, it didn't filter out the afternoon chill. Late in the day, Zip visited the necessary. As he reached for the door latch, a white man jumped from the bushes at the back of the lot.

"Good afternoon, boy. I'm detaining you. Come along without a struggle, and you won't be harmed."

Zip scowled. "I seen you before."

"But you haven't seen this, have you?" From the pocket of his green overcoat, Isaiah Fleeg drew his Colt hideout pistol with his yellow-gloved hand.

"Step around behind the privy. My assistants are waiting with transportation."

Tempted to run, or at least yell, Zip's intentions were balked by the intimidating weapon. "I don' know what this is about."

"All will be explained, and to your advantage, I guarantee. I don't want to lose my temper with you, boy, so humor me. Get moving."

Zip spied a tall Negro with amber skin lurking among low palmettos bordering the alley. Surely these bad men had mistaken him for someone else; he'd convince them of it when the leader was less impatient. On that thin justification he stepped into the shrubbery, where the amber man seized his arm and shoved a rag into his mouth.

A third man, white, with a gold earring and a livid facial scar, forced Zip into an old one-horse rockaway with its black side curtains rolled down. The white man fastened Zip's wrists behind his back with baling wire. The two henchmen took the high front seat; the scarred man picked up the reins.

Zip's chief abductor climbed in. "Lie on the floor."

Zip obeyed. Isaiah pressed the sole of a black ankle boot on Zip's neck. Get these devils to admit a mistake? Zip suddenly doubted it. The carriage rattled off while he contemplated the enormity of his misjudgment.

East of the City Exchange, Bay Street petered into an unlovely neighborhood of failed and empty shops and, down the slope, beside the river, abandoned storehouses with grime-streaked windows. Here there were no street lamps, and few respectable people. The address was the same for all the riverside properties — "Under the Bluff."

In a nameless ballast-stone building full of dust and wispy cotton linters, lively spiders and lethargic brown skenks, Zip met two other prisoners of his race. Both were in their early twenties. The stouter of the two, introduced as Nehemiah, bore bruises and abrasions that showed his resistance to captivity. His wrists were manacled around a wooden pillar supporting a rickety stair; above, a loft door opened on a path leading to the top of the bluff. Isaiah used this obscure exit to slip in and out unseen by loiterers along the river.

His other prisoner, Ralf, wore leg irons. He sat on a pallet of ticking, head between his knees. He barely glanced at the new arrivals.

"Put the leg irons on this one, boys," Isaiah

instructed his men. When Zip was secured, Isaiah squatted by him, though not so close that he could be seized. "Your name, boy."

"Zip."

"Zip what?"

"Zip — uh — Zip Winks."

Isaiah made a sucking sound between his teeth. He walked into the vast darkness — the storehouse was lit by a single hanging lantern — and returned with paper and pencil. "Make your mark on this, please."

Zip's eyes gleamed with defiance. "Can't read that."

Isaiah sighed. "Are all you niggers ignorant? What it says is very simple. You willingly consign yourself to me in return for free transportation to a northern city. There you will be given a monthly salary, food, clothes, and a prideful place in the United States Colored Troops."

"Slow down. You telling me I be a sojer?"

"I am."

"Sojer with a gun?"

"That's it exactly."

"Gen'l Sherman don't want coloreds for sojers."

"Uncle Billy may be the hero of the hour, but on the issue of arming the Negro, he's one hundred eighty degrees away from General Grant and Mr. Stanton, the secretary of war. They welcome coloreds into the ranks of fighting men. Sherman will come to grief if he bucks them."

He leaned forward to whisper, "Sherman's a bigot, in case you didn't know."

"No, I didn't."

"Up north you will be a draft substitute for some white gentleman who doesn't care to risk himself in combat. You will bring dignity and honor to your race." And to Isaiah, a three-hundred-dollar substitute's fee, unmentioned. Of course he had expenses — the two street ruffians he'd hired, the rented rockaway, steerage fare on a coastal steamer — but if he collected just five Negroes, he'd clear a thousand to twelve hundred dollars.

"Doesn't that sound fine, boy?"

"I wanted to be a sojer a long time," Zip admitted. "But this is fishy. If I bring dignity an' honor to my race, how come I got to be chained up?"

"For your own safety. Savannah's full of Johnny Reb hotheads eager to hang any nigger willing to bear arms against white men. The whole town fears occupation by colored troops after Sherman leaves. Better you stay out of sight until we can ship you and your friends to New York. One of my men will be back with a bucket for your personal needs. Breakfast arrives bright and early."

Nehemiah gnashed his teeth. "Biscuits hard as rocks. Weevily, too."

Ralf sobbed.

The tall amber man gratuitously kicked Zip's ribs and walked away laughing.

December 27 and 28, 1864

Miss Vee's — Searching

After the disappearance, Adam circulated through the downtown, then Forsyth Park. On neither expedition did he sight Zip or any clue to his whereabouts. He reported his bad news when he returned to York Street.

Hattie slept poorly. Half-human creatures with fiery eyes chased her through nightmares. Vee and Sara sat in the parlor, fretting. When the clock rang midnight, Sara excused herself. Vee remained and nodded off in her chair. She slept so soundly the next hour, she failed to hear the bells and horns signaling a sizable fire to the west. Ultimately two hundred houses burned, and tons of gunpowder nearly exploded in an arsenal. This they learned from neighbors next morning.

Winks woke at 3 A.M. complaining of pain. Sleepy-eyed, Sara rushed to his bedside with a lamp. She changed his dressing while Vee spooned medicine into him in such an agitated way that he choked. Vee soothed him by patting and stroking his hair until she realized what she was doing.

The regimental surgeon called at nine o'clock. He rigged a sling for Winks's arm, advised that the sergeant was recuperating without difficulty, and complimented the ladies on their care. He left asking himself why they were so dour and drawn, as though their minds were elsewhere.

Adam visited the newly opened military food store. With a basket on his arm, he joined an amazing assortment of men and women, old and young, queued up outside the hall. Some wore silks, some linsey-woolsey, some garments sewn from cornmeal bags. Adam saw a one-legged grandfather in army butternut, and a lad in a coatee cut from flowered drapery material. He saw grand dames in feathered hats and care-worn women in country bonnets. Blacks stood next to whites without comment or complaint from either.

He waited two and a half hours to have his ticket examined by a guard who then admitted him to the hall. Along crowded aisles he col-lected rations of rice and black-eyed peas, salt pork, coffee, and a small packet of sugar. Back at York Street, he described the leveling power of hunger that he'd witnessed.

Thursday afternoon, the mood in the house-hold sank further. Sara expressed it: "I fear he isn't coming back."

"The colored people are in a state of agita-tion," Vee said. "He's run off."

"Doubt that, ma'am," Adam said. "He told me he liked it here." Hattie added her voice to his; she'd heard the same sentiment.

"Then something nasty's happened to him," Winks said during an impromptu bedside con-ference. "By thunder, I wish I could crawl out of here. I'd find him."

Vee and Sara debated the wisdom of attending a public meeting called for half past four at Masonic Hall. "What's that about?" Winks wanted to know.

Vee explained. "Fifty or sixty local folk petitioned Mayor Arnold, requesting a meeting with the city fathers. Apparently there's broad support for some sort of declaration of loyalty to the Union and Constitution. I suppose it wouldn't hurt to attend. Stay or go, it won't return that poor boy any sooner."

Sara agreed, and Hattie too, although Hattie felt the situation called for something more positive than inaction.

Legrand dropped in to visit just as Sara and Vee left for the Masonic Hall. Legrand paid his respects to Sergeant Winks in the bedroom, albeit cautiously. Then he and Hattie sat in the kitchen sharing a stone jar of root beer he'd brought. "Sparks concocted it. Not half bad."

Hattie replied with a listless nod. The gloom of the winter afternoon oppressed her. She cudgeled her brains about Zip, whom Legrand suspected of disappearing over the horizon for good.

A memory clicked in place. "Legrand, I don't think so. I suspicion he was kidnaped, and I'll bet I know who took him."

"Who?"

"A strange man who watched Zip and me when we walked Amelia on Christmas afternoon. I saw him twice, once in Johnson Square, then again just down the street."

"He followed you?"

"I presume so."

"Was he a local gentleman?"

"More likely a Yankee. He had a purple nose, like a cabbage, and was dressed up like a circus clown, in a green overcoat with black checks big as windowpanes." Hattie licked the rim of her empty glass and savored the last sweetness. "I can't understand why he'd carry off a poor darky like Zip."

"Zip's young, isn't he?"

"Not even twenty."

"Pa said that up north, they're selling colored boys for the army — substitutes for men who are drafted and don't want to serve. Pa read about it in an old Washington paper yesterday. Men calling themselves recruiting agents headed for Savannah when the city surrendered."

"My heavens." Hattie hopped off her stool. "We must find him."

"How? He could be locked up out of sight. Wouldn't you stand a better chance of finding the man who followed you?"

"Well, that's true, but if we can't find him, I know a way to signal to Zip."

"You do?"

In reply, Hattie whistled.

Hattie donned her bonnet, shawl, and mittens. She and Legrand left the house without informing Adam or Winks. In Wright Square, soldiers were stoking a bonfire and singing "Sweet Betsy from Pike."

Legrand was still skeptical: "Savannah's a big place. Zip could be anywhere."

"Use your brains, Legrand. Do you think a man who looks like a clown will be locking up nigras in someone's mansion, or a hotel room? Too public. We'll start with the rail yards. I'll signal every few minutes." She repeated the odd whistle she'd identified as that of the red cardinal.

"Hattie, you can't go places like the rail yards. All kinds of desperate people are camping there. You're a female. Just a child."

Hattie stopped in the middle of Bull Street and put her hands on her hips. "Take that back."

"What part?"

"The part that isn't true. The child part."

Seeing her dudgeon, Legrand muttered, "All right, I take it back, but —"

"No more argument. I can go anywhere in Savannah with you to guard me." She seized his hand and folded it tight in her mittened fingers. "You're a war veteran, Legrand. Come on."

Born and brought up in a religious household, Hattie had listened to Bible readings and Sunday sermons that included alarming descriptions of Hades. Here on earth, she never expected to see anything resembling that dismal place, but she found it on West Harris Street, where bonfires burned in the wreckage of Savannah's once-busy rail yards.

Legrand held her hand as they wove through the maze of rolling stock converted to shelters or chopped to pieces to stoke fires. Animal bones boiled in reeking kettles. Starving families stared from abandoned cars of the Central of Georgia, the Savannah & Albany, the Ocmulgee & Flint Rivers. Begging hands stretched out to them in the Central's gutted roundhouse. Pleas and whimpering, cries and cursing pursued them.

Repeatedly, Hattie whistled and listened, whistled and listened, without a response. She wanted to run from the dreadful place, but Zip's plight kept her searching. Finally, after an hour, she said, "He isn't here." They hurried away on Harris Street.

Hattie sank down on someone's cement stirrup block. Legrand listened to the trees soughing in the wind. He turned up his coat collar. "Where now?"

"The docks. Plenty of empty cotton warehouses down there."

"Plenty of evil dram shops, too."

"We'll go anyway. It's still hours till curfew."

They descended the bluff at Barnard Street. Lights on moored vessels made pretty reflections in the water. Less pretty were the raucous shouts and arguments issuing from dingy groggeries. Legrand refused to let Hattie enter any of these. She shivered on the cobbles, warily watching to left and right, while Legrand went in, kepi in hand, to describe the odd-looking stranger. He emerged each time with the same negative shake of his head.

A little farther on, the taverns gave way to lightless buildings where cotton had been stored for shipment through the blockade. Legrand found crates or hogsheads for Hattie to stand on so she could peer into ground-floor windows. These were uniformly dark, caked with dirt and salt spray. Climbing down, she shook her head just as he had.

Presently they reached a storehouse whose grimy windows showed pale lantern light. Hattie squeezed Legrand's hand excitedly. "What can I stand on?" He surveyed the area, found nothing convenient, formed a stirrup of his palms and boosted her.

Hattie clung to the brick sill. She gasped. "Hsst! Let me down."

He jockeyed her to a safe landing. Hattie whispered, "I saw a colored man, chained to a pillar with manacles."

"Zip?"

"No, but there are other nigras in there, I just couldn't see them clearly."

She stepped into his cupped hands a second time. She pressed against the building to the right of the window, not immediately visible if someone looked her way. Her throat was dry, and her lips. She worked up a supply of spit and after two attempts, got off a successful cardinal call.

She listened. Heard the river lapping, men bellowing a chantey in the distance. She started to fall, clutched the sill. Legrand balanced her like a circus acrobat. Secure again, Hattie risked showing herself in the window. She whistled.

In the warehouse, a caged bird answered.

"He's there, Legrand." She heard commotion inside, saw a lantern's beam flash on the grimy glass as she jumped down.

A door at the end of the building banged open. A lanky Negro with skin Hattie thought of as saffron raised his lantern over his head.

"Run, Legrand. He's armed."

The Negro spied them. Legrand snatched her hand and almost jerked her out of her shoes. The Negro didn't bother to chase them. He shot at them instead.

Masonic Hall — Searching, Cont.

4:30 P.M. and Later

Nearly seven hundred souls crowded into smoky Masonic Hall at the corner of Bull and Broughton. Mayor Arnold brought the meeting to order. He introduced the first speaker, old Bettelheim, one of the petitioners. The hardware merchant hobbled to the platform.

"Friends and fellow citizens of Savannah. Tonight I appeal to your reason and your compassion for your fellow man. The South, and our fine city, have endured four years of devastating war. We have seen loved ones killed and maimed on distant fields of battle whose names remain foreign to us. We have suffered hunger, pestilence — personal privations of every kind. Those whom we feared — those who came to subdue us — are not, by and large, the despicable vandals and desecrators they were portrayed to be."

Stentorian booing erupted in the gallery. Others quickly silenced the protester. Someone yelled, "Go on, Bettelheim."

"I have little more to say other than to plead for a return to normalcy, and for willing submission to national authority under the Constitution. The time has come to bury bygones in the grave of the past."

Applause followed, but Vee withheld hers.

One by one, men and women rose from the audience to repeat Bettelheim's appeal in different words. Mayor Arnold took the podium to thank all who'd spoken. His face showed strain, even anguish, but he endorsed what the speakers had said. More booing; half a dozen walked out. An alderman called for the question.

Sara glanced at Vee and raised her hand when the vote was taken. Seconds passed. Then Vee did the same. Cries of, "Traitors," and "Miserable sycophants," rang from scattered places in the hall, but the peace vote carried overwhelmingly.

Judge Drewgood, seated with Lulu in the first row, stood up and ostentatiously called for silence. Nine rows behind him, Sara pulled a face. Just like him to wait for the outcome before declaring himself. Finger pointing heavenward, the judge lauded the assembly's decision as "a milestone on the road to renewed peace and prosperity."

His oratory, belated as it was, nevertheless generated an ovation. Courthouse cronies surrounded him to congratulate him. Vee started, ducked as something sailed overhead. The rotten egg broke on the judge's brow and dripped down.

"Phew." Sara held her nose as others were doing. Vee fanned herself. The judge immediately became a foul-smelling island in a sea of rapidly retreating well-wishers.

On the way out to Bull Street, Vee said, "I'm not sure it was the right outcome."

"It was the only possible outcome, Vee. The war's over. We must bind up the wounds and start afresh."

Sara and her friend returned to York Street at six. From the parlor, Sara called, "Hattie?" There was no response. Adam walked out of the kitchen, long-faced.

"She's not been here in some while, Miz Lester."

"Do you know where she went?"

"Ma'am, I don't. Sergeant might."

The ladies hurried to Winks's bedroom and unceremoniously woke him. He rubbed his eyes. "That friend of hers, Lamar —"

"Legrand," Sara said. "He dropped in just as we left."

"Guess he and Hattie left soon after. I must have been asleep."

Sara looked stricken. "I pray nothing's happened to them."

In the silence, Winks's grim expression echoed the same fear.

"Through here," Hattie cried, leaping into a doorway.

Legrand warned her that she mustn't enter the place, but she didn't hear or didn't care. She was already dashing toward a front table, where roistering sailors goggled at Hattie's skirt and bobbing curls. A man in a striped jersey caught her wrist. "No ladies permitted on these premises, missy."

"An' there's the door." The florid barkeep snapped his towel toward the entrance. Hattie pulled and yanked, but the tipsy seaman wouldn't release her, in fact found her struggles hilarious. Legrand leaped forward, snatched a glass off the table and poured beer on the sailor's head.

He sputtered and spat; everyone else including the barkeep laughed at his expense.

Hattie broke away. "Must be a back door," she cried, rushing on.

At that moment their saffron-hued pursuer entered from the dock, pistol in hand. He'd fired two shots at them, both of which missed. The barkeep waved a hickory billy.

"No niggers allowed. Get out."

He flung the billy. It sailed end over end, forcing the saffron-colored man to duck and dodge out of sight to avoid it. Hattie and Legrand reached the back door.

"Did you expect that to happen?"

"I thought it might," Hattie said. "This way."

A dark, fetid passage led to a rickety stair. They climbed at top speed, arriving in a similar passage that opened on Bay Street, between deserted offices. Hattie leaned against the bricks, caught her breath.

"You were very brave, Legrand. Thank you."

Legrand bent over, hands on his knees, nearly fainting from the strain on his wound. "I think we lost him."

"Yes," she said.

"We can go home."

"No."

"No? Then where — ?"

"Madison Square. Someone has to rescue Zip before they move him and hide him where he can't be found." She darted into Bay Street, running. Legrand rolled his eyes and limped in pursuit.

"I suppose I'll have to be sassy to get us in the door," Hattie speculated as they neared Union headquarters.

Legrand didn't disagree. "I'll wait outside. Couldn't hold my head up if anyone saw me in that den of blue-bellies."

Hattie was right about the need for audacity and a sharp tongue. The sentries at the Macon Street door of Charles Green's house crossed their bayonets to bar them; the steel gleamed in the light from porch lanterns.

"No admittance to civilians after six P.M.," said the private, who looked too young to shave.

"I'm here to see General Sherman about an urgent matter."

"Girlie, didn't you hear him?" said the other sentry.

"I heard, but if you don't stand aside, I promise the general will have your scalps."

The soldiers exchanged looks. The second told the first, "Fetch Major Hitchcock, Daniel. We'll see what he makes of this."

The bayonets uncrossed. The first private about-faced and marched into the house. Legrand retreated to the street, folded his arms, waved Hattie on when the sentry returned to admit her to the downstairs. Hitchcock met her there.

"Miss Lester." The major couldn't conceal amusement. "When Private Daniel said a young lady insisted on seeing the general, I should have suspected it was you."

"I wouldn't be here if a man's life didn't depend on it."

"What? A man's life?"

"Possibly more than one."

The major glanced toward the stairs. "The general's at supper. He routinely works until midnight or later. I hesitate to interrupt him."

"In this case, I think he'll appreciate it."

Skeptical, Hitchcock said, "We shall see." He disappeared upstairs.

Hattie walked to and fro in the lavishly appointed hall. Two clerks busied at their desks; somewhere a telegraph key tapped. Otherwise the mansion seemed asleep — much quieter than when she'd visited the first time.

Boots on the stair announced Hitchcock, then Sherman, coatless and in disarray as usual. The general's old suspenders showed, and a napkin was tucked into his collarless shirt. Sherman greeted her with a mock bow.

"Miss Lester. Do you always visit at mealtime?"

"Mr. General, the matter won't wait."

"The same could be said of the excellent broiled catfish I left on my plate. Never mind, come along to my office. That will be all, Henry." The major quietly retreated.

Seated in the second, inner parlor, a desk between them, Sherman tugged the napkin from his shirt, heedless of scattering crumbs. Hattie had planned her strategy on the dash to Madison Square, but a sudden premonition of failure unsteadied her. The general was a commanding and impressive figure, not unfriendly, but watching her with a steady gaze that demanded an explanation.

"Major Hitchcock used the word *urgent* when describing your visit."

"Yes, sir. I'm here because of a warehouse down on the river. A Negro named Zip is being held prisoner there, and other Negroes may be confined with him. My friend Legrand suspicions it has something to do with selling colored replacements for white soldiers up north."

"That noxious trade does exist. I despise it. Continue."

"Zip is a brave person. He helped rescue my mother and our friend Miss Rohrschamp when looters broke in. He saved the life of one of your own men, Sergeant Alpheus Winks, of Indiana, when a looter threatened to shoot him."

Sherman scraped a wooden match on his sole, lit his cigar, and flicked the match into a spittoon. "I think I am ahead of you, Miss Lester. You want me to send some men to rescue your colored acquaintance."

Hattie gulped and nodded, not personally intimidated by this fabled enemy so much as fearful of his power to deflect or crush her plan. "Yes, sir, that's what I came to ask."

"But you don't really know why this Zip fellow is being detained?"

"Only what I told you, sir. The purpose must be illegal, because one of Zip's jailers fired shots at my friend Legrand and me after we discovered the warehouse."

Sherman leaned forward, more the father than the soldier. "Not injured, were you?"

"No, sir, thank you for asking. We came right here so I could appeal to you for help. I can offer something in return."

That startled him. "What, precisely?"

"Well, everyone's heard about your message to Abraham Lincoln —"

"Very well received, it was," Sherman said, nodding behind a veil of smoke. "The president was gratified that the lost army, as the papers referred to us during the march, had turned up found at last. Exactly what is this quid pro quo you have in mind?"

Hattie sat up straighter, hands in her lap, striving to imitate her mother's calm and reasoned demeanor. "I am a good Southerner, general. An ordinary person."

Sherman interrupted. "I mean no discourtesy, but permit me to stop you."

"Sir?"

"A match I use to light this cigar is ordinary, and it burns brightly. Professors of science tell us that every seventy-five years, Halley's Comet streaks across the cosmos. It, too, burns brightly. But it is not ordinary. Do be careful how you use the word *ordinary* in reference to yourself. In my lifetime I have met scores of ordinary people, and I cannot possibly classify you as one of them. Do you take my meaning?"

"I think so. May I go on?"

His nod granted permission.

"I propose to write a letter to Mr. Lincoln. Your message gave me the idea. I'll say to him that the South is beat for good, anyone with a thimbleful of brains should face it, and the country must come together again. You called me a — a certain kind of rebel, but it's time for me to put that away. I will try to be a good American. I'd like the president to know my feelings. They say he's a kind and understanding man."

"Even in Dixie they say that?"

"Well — some do."

The general studied the end of his cigar. "You want me to see that your expression of new-found loyalty reaches the White House, in return for which I'm to send men to rescue your friend and any other colored gentlemen held against their wills at this mysterious warehouse?"

"That's the bargain I came here to propose, yes, sir."

The general remained silent for nearly a half minute. Hattie wiggled on her chair, palms perspiring. Sherman tapped ash from his cigar but missed the spittoon's brass rim by inches.

"I'm willing to entertain part of your proposal, even endorse it. But I can't endorse the whole of it."

Hattie felt failure like a stone in her middle. "You can't?"

"I cannot sit idly by while brave soldiers expose themselves to uncertain dangers, in your behalf." Hattie fought the impulse to weep.

Sherman rushed to the door, flung it wide.

"Orderly. Ready my carriage. I want an armed squad to accompany Miss Lester and myself to the river, at once."

The Warehouse — 9:10 P.M.

Abruptly awakened from a whiskey-induced doze at his hotel, Isaiah Fleeg was not in a gracious mood, or anything near. His shadow advanced and retreated as he stomped back and forth, showing his minions, and the prisoners, how incensed he was.

His henchman hung back. The squat man with the earring had lost a coin toss and thus drawn the duty of rousing Isaiah. The yellow-skinned man had stayed to watch the prisoners: Ralf and Zip immobilized on their pallets with leg irons, rebellious Nehemiah still manacled to the stair pillar.

Isaiah pulled up short to revisit the errors of his Negro helper: "Let's go over this again. You saw a youngster through that window. You gave chase and discovered two spies instead of one. You shot twice, and both rounds missed. You, a strong man, couldn't catch two children."

"I tol' you, boss, they ran into a saloon down the way. Coloreds cain't go in there."

Isaiah slapped his yellow gloves in his palm. "Don't hand me excuses. What I want is the identity of those spies."

The craven prisoner, Ralf, pointed to Zip. "He know who they are. He say so when the girl looked in the window. He kind of spilled it out, then took it back."

Isaiah planted himself in front of Zip's chained legs. "That true, boy?"

Zip shook his head.

"You deny you know your would-be rescuers?"

"Yes, I do."

Ralf said, "He lying to you, boss."

"Hear that, Zip? One of your fellow recruits insists you aren't being square with me. Perhaps we should test your veracity."

Zip glared at Ralf. Isaiah motioned the tall Negro to his side. "Make amends for your blundering, Gabriel."

"Yes sir, boss, how can I do that?"

"Persuade this nigger to be more candid." Isaiah put a finger to his chin, striking a pose suited to a stage actor conveying deep thought. "Start by breaking his fingers. Left hand first, I'd say. One finger at a time."

"Ought to work," Gabriel said eagerly, kneeling. Gabriel seized Zip's left hand. Isaiah tossed him a dark blue kerchief. "Stuff that in his craw. We don't want a lot of caterwauling."

Zip tried to scoot away, his leg chain clinking. The white henchman ran behind him and hooked an elbow around his neck. Gabriel seized Zip's left hand, said, "Hold his mouth open."

The other man reached for Zip's jaw with his free hand. Zip bit his thumb. The white man squealed.

Isaiah purpled the air with oaths. He booted Zip's ribs. With Zip groggy, stuffing the kerchief between his teeth proved no problem.

"Proceed, Gabriel. You can break all his fingers if need be. Just make him talk."

Gabriel bent Zip's little finger backwards. The bitten man forcibly restrained Zip's other hand to prevent further interference. Zip's cheeks popped with sweat. Gabriel bent the finger more. Zip unsuccessfully stifled a moan. Isaiah said, "That's the ticket."

Furious pounding on the river door diverted the torturers. The door shook alarmingly, although a large horizontal beam held in two iron brackets prevented it from being opened.

A greasy window broke, showering glass into the warehouse. The barrel of an 1861 model Springfield rifle appeared, behind it a boyish face and blue forage cap. Other voices demanded entrance.

Isaiah Fleeg believed in bold play when he held high cards, but Savannah, this miserable putrid backwater of the decadent and disloyal South, had dealt him deuces and treys. He snatched his hideout pistol from his overcoat pocket. "Leave the niggers. Every man for himself." He fired at the thick door.

Isaiah's bullet failed to pierce the door, which fell inward suddenly, hinges broken and the bar snapped in two by a log ram in the hands of soldiers. Isaiah saw torches streaming and smoking in the dark, enough of them to suggest an entire regiment come to thwart him. A bearded man wearing a long blue coat without insignia leaped into the room.

Isaiah's response was to shoot again, without careful aim, then dash for the stairs. Nehemiah stuck out his foot, but Isaiah dodged. He scrambled up two, four, six steps. Yankees spilled into the warehouse, bayonets flashing, torches fizzing. The bearded man ran halfway to the stair and shouldered a regulation Colt Army .44 revolver mounted to a glossy stock.

"You on the stairs. This piece is cocked. Throw down your weapon or you'll be dead meat for breakfast."

Isaiah whipped around and fired at the bearded man, who fired almost simultaneously. Splinters flew up between the soldier's shabby shoes. Isaiah's soft hat blew off, the left brim pierced. A burly sergeant shouted, "You boob, you attacked General Sherman. That's a hanging offense."

"Let him be, Sergeant. He's in my sights. One more twitch, and I'll drill him between the eyes."

Isaiah peered at the flint-eyed soldier; his courage, never in large supply, ran out faster than sand from an hourglass pulverized by a coffee mill gun. The hideout pistol fell from his fingers. He raised his hands. Sherman signaled the sergeant.

"Chain him. Don't bother to be gentle about it."

A moppet with golden curls appeared behind the general. "See your gentleman in here, missy?" he asked, never letting his eyes stray from Isaiah.

Hattie pointed. "Right there, Mr. General."

"A good night's work, then."

Hattie hugged Zip. Sherman's men dragged Isaiah off the stairs. Others subdued his hirelings, neither of whom was anxious to fight. A corporal searching Gabriel discovered a ring of keys. He freed Zip from his leg irons and Nehemiah from his manacles. No one bothered with Ralf, who continued to hide his face in his hands and sob. "You a disgrace to your race," Zip said to him.

Legrand, largely relegated to inaction in the background, marveled at the remarkable scene. W. T. Sherman took his .44 off cock and grounded the stock next to his leg. Hattie, still with her arms around Zip, cried almost as noisily as the humiliated Ralf.

New Year's Eve

Miss Vee's — 3 P.M. and Later

A pot of white rice and black-eyed peas simmered on Vee's iron stove. Adam had waited three hours at the military store to bring home extra peas and rice so the household could enjoy hopping John at New Year's. The dish supposedly generated good luck, which might include a resumption of peace.

A desiccated wedge of red pepper and a large Georgia onion lay on the chopping block, to be diced and added to the pot along with a skilletful of country bacon; Zip had found the bacon without saying precisely how or where. Amelia avoided the kitchen, as if porcine instinct told her of a less fortunate pig making the ultimate sacrifice for the meal.

Winks was out of bed, dressed in freshly laundered clothes and resting in the parlor. His hair dangled over his shoulders, badly in need of attention. His luxuriant beard, untouched by a razor for days, gave him the look of one of the war's more patriarchal generals. At three o'clock, Vee paid another of her frequent visits to check on him.

"How are we feeling today, Alpheus?"

"I don't know who else is here, but I'm feeling pretty fair. Yesterday the surgeon said I could be rid of this sling in another week."

"And follow your regiment then?"

"Not just yet. Can't fire a gun with a hope of hitting anything." To demonstrate, he flexed the fingers of his right hand, albeit with difficulty. "Whatever's cooking in the kitchen smells good."

"Hopping John. A Southern specialty. It wards off evil spirits. Tell me, Alpheus — if you don't march to Carolina, where will you go?"

"Back to Indiana, I expect."

Her eyelids fluttered, a possible sign of dismay.

"I seen the elephant, Miss Vee. I don't need to see him again. With my poor brothers laid to rest, I don't suppose Mama can run the farm alone." He coughed and fiddled with the coverlet on his knees. "Now, I would say we're friends, wouldn't you?"

"Yes, I would agree with that."

"So, friend to friend, I can tell you something that's been on my mind ever since Christmas?"

"What is that, Alpheus?"

More fiddling. "Um — well — when the war's over, the trains'll run again. You could come visit."

"Indiana?"

"Putnam County's mighty pretty in the spring and fall. Pretty when it snows, too, though if I don't see another blizzard till I'm ninety, that's fine."

The redness in her round cheeks grew brighter. "I've never been north. I've never been out of Georgia except for trips to Charleston when I was a girl. Wouldn't I stick out?"

"Why, I don't believe so, not when the country's put back together. Fact is, I think you'd be right at home. Lots of people say Indiana's the most Southern of all the states. We could arrange it so you could stay awhile if you liked. I've got friends who'd put you up in a nice spare room, all legal and proper."

"That's a tempting offer. My students have deserted me, so I needn't worry about their lessons."

"Once life's back to normal, there's sure to be a call for piano lessons in Putnam County. It's not the back woods, y'know."

Vee's eyes danced. "I could give my piano a good home at Silverglass. If Sara's captain comes here again, he could sit down and play."

"It all sounds mighty fine," Winks agreed, though he couldn't be sure whether she meant yes, she'd visit, or no, she wouldn't. To spare her embarrassment, he shook his injured hand in the general direction of a folded news clipping she carried in a nonchalant way, as though she didn't have it. "Say, what might that be?"

Fresh color filled her cheeks. "Just an old poem from the *Savannah Republican*. Last year I copied out a stanza I liked, and this morning I chanced across it in my bureau."

Winks detected an obvious shading of the truth but didn't call attention to it. He leaned back in his rocker. "Suppose I could hear it?"

From the pocket of her skirt she pulled pince-nez reading glasses which she fitted on her nose. Avoiding eye contact, she read to him:

War is ruled by men,
Love's ruled by the fair.
War needs many soldiers,
Love needs but a pair.
War makes foes,
Love makes friends.
War's soon over,
Love —

She muffled the concluding words.

Winks leaned forward. "Could I have that again?"

She drew a long breath, as though poised on a rock for a dive into a deep pool. " 'War's soon over, love — never ends.' Oh, I think they called me in the kitchen."

"Miss Vee." His voice held her at the door. "Will you come visit?"

A prolonged silence followed the exchange. Then she whispered. "I will."

Winks and Vee shared a moment of perfect understanding before she floated away to the kitchen in an unfamiliar state of bliss.

Thirty minutes later, Stephen climbed the front steps and knocked. Sara admitted him, took his hat. "What a surprise, Captain."

"I hope I'm not interrupting. I wanted to extend New Year's greetings to the household. And I surely would like permission to play the piano a little."

"I don't believe Vee would object. I'll tell her you're here. Meanwhile, why don't you sit and play?"

After a few practice arpeggios, he began "Tenting Tonight." Sara returned, without Vee; Adam said she was visiting the necessary. Stephen sang the ballad in a pleasing baritone.

Many are the hearts that are weary tonight,
Waiting for the war to cease;
Many are the hearts looking for the right,
To see the dawn of peace.

Sara was touched and overcome by the sentimental song. Hattie appeared, Amelia cradled in her arms. Stephen didn't see Hattie as he lifted his hands from the keyboard and swung around on the iron-braced bench to face Hattie's mother.

"The new year seems an auspicious time to say this to you. My heart is one of those the song describes. Has been since the hour we met. When we're all Americans again, I'd like permission to come back and call on you. One day I'd like to show you the lights of New York. It isn't as backw— quiet as Savannah, but neither is it entirely a den of iniquity. Yankees are not all horned devils. I hope you'll let me return and extend an invitation."

Stunned, Sara found it impossible to answer.

He took it as rejection. He reached behind him, closed the cover on the keys. He strode to the table where Sara had placed his hat. He bowed. "Well, ma'am — good day. And happy New Year too."

His footfalls faded rapidly on the outer stair.

Sara slipped into a chair, bowed her head. Hattie set Amelia on the floor.

"Mama, you know that captain likes you. Papa's been gone a long time. We all miss him, but I think you should let the captain call on you."

"I thought you despised Yankees."

"As a class I guess I still do. But I suppose we must take them one at a time now. Wouldn't you like to see New York City?"

Sara vigorously wiped her eyes. "I might. However, I don't know where the captain is quartered, and I certainly won't chase through the streets like some ill-bred hussy, trying to locate him."

Hattie beamed. "Oh, Zip will do that, Mama. I already asked him."

They sat down to supper at five. Scarcely had Vee offered the blessing and passed the corn bread she'd baked with ingredients from the military store, than a clatter on the outside stair announced one more visitor. "Maybe the captain came back," Vee said as she went to answer the knock.

But he hadn't; a caped lieutenant stood there. "Beg pardon, ma'am. I am looking for a Miss Lester."

"I am Miss Rohrschamp. Do you want Miss or Mrs. Lester?"

"The former. General Sherman requests the young lady's presence at headquarters."

"This minute?"

"Yes, ma'am."

"We have just begun our meal."

"The general will see the young lady's returned in ample time to finish."

Sara appeared. "Does she have a choice in this matter?"

"Well, ma'am, seeing that General Sherman is in command of the city, not to mention this whole section of the state of Georgia, I would say no, she doesn't."

Charles Green Manse — 5:30 P.M.

So once more, Hattie arrived in Madison Square in a military carriage and was shown to the general's untidy room on the second floor. Sherman wasn't seated with food this time, but stood before a pier glass, buttoning the collar of his uniform blouse.

"Ah, Miss Lester. Do sit down, please, and be comfortable." Hattie did the former but couldn't accomplish the latter.

"Thank you so much for responding to the

summons, and for honoring our bargain. I received your letter, which I have already dispatched to President Lincoln. The colored chap we rescued delivered the letter."

"Zip Winks."

"Winks, you say. Is he related to the sergeant?"

"An admirer only."

"There's a place for him in our pioneer corps whenever he desires. He brought a small food crock along with your letter. A savory treat, one I remember from my days superintending a military school in Alexandria, Louisiana."

"Hopping John. My mother and Miss Vee sent it. Eat some tonight or tomorrow, you'll have good luck for a year."

"I can certainly use it. Secretary Stanton will arrive in a few days to debate whether my opinions about colored men as front line troops are correct." He drew up a chair opposite her. "I would like to say again how much I admired your courage and audacity in helping to free the illegally detained Negroes. Fleeg's in the county jail, as you know. The civil authorities will punish him. However, I wanted to tell you personally that Sergeant Winks will receive a commendation."

"Thank you, Mr. General. He'll appreciate that."

"You still don't like me very much, do you?"

"I can't say I do, sir. I'm truly grateful for your help with rescuing Zip, but it doesn't change one thing. You made war on old men and women and children. And horses. And chickens. Hogs too."

"War is cruel, Miss Lester. You can't make it anything else. I marched from Atlanta, off the map and all the way here, so the Confederacy would understand it was whipped, and give up that much sooner. Only then could we put the Union back together."

In the street, celebrants sang "Auld Lang Syne." Sherman said, "Please convey my news to Sergeant Winks."

"I will, Mr. General. May I say, I heard about the passing of your infant son, and I am very sorry for it."

"Kind of you to say so. I never saw baby Charlie. War punishes all of us one way or another."

"Yes, sir, I believe you. Is there anything else?"

"Just this. Where you kicked me?" Sherman rubbed his right ankle. "When the weather's cold or damp, it still hurts. Plenty."

Hattie wished him happy New Year and went out smiling.

January 1, 1865

Miss Vee's — 7 A.M.

Hattie woke on her trundle bed on the first morning of the new year. Sara had taken over the upper bed, Vee returning to her own room. Winks had spread blankets in the parlor; Adam still bedded in the kitchen. Dr. Rohrschamp's house was crowded, but somehow all the more pleasant because of it.

What Hattie discovered when she woke up wasn't pleasant. She wasn't grief-stricken; Sara, never priggish, had prepared her daughter. Yet the knowledge of irreversible change brought a rush of tears. Sara heard, and awoke.

"What is it, Hattie?"

Hattie drew back the comforter for her mother to see. Sara put her bare feet over the edge of the bed and stood.

"Girls embark on the road to adulthood at many different times. I promise you this. Growing to be a woman is a wonderful thing. One day, you'll know."

Tears of her own flowed as she hugged her daughter against the warmth of her flannel bosom.

"Oh, my dear child. What a momentous year this has been, for all of us."

January 19, 1865

Outside the Exchange, Broad Street

In the bright winter sunshine, General Slocum's left wing passed hundreds of spectators gathered along Broad Street. Over New

315

Year's, the last mines had been cleared from the river, and sunken obstructions removed. Elements of General Howard's right wing had already boarded steamers for Beaufort, South Carolina. The left wing intended to march up river, presumably to invest Augusta, but Winks dismissed this as a feint. "The real target's Columbia or Charleston, you watch."

Miss Vee hadn't joined the crowd, preferring to remain at home and fuss over the sergeant, to whom she seemed permanently attached; nor did he act unhappy with the arrangement.

National and regimental flags splashed color along the broad avenue. Bayonets shone, silver spikes of war on the rifles of passing companies. Caissons rumbled, and a regimental band serenaded marchers and onlookers with "The Girl I Left Behind Me."

Hattie stood between her mother and Legrand Parmenter, watching the resumption of the war. Hattie thought Sherman's lean and sunburned Westerners very fit from the Christmas respite. She pitied the civilians who were about to feel Yankee wrath, whether in Augusta or the Palmetto State.

Slocum's pioneer corps passed, smartly turned out in blue. Among the proud faces she saw Zip's. She waved and waved until she was sure he'd noticed. She would miss him, but he'd promised to return. He liked Augusta, he said, and might like to settle there as a free man of color.

Among a ragged formation of reporters and sketch artists, Stephen appeared riding Ambrose. He blew a kiss to Sara. She wanted to respond in kind, but her girlhood training kept her from it. She waved with great enthusiasm. If Mr. Wordsworth had a line appropriate to the moment, she was too giddy to recall. Hattie joined her mother in waving until Stephen passed from view. She had no doubt she'd see him again.

Then Uncle Billy rode by with his staff. He was going as far as the river, and would travel to Beaufort by water. Hattie's mother had called on the general shortly after New Year's, old Adam accompanying her. Adam repeated his account of the conversation at Judge Drewgood's dinner table. Next day Sherman canceled the auction of the rice plantation and ordered General Sensenbrenner to an obscure post in east Tennessee, punishment for his connivance.

The general recognized Sara, her daughter, and Legrand. His blue coat seemed less shabby — crates of new uniforms had arrived — but his gloves and collar were dingy as ever. He tipped his old slouch hat to the Lesters and Legrand, on his face a curious bemused expression. He squared his shoulders and rode on.

"What an odd look he gave you," Sara said to Hattie.

Legrand said, "I think Uncle Billy met his match."

Down where her mother couldn't see, Hattie

slipped her hand into Legrand's. Christmas was over, the mistletoe put away, but she felt very grown-up, even ardent. Perhaps she'd let him steal a kiss when they said good-bye.

Before dark, Legrand helped Sara and Hattie load their belongings into their dilapidated wagon. Winks and Miss Vee saw them off from the front stairs. Sara took the reins, Hattie beside her. Amelia squeezed between them, snout wrinkling, as if she already smelled the salt marshes on the road home to Silverglass.

Afterword

Writing a story about a Christmas that occurred in the midst of the bloodiest war in American history may be both rash and dangerous. Still, many people encouraged me to go forward, and I was heartened by certain words of the playwright and director Alan Ayckbourn in his recent book on his craft.

"Without light," Ayckbourn observes, "how can we possibly create shadow? It's like a painter rejecting yellow. . . . The darker the drama the more you need to search for the comedy." In planning and writing *Savannah*, I searched for light to contrast with the war's hours and hours of darkness.

The novel began as a discussion in the office of my publisher on Hudson Street, New York, one warm May afternoon in 2002. Present were yours truly and four people knowledgeable about publishing: Carole Baron, the head of Dutton, one of those business associates who turns into a friend; Dutton's editorial director, Brian Tart; my own talented editor, Doug Grad; and my literary representative and legal adviser, Frank R. Curtis Esq.

It was Carole who suggested a Christmas

story done somewhat in the manner of one of my historical novels. Carole didn't ask for another Civil War novel, but my mind jumped at once to the famous telegram, or *telegraph* as they said in 1864, from General Sherman to President Lincoln, following the capture of Savannah. Here was an opportunity to write about a city, and a locale, an hour from where I've lived for a quarter century. I needed no persuasion. You have read and, I hope, enjoyed the results of that New York meeting.

Now, a few explanatory notes:

For purposes of the story, the 81st Indiana regiment is fictitious. Some of Winks's conversations with civilians have been adapted from contemporary accounts that appear in primary and secondary sources.

The Union "sleigh" distributing toys and foodstuffs in Savannah on Christmas Day, 1864, may be apocryphal, but it is documented in at least two places. I liked it and used it.

Sherman and Grant did recommend "Jef" Davis for promotion from brevet major general to regular rank, but promotion was denied. The killing of a superior and the incident at Ebenezer Creek made him suspect at the War Department, where Secretary Stanton was only one among many fervent abolitionists. Davis continued to serve in the regular army in Alaska and the Modoc Indian war. He died in 1879.

William Tecumseh Sherman lived a long life as a Union hero and notable public figure. He repeatedly turned aside pleas that he enter politics and run for president. His refusal is famous: "If nominated I will not run, if elected I will not serve."

Isaiah Fleeg calls Sherman a bigot. It's one of the few trustworthy statements made by the shifty Mr. Fleeg. Scholars generally regard this view of Sherman as correct, though he was not unlike millions of others of his time. He expressed liking for blacks generally; he loathed slavery and slave owners, but he didn't believe black men capable of bearing arms as front-line troops, even though, as mentioned in the story, they had already proved themselves, notably in the attack on Battery Wagner during the siege of Charleston in July 1863.

Yet Sherman can't be dismissed simply by playing the race card against him; there is much more to him. He was an effective leader, more interested in results than display. By nature or inspiration, he was also a military genius. When he struck out from Atlanta in the autumn of 1864, at age forty-four, he conceived and led a march that is considered a sort of masterpiece in the art of war.

Capturing Savannah, he treated the city relatively gently. The record shows that he enjoyed himself there. Children did like him, and called on him, as did wives and relatives of Confederates who were his battlefield foes. We can speculate that the Christmas season had much to do with it.

In South Carolina, Sherman willingly returned to his role of "the new Attila," climaxing his rampage across the state with the great Columbia fire, which Southern partisans accuse Sherman's men of setting. Those on the other side blame troops of the retreating Wade Hampton. Whatever the truth, Sherman is largely excoriated in the modern South, although this doesn't prevent his familiar bearded face from being used freely to advertise many a commercial tour in Savannah and elsewhere in Georgia.

Sherman rose to the rank of full general in 1869, and succeeded Grant as commander of the army. He continued in this post for fourteen years. In that time, ironically, new postwar regiments of black cavalry on the Western plains, the so-called buffalo soldiers, distinguished themselves not only for their courage and fighting ability, but also for their discipline, statistically the best in the Army then and for years afterwards.

The Negro regiments were commanded by white officers, many of whom resented the duty. One who didn't, and proudly acknowledged it with his nickname, was Gen. John "Black Jack" Pershing. I dealt at some length with the buffalo soldiers in *Heaven and Hell*, the final volume of the North and South Trilogy.

Sherman's *Memoirs* were published in New York in 1891, the year of his death. The book remains in print today; the Library of America publishes a fine edition of the text. Of course Sherman looms large in every major work about the Civil War, but several shorter books are devoted to "the march" as it has come to be called. Both Burke Davis and Lee Kennett have written good accounts of the campaign. Richard Wheeler covers the same ground with a documentary approach utilizing statements and writings of participants. Equally valuable, especially for those who want to revisit sites of the march, is *To the Sea* by Jim Miles, a combined history and travel guide.

Language is constantly in flux, as anyone trying to decipher contemporary adolescent slang will recognize. It was so in the nineteenth century too, and I hope I can be forgiven the use of a few now-obsolete words that delight me: *slantindicular* ("slanted or distorted"), *snollygoster* ("a term of opprobrium frequently applied to politicians"), and my favorite, *sockdologer* ("a particularly lethal punch").

In the spring of 2003, my wife and I explored the fascinating waterways and abandoned rice fields of the Ogeechee and Little Ogeechee Rivers, as well as the many canals dug between small, lush islands in the streams. Our flat-bottom boat came from the University of Georgia Marine Extension Service in Savannah. John A. Crawford of that service, as good an ecologist as he is an historian, piloted the boat. Our company included the man who had arranged the trip, Capt. Rusty Fleetwood of WGB Marine, Tybee Island, Georgia. Rusty is a boat builder, charter captain, and author of his own encyclopedic book on water craft of the Southeast coast. With the help of Rusty and John, I found a likely location for Silverglass. I thank them both, as well as our hosts at Coffee Bluff Marina, Harold and Rochelle Javetz.

Maj. Len Riedel, executive director of the Blue-Gray Education Society, provided specialized information for the story, as did my longtime friend and former Hilton Head Island resident John Lawless, an organist and musicologist without peer. (He also knows where to buy the best wines.)

For generously sharing his expertise on Civil War wounds, I am indebted to Richard W. Hertle, M.D., head of ophthalmology at the Children's Hospital, Ohio State University.

Very special thanks are reserved and hereby rendered to Dr. Stan Deaton, the unfailingly helpful director of publications for the Georgia Historical Society, which is headquartered in a marvelous old building opposite Forsyth Park. It was Stan who introduced me to Rusty Fleetwood and provided facts large and small whenever I asked (probably too often). I am also indebted to Roger Smith, Stan's colleague at the Society, for valuable help.

Of course, none of the people thanked is in

any way responsible for the use I made of the information they so generously provided.

As I have done many times before, I thank my always-supportive friend and adviser, Frank Curtis, and my wife, Rachel, who manages to live through each of these novels with enthusiasm, encouragement, and unfailing affection.

Lastly, I thank you, the reader, and wish you happy holidays, this year and for many years to come. We must not forget the lesson of the Savannah Christmas: Regardless of our many differences, we are all members of one family.

John Jakes
Hilton Head Island, South Carolina;
Greenwich, Connecticut; Savannah, Georgia
December 1, 2003

About the Author

John Jakes is the bestselling author of *The Kent Family Chronicles*, *The North and South Trilogy*, *Charleston*, *On Secret Service*, *California Gold*, *Homeland*, and *American Dreams*. Among his works for the stage is a widely produced adaptation of *A Christmas Carol*, based on the script used by Dickens himself in his famed platform readings. His love and knowledge of American history is a reflection of his own heritage. His maternal grandfather emigrated from Germany in 1861 and settled in the Midwest. On his father's side, he is a descendant of a soldier of the Virginia Continental Line who fought in the Revolution. He divides his time between South Carolina and Florida.

The employees of Thorndike Press hope you have enjoyed this Large Print book. All our Thorndike and Wheeler Large Print titles are designed for easy reading, and all our books are made to last. Other Thorndike Press Large Print books are available at your library, through selected bookstores, or directly from us.

For information about titles, please call:

(800) 223-1244

or visit our Web site at:

www.gale.com/thorndike
www.gale.com/wheeler

To share your comments, please write:

Publisher
Thorndike Press
295 Kennedy Memorial Drive
Waterville, ME   04901

LT JAKES
Jakes, John, 1932-
Savannah, or, A gift for Mr.
    Lincoln

DATE DUE

LP
LARGE
PRINT